Undaunted Lovers

Undaunted Lovers

A Tale of Forbidden Love

Doctor Jac

ISBN-13: 9780996292122
ISBN-10: 0996292128
Library of Congress Control Number: 2016907033
DUNIS PRESS, San Jose, CA

*To the men and women of our armed forces and their families;
especially to those who risk their lives undercover
and are unable to receive honors or rewards.
Thank you all for your selfless service.*

Acknowledgements

As always this book would never have been completed without the constant advice and recommendations of my story editor, my lovely wife, Laura. Insights and data on military topics were provided by my brother, Col. David Fitzenz, US Army, Ret.; Maj. Harrison Peoples, US Army, Ret.; and Capt. Robert Coon, all Vietnam heroes. Drs. Harvey Slater and John Rashkis guided me through medical issues. My 93 year old, mother-in-law, Laura Sanchez Dubois, helped with Spanish, as did Derek Ling with Chinese language and customs. The team at Create Space was very patient and responsive during the publishing process. Beta readers offered ideas and pointed out problems. Publicist Jill Lublin led us in designing a marketing plan and program that helped immeasurably to launch this series. Paul and Pierce Jamieson, Sara Palmer and Doug Brown did a splendid job carrying out the marketing plan. Writing and publishing a book is truly a long and sometimes lonely trek. No one succeeds alone. Thanks to each and all.

Contents

Chapter 1

Chance Encounter

July 1967
NAS Barber's Point
Oahu, Hawaii

When Mike was growing up, he never imagined doing anything as exotic or dangerous as spying. That changed one day when his dad advised him, "Mike, if you want a happy and successful life, you have to go where your talent is recognized and appreciated. Eventually, you'll have to get out of North Dakota."

Twenty years later Michael Holmes is a naval air intelligence officer at Barber's Point Naval Air Station. It's on the leeward side of Oahu in the tropical paradise of Hawaii, light-years away from the frigid hills of North Dakota.

One Saturday night near the end of his tour, he's invited to a party at the home of Louis and Celia Cravino. Lou is a lieutenant commander and a pilot. They're a wild couple in their midthirties.

To give you a taste of their style, one evening Mike was at a party with the Cravinos, and it was time to leave. Lou and Mike were on the front lawn chatting with another couple for several minutes. Finally, Lou turned toward the house and yelled impatiently, "Celia, are you coming?"

To which she yelled back, "Hell, no—I'm not even breathing hard."

This party is a sizable affair of about twenty-five people. Most of the ladies are in muumuus with flowers in their hair and pikake-shell necklaces. Women like muumuus because they're comfortable and colorful and conceal figure flaws. The men have on Hawaiian shirts and white shorts, some with battered straw beach hats. The house is decorated in a tropical theme with flowers everywhere and a couple of torches and tiki god statues on the lanai.

They mingle, eat, drink, chat, and have relaxing fun playing charades. Celia points out Grace Donaldson and suggests that Mike should talk to her. Despite the last name, she's a Chinese girl probably in her midtwenties, a neighbor of the Cravinos. She has a strong presence that is quite compelling. She's tall and very pretty with skin like porcelain. Her red-flowered muumuu hides what appears to be a slim figure. Even when she's standing at ease, she gives the impression of being very focused. Most amazing are her blue eyes. When Grace talks to someone, she gives them her full attention. She's smiling, soft spoken, but direct. Although it's obvious from remarks during charades that she's quite intelligent, she's also very approachable. Her smile envelops and warms you like sunshine in the morning. Her presence draws you in. It might be his imagination, but she seems to be watching him. Clearly, it's time to move in and cut her out of the herd.

"Hi, I'm Mike Holmes. Did I hear your name is Grace?"

"Yes, I'm Grace Donaldson. Donaldson is my husband's name. I'm here alone because his unit is deployed to WestPac. My Chinese family name is Liu, and my given name is Chan-juan." She laughs deliciously when she explains that it means "graceful" in Chinese. "Are you related to Sherlock Holmes?"

"No. Not at all. He was English, and I'm primarily a Luxembourger."

"When you say 'primarily,' what does that mean?"

"It means I'm three-fourths Luxembourger and one-fourth Sioux Indian."

"You don't look Indian."

"How do the aboriginals of your imagination look, may I ask?"

"Actually, I don't know, but you do look a little Mongolian, Are the Sioux and Mongols related?"

"I suppose it's possible that the prehistoric Mongols traveled across the Bering Land Bridge and met or became my ancestors. But perhaps we might move on to another topic of greater promise," he says with a sly smile.

Despite this frosty opening, there seems to be some unexplainable connection between them. He decides to test it. "May I obtain a libation for you and invite you to accompany me to the lanai, where we might separate ourselves from the flock? Once there we may be able to converse without megaphones."

"Such a gracious invitation certainly cannot be refused. Do you always speak so correctly?"

"It's a by-product of three years at Oxford. I was on a Rhodes scholarship and I picked up their more formal way of speaking sometimes, just for fun. But let me assure you, dear lady, that whilst I admire the post-Edwardian syntax of our British cousins, I am not what you colonists call a 'stuffed shirt,'" he proclaims with a mock-pompous tone.

"Well, ya coulda fooled me, brudda," she replies in beach-boy patois. "What else can you tell me about yourself?"

"An abridged biography would reveal that my grandfather emigrated from Luxembourg in 1898 and settled in North Dakota. He married a Sioux Indian woman. I grew up next to the reservation, where I learned a lot from my Sioux cousins about sharpening your senses—focusing and concentrating on all the sensual signals around you." Pausing slightly to test the effect, he continues, "I say, madam; I believe I detect a very slight Asian accent, which suggests you are not a native of this splendid isle. Am I correct that it is most likely from central or perhaps northern China? If you were to speak Chinese, I believe I should more closely identify the region."

She pulls back in surprise. "You're good. You're a smart-ass, but you're good. Yes, I was born in China and grew up in Henan Province. How could you tell?"

"It's simple. At Oxford I concentrated on Asian studies. Chinese language was part of it. By listening closely, I learned a bit about the tonal differences within Mandarin dialects. Plus, I heard a very slight tick when you said some English words. There are certain sounds that are difficult for northern Chinese to make. Please continue."

Smartly brushing away her lustrous, gardenia-scented black hair, she throws her shoulders back and lays into him. "Mr. Holmes you are something special. However, it is abundantly clear that you are uneasy and overplaying your hand. This is probably an outgrowth of having encountered an intelligent woman of taste and beauty who is not overwhelmed by your pretentious manner. I must exercise a high degree of forbearance if we are to find a common ground on which to converse."

Mike is momentarily knocked off center by her. This girl doesn't take crap from anyone. This could be fun, if he doesn't screw it up.

Taking a sip from her tall, frosty drink, she continues, "For your information, sir, my family has a military background. My father, General Liu, was Chiang Kai-shek's chief of staff. When the Kuomintang lost the mainland to the Communists, we left with Chiang to Taiwan," she goes on to explain. "My father eventually had a falling out with Chiang over his brutal rule of Taiwan. Secretly, the CIA helped us obtain visas, and we escaped once more, this time to Hawaii. Since my father had extensive knowledge of China's military capabilities, we were welcomed and put on an accelerated citizenship track. Within a month we were citizens. I was twelve when we arrived. I didn't have a problem quickly learning English. However, the bruddas sometimes don't enunciate very well, so I may speak a bit of three tongues simultaneously.

"A few years after we immigrated, I attended Stanford, where I completed my bachelor's degree in Asian political economics in three years. It wasn't difficult since I had grown up in the middle of it. I was nearly finished with my master's, when my father suddenly became quite ill. Having no siblings, I came home to help my mother. Is that sufficient to satisfy your inquisitiveness?"

He thinks, "What an explosive start. I'll have to choose my words carefully in the future. It's clear she's a very insightful woman."

After an hour they're into a more comfortable flow. Starting with typical cocktail-party news of the day, squadron gossip, and the weather, gradually and easily they shift toward more personal issues such as interests, hobbies, and experiences. She reveals a quick wit and an appealing sense of humor. Although she's very relaxed and somewhat open, Grace isn't flirting. There is a boundary. There is something about her that he's never encountered. Growing up in China during the civil war and Japanese occupation, fleeing to Taiwan, experiencing Chiang's harsh dictatorial rule, and then escaping again to Hawaii—all have left their mark. This is an extraordinary person.

Too soon she says she has to leave because she's doing some modeling the next morning. Mike's more than disappointed. He needs to spend more time with this remarkable woman. She's the epitome of what he's dreamed of since he started thinking about girls. Celia had introduced Grace as a neighbor who lived just a few doors away. Mike offers to walk her home, and she doesn't refuse. They say good night to Celia. As they leave, Mike tells Lou that he's taking Grace home and will be back shortly. Lou nods with a lascivious smile. Dirty old man.

They step out into a gorgeous tropical night. The air carries the scent of hibiscus, gardenia, and orchid. A soft breeze rattles the palm fronds. The sounds of the night are soft, mystical, and exquisite, and so is she. Some invisible night bird calls, and its mate answers. A three-quarter moon paints the sky a deep-velvet-blue backdrop for a million stars while casting shadows along their path. The soft light on her perfect skin is mesmerizing. Mike strolls as slowly as he can without being too obvious. He wants this evening to last forever. As they near her house, he tries to find some way to keep the conversation going that isn't totally stupid or maudlin. Eventually, he has to say good night in a way that's sincere and won't be a cliché. He doesn't hint at coming in, and she doesn't offer. Finally, he says, "Grace I've had a delightful evening with you. You're an extraordinary woman. I hope we have a chance to meet again. I would ask you out, but you're married, and I respect that."

Grace listens without a word. Then she reaches out her right hand. He moves a half step forward and takes it, not knowing what to do next. After a second, he expects her to pull away, but she holds on and looks deep into him with those crystal-blue eyes. Without thinking, he pulls her hand up and kisses it.

She smiles with a look that reveals pain somewhere inside. Then, she says, "Michael, I'm usually not this bold. But I want you to know how memorable this evening has been for me. You're a remarkable man. I've never done this before, but I would like very much to keep in touch with you. We can't be together, but do you see any reason why we couldn't just be pen pals? If you feel the same way, and you have time to send me an occasional postcard or note from your travels, it would make me very happy. Address it to C. J., and sign it Sherlock, just for fun. Send it to my mother's address on this card," she says, handing him a card from her purse.

While he's still holding her right hand, she reaches out with her left, touches his cheek, and gives him a light kiss. She turns quickly and walks up the path to her house. When she reaches the screen door, she turns, pauses, gives him a little smile and a small wave before opening the door and disappearing. He's transfixed.

Finally, he turns and walks back to his car thinking, "Wake up, Michael. She's not a mirage. She's real." His two years at Barber's Point had been taken up with work and competitive golf, so there wasn't much time for romance. Now, suddenly his old, primeval impulses emerge. It's almost like hitting puberty again. Unfortunately, there is that insurmountable problem. No matter how he slices it, she's married, and nothing is going to change that. Celia told him that Grace's husband is a playboy, and she thinks their marriage is not especially happy. That only makes it worse.

The following Tuesday Mike receives orders for his next duty station, Washington, DC. He's to leave in two weeks. As much as he would like to call Grace to say good-bye, it seems inappropriate. He decides he has to write it off as a wonderful night but an impossible situation. All he can do is exchange notes with her from a distance, almost like grade school. Perhaps over time she'll drift away, and this will be just a beautiful memory.

On Sunday morning, Mike's phone rings, and it's Grace. "Michael, I have to talk to you. Can you meet me at Maili later today?"

"Yes, what's the matter? Are you okay?"

"I'll tell you when I see you. Don't worry. I'm all right. Park in the Maili Beach parking lot and walk north along the beach. I'll watch for you. I'll be waiting at six o'clock. There shouldn't be many people there at that time. "

As he hangs up, he racks his brain. What could this be about? "I don't think I did anything to hurt her. All I did was kiss her hand."

By 1745, he's at Maili. He takes off his sneakers and walks barefoot northward along the tide line. In about a quarter mile, there are no people except for one woman sitting on the beach a hundred yards ahead. As he gets closer, she stands up and waves.

She takes his hand and leads him to a sheltered niche. "Let's go over here."

"What's the matter, Grace?"

She pauses, looks at him in a vexed manner, and blurts out, "It's you. We have a word in Chinese for people like you. It's *hundan*. Do you know what that means?"

"Yes, it means 'bastard,' doesn't it?"

"That's what you are—a *hundan*, a big, bad *hundan*."

"What in the world are you talking about? What did I do?"

"You messed up my life. That's what."

"How did I do that?"

"I was going along comfortable in my marriage, and then you came along and upset everything."

"I don't get it."

"Look, stupid. I'm married. Maybe it isn't as hot as Romeo and Juliet, but I was content. Now you show up and…and…and mess with my head. Don't you get it? I've fallen for you, or at least I think I have. Kiss me, you bastard. Maybe that will break the spell."

She looks around and sees no one. Then, she puts her arms around his neck and lays one on him. Wow. She means it. His lights go on, and bells go off. He can feel that they do for her as well. Gradually, she pulls back and looks intently at him, seeking an answer. Then, she makes another run, and this one is more serious than the first. Finally, she steps back again, takes a long, deep breath, looks around the empty beach as though expecting something, and then starts to cry. "You see what you've done? You've totally messed me over, you bastard."

"I should sincerely appreciate it if you would choose another appellation, madam."

"Don't give me any of that British crap. I'm serious."

"I can see that."

"So, don't just stand there, sailor boy. What are you going to do about it?"

"Me? I'm upset too, but I figured I just had to get over it in the next ten years or so."

"Well, it's not that simple."

"Have you talked to anyone about it—maybe your mom?"

"Yes, I did. She understands but says this might just be a hot flash. She says I should let it go for a while and see if it wears off."

"You mean like a bad rash?"

"Don't trivialize this. I'm hurting, and you caused it. You kissed my hand. Who do you think you are...you hand kisser?"

"Grace, I've run all sorts of scenarios through my head, and none of them work. I want to be with you, but I don't see any way for it. You're not going to get a divorce over a two-hour conversation, are you?"

"Just shut up and hold me. You can do that, can't you?"

Chapter 2

What Have I Done?

September 1967
Honolulu, Hawaii

"What have I done?" Grace asks herself. "Am I out of my mind? Why am I encouraging Michael? There's no way this can work out. This is crazy. I'm married, and that's not going to change any time soon, if ever. Get a grip, girl. I need to call Diane."

"Hi, Diane, how are things in California? The last time I talked to you, you had a new boyfriend. Is he still around?"

"Grace. It's so good to hear your voice. No, I struck him off the list; too possessive. What about you? How's Jerry? Has he calmed down at all? I never met anyone who liked to party as much as he does."

"No, ever since your visit last year, nothing has changed. He still thinks he's God's gift to women. Right now he's in WestPac. He'll be back in a couple months."

"So, how are you? What are you doing? How's your momma? Tell me what's going on in paradise."

"That's why I called. I've gotten myself into a real mess. I'm so stupid."

"Sounds juicy. Is there a man involved, I hope?"

"Yes, that's the problem. I met this naval officer at a party a couple weeks ago. He's really special. I've not met many men as interesting and real as he is. He's from North Dakota, of all places, and he's part Sioux Indian."

"Hey. That's a great start. Tell me all about him."

"He's about twenty-eight or twenty-nine, I guess, a hair over six feet, with thick black hair, luscious dark eyes, and a great smile. He's really intriguing. He was a Rhodes Scholar and he speaks Chinese—can you believe that?"

"Don't breathe. Just keep talking. This is getting exciting."

"It's exciting, all right. I think I've fallen in love with him."

"Oh my god, I've never heard you talk about any man except Jerry. You're always saying nice things about him…always defending him. You think your glass is half-full, but I have to tell you something straight out, dear friend. It's half-empty. Let me tell you how it is. What you have to realize is that the world is changing. We don't have to stay in a bad situation. Time is flying. Your clock is ticking. You're a great girl. You need to come down from the clouds. Life is too short to waste it on someone who doesn't appreciate you."

"Diane, you're right. I know it, but it's hard for me to go back on a promise I made to love and honor till death do us part. I know Jerry's not the perfect husband, but frankly, the more I look around, the fewer great husbands and good men I see."

"Don't get down on all men, dearie. I love 'em. You just have to manage them. So, tell me more about Mr. Wonderful. What is it about him that gets your motor running?"

"I'd forgotten what it's like to talk to a man whose really interesting, one who actually listens to you, who can easily talk about all kinds of things without having to show off. We talked for a couple hours, and he wanted to know all about me—where I came from in China, about my father and Chiang, what it was like during the war with the Communists, which I didn't remember 'cause I was just a baby. We talked about Asian political economics, can you imagine that? We discussed hobbies and playing golf in Hawaii. He's a scratch handicapper. We seemed to have a lot of things in common, some things I can't describe. I just feel it."

"Oh, girl, you've got a live one. Reel him in."

"Diane, I'm serious. This is the rest of my life we're talking about."

"Oh, honey, I know, and I'm so happy for you that you've found a great guy."

"Well, I've found him, but I don't know what to do with him. I just know I want him in my life right now. I asked him if we could be pen pals, if he would send a postcard from his travels to my mother's house. I'm leading him on, and I feel guilty because I don't see a happy ending for this."

"Okay, missy, this is the first step. Is he going to do it? That's the test. If he follows through and writes to you, then you know he's for real. That's all I can offer at this point. Just go with it, and see what happens. I'm always here for you, but I'm late for an appointment now. Call me any time. I want to know how this goes. It's so juicy. Good luck."

After hanging up Grace thinks, "Diane's right. I have the right to be happy. Maybe Michael is all I think he is at first impression. But now all I have to go on is a two-hour cocktail party conversation and fifteen minutes on the beach where I was hysterical. I'm really confused. I don't know how deeply he feels for me. It can't be too deep after just this.

He said he respected her marriage, so he wouldn't ask me out. Yet he seemed genuine when he said he hoped he would see again. This thing is like a bouncing ball. One minute I'm up, and the next I'm down. I need to stop for a while and just wait to see what he does. He might write a couple times before finding a girl in another port, and that would be it: a bittersweet memory and nothing more."

Grace thinks back. "What attracted me to Jerry in the first place? He's tall, handsome, and fun loving, a little too much there sometimes. He was attentive to me, but I learned later he is to all females. He's a fun guy, but that's not enough to build a marriage on. I know what did it. It was those beautiful golden wings. He's a pilot with all the glamour that goes with that. He just swept me off my feet. I was young, right out of college, and a bit naïve. I need to talk to mom when I see her tomorrow. She's been through a great deal in her life with dad. She's got her feet on the ground."

"Zăoshang hăo, Mama (Good morning, Mama). Nǐ hăo ma (How are you)? You look very nice today. Are you going to the cultural center for mahjong this afternoon? Mom, I need to talk to you. I'm a little mixed up over something that happened recently."

"What's troubling you, daughter?"

"I met a young man at a neighborhood party a couple weeks ago. I told you about him. He's a naval officer. We spent a couple hours talking. By the way, he speaks Chinese. I don't think I told you that. He knew I was married, and he didn't make a pass at me. He's quite respectful. I really like him. You told me to relax and see how I feel over time. As you said, it might just be a hot flash. Actually, it's more than that, Mom—much more. The night I met him, he walked me home and kissed my hand. That was it. After I talked to you, I called him and had him meet me on the beach at Maili. I told him how I felt. I called him a *hundan* for messing with my feelings."

"What did he say to that?"

He said he had thought a lot about us and really cared for me but couldn't see any way to solve the problem. He's levelheaded. He said that I wasn't silly enough to get a divorce based on a two-hour chat at a party. I asked him to be my pen pal even though we can't be together. Maybe that was a mistake. It might just prolong the agony. He said he'd write, and I gave him your address. Obviously I can't have his cards come to my house. Maybe he won't write, and that will be the end of it."

"My dear, sweet girl, I see you're very upset, and it may take a long time, or forever, to get over him. But you must. I know I'm old fashioned, but there is wisdom in that. Let me tell you a story.

"When I met your father, he and I had already been engaged by our parents. That is the way it was in China before the war. Fortunately for me, he was a good and kind man, and he loved me as much as he could. You know men don't love like women do. Our life is our family. Their lives are divided between work and family. Anyway, you know we went through difficult times: first the war with the Communists, then the bad time in Taiwan, and finally, having to come to Hawaii. This is a beautiful place, and our life is very comfortable, but it isn't China. I am Chinese, a daughter of the Middle Kingdom.

You know we believe that China is the center of the world. We have invented most of the basic tools of civilization. People outside China are barbarians. They are *bai youling*, white ghosts. I will never be entirely comfortable living outside of China among the *bai youling*.

"I believe that a woman must make a commitment to her man, and, so long as he provides for her and does not abuse her, she belongs with him…forever. I cannot advise you any differently. This is who I am and what I believe in my soul. I will do anything you ask me to do except help you end your marriage. Think deeply and clearly about this, my girl."

Chapter 3

The Making of a Spy

September 1967
Washington, DC

The last year at FAD Mike pressed hard to attend naval intelligence school in DC. His CO went to bat for him through his contacts at BuPers and it worked. He received orders to proceed to the Naval Intelligence Training Center, Anacostia, Maryland, just east across the river from Washington, DC. Like they say, it's who you know that counts. In the military there are always more qualified people than there are positions available. Knowing someone who supports you can be the tiebreaker when your file comes before the promotion board.

Mike arrives for school in September and finds an apartment in Alexandria, Virginia. Alexandria is across the Potomac River, six miles directly south of the center of the District and adjacent to the Pentagon. It's an historic area filled with colonial-style red-brick buildings dating back almost two hundred years. Plaques adorn many structures describing people and events as far back as 1812. Alexandria's also close to some of the better public golf courses in the DC area. Two of the best are the Army-Navy Country Club and East Potomac. There is a seven-to-one ratio of women to men here. Maybe that will lessen some of the pain over Grace's unattainability.

The intelligence school is a demanding program of broad, strategic issues governing the country's intelligence policies as well as daily data-gathering techniques. This is a spy school. They learn everything about espionage from how to pick a lock to data acquisition and management, asset recruitment, surveillance, and regulations regarding our country's views about interrogation to escape and evasion. The emphasis is on command issues and on how America has to play that game. The basic idea behind intelligence is to gather useful information that is not accessible through other means. It can be intriguing, exciting, and dangerous part of the time. Still, other times it is tedious administrative work.

About a month into the course, there is a lecture on espionage policies given by an attorney from the Justice Department. She introduces herself as Florence Weintraub. She looks to be in her early thirties; she is about five foot eight and firmly built. She has short black hair and minimal makeup. Her heels are a sensible one inch. Her blue suit is obviously expensive and very businesslike. One might classify her as handsome rather than pretty. She has an upper-class aura. It's clear that she's quite intelligent and has a thorough knowledge of her topic. During her lecture, she mentions issues of penetrating the sovereign territory of friendly as well as enemy nations. "On the enemy side, we do whatever we deem necessary to further the interests of the United States." She indicates with a very small smile that we have to make those decisions while in the field. After she finishes, Mike waits for a few people who want to ask questions. When it's his turn, he can see she's tiring.

"Excuse me, Miss Weintraub. I'd like you to know that I appreciate the effort you've put into this lecture and its delivery. It's quite clear that you're well versed on the subject. You could see how much the class enjoyed it. I won't keep you, but I have one question regarding the limits of interrogation. At what point must the interrogator cease intimidating the prisoner?"

"Mr. Holmes," she says reading my name badge, "that's an extremely difficult and broad question to answer simply. It's not without numerous permutations and exceptions. But it's after five o'clock, and if you're available, I could really use a drink," she adds with an almost flirtatious smile. He sees immediately that this lady likes to be in charge. It's the end of the day, yet he didn't expect to receive such an invitation.

"If that suits your schedule, I should be delighted to discuss this over a libation of your preference."

"My, what a gentleman. Let's go, Mr. Holmes."

At a local bar, over the next hour, they cover the interrogation topic in great detail, actually more detail than necessary, but she doesn't seem to be in a hurry. At last she asks, "Would it be too forward of me to suggest we find a place to have a little dinner? Justice gives me an expense account, so dinner would be on Uncle Sam."

Again, he's taken aback by her assertiveness. "I suppose it is a hallmark of attorneys," he thinks. "Yes, ma'am, if you have the time, I should be delighted. However, this will be my treat, since you're laboring overtime on my behalf."

"Please just call me Flo. It's after hours. Miss Weintraub goes home at five."

They both live in Alexandria. Typically Mike takes a shuttle from NIS to his apartment. Flo has a car and offers to drive them to Il Porto, a new Italian restaurant on King Street in Old Town. The drive takes about forty minutes through heavy traffic. As they go, they make small talk. Once settled in a booth, they relax and share a bottle of wine while ordering appetizers and then prawn cocktails. Flo bites into a fat prawn dripping with red cocktail sauce. When some dribbles over her lower lip, she slowly licks it off while squinting at him with a little smile through half-closed eyes. The conversation gradually shifts from naval intelligence to personal topics. The evening goes smoothly with Flo doing much of the talking. She sucks a piece of her chicken cacciatore into her mouth and looks directly into his soul. He takes a large gulp of pinot grigio and feels the cold sharpness of the alcohol cleanse his throat. He thinks, "If I didn't know better, I'd say she's coming on." By the time they finish dinner and share a flan with espressos it's almost closing time, and the big question is about to be asked.

"Would you like to come up to my place for a nightcap?" she probes.

At this point the question is not startling. This is his first "date" since Hawaii. Immediately he flashes back to Grace.

"Excuse me for being so forward," she says. "It's just that we seem to be compatible. It's not easy in this town of high achievers to find a real mensch."

"Well, I must say this is a most enticing invitation, and you, my dear, are a most attractive lady. Unfortunately, I'm scheduled to deliver a presentation at school in the morning and I am less than well prepared. I shall be burning the midnight oil, as they say. Perhaps you might grant me a rain check for a future assignation?"

"That's disappointing." Then, in her direct manner, she lays it out: "By the way, you're not gay, are you?"

"No, madam. Most assuredly not. It's just that the navy has preempted this evening for its own purposes."

"Very well. I'll take you home, if I must. Here's my card. As soon as you have a free evening and would like to see some interesting sights, please give me a call," she says slowly with a sly smile and holding onto her card for a long moment.

"Why didn't this happen before I met Grace? Now I'm so perplexed about her that I can't think of being with another woman. When it comes to women, I am such a cherry."

October 1, 1967
Dear C. J.,

I'm settled here now and have time to reflect on our last meeting. I still believe it's inappropriate for a single man to tell a married woman that he is in love with her. However, your colloquial "mess with my head" pretty well sums it up for me as well.

I've been thinking about you constantly. Our talk on the beach at Maili was unforgettable, the emotions undeniable. Your face and voice are a part of me now. I run fantasy scenarios through my mind daily. Still, I have no peace, no solution. There seems no way around it. Propriety be damned, I am clearly in love with you. Honestly, I don't know what to do now. I guess I'll wait to hear from you to learn what you're thinking, and feeling.

I hope you're well and that your head is clearing. I'll write again if you let me know you still want to hear from me.
Miss you,
Sherlock

The next Friday after work, Mike decides to go to a local golf practice range and work on his game a bit. As he's hitting balls, it occurs to him that he's hitting down too hard. He should relax on the downswing and sweep the ball off the turf with just a thin divot, keeping the face of the club moving down the target line as far as he can. He doesn't "trap" the ball as the pros do, but for him the sweeping stroke works better. As he starts over, the change is instant. He's hitting long irons like bullets, and his swing is effortless. When he pauses to check his grip, someone behind him says, "Wow. I haven't seen anyone outside of the pros hit long irons like that. Are you a professional golfer?"

Mike turns to see a fellow of about fifty smiling at him. He's leaning on a club. He's over six feet tall and carries 180 pounds in a little paunch. The man is very nicely dressed in a dark Ralph Lauren golf shirt and neatly pressed khaki slacks. This fellow exudes class. He repeats himself, "How do you do that? Long irons are very hard to get off the ground and control."

Almost laughing, Mike admits, "They don't go that way all the time. That's why I'm here."

When the fellow smiles you could take him for a Cary Grant double. "Well, could you look at my swing and give me a couple tips?"

Mike watches as he hits several balls. His swing isn't that bad. His handicap is probably in the mid-teens. He just doesn't seem to be consistent due to a weak left leg that tends to bail out and a rather quick transition between his backswing and downswing. Mike suggests he firm up his left side and make a very slight pause at the top. Immediately, his shots improve. He'll hit four or five in a row well and then miss one a bit. Mike points out that now the man has some checkpoints to focus on that should give him more consistency.

"Thanks a lot. This will drop my handicap a couple strokes. How can I thank you? Can I buy you a drink?"

Mike agrees, and they pick up their clubs and head for the nineteenth hole. It turns out the fellow is as pleasant as he looks. He's very smooth, relaxed, and easygoing but with an air of confidence about him. Mike asks him what he does when he's not on the driving range.

He says, "I work for one of the beltway bandits—you know, defense contractors."

"What do you do for them?"

"I'm in cryptology. We make coding and decoding systems. We work with the NSA, ONI, FBI, and CIA. What do you do?"

"I'm a naval officer going through intelligence school."

"Well, if you haven't heard yet, you'll learn a lot about the covert agencies and their operations. Many Americans think that spying is a dirty game, and it is—dirty and dangerous. But we have to protect the interests of Americans against foreigners who try to harm us."

"I'd like to know more about cryptology. It's coming up on our curriculum in the next couple of weeks."

"At one level it's pretty simple. Cryptology is split into two subdivisions. Cryptographers try to develop methods to ensure the secrecy of messages using computers and high-level math for encoding. Cryptanalysts try to break the cryptographer's work to find the meaning of the message. They're both based on very complex mathematical operations. We work on both sides to help agencies do one or the other jobs. It gets pretty interesting when you're involved in a real case. But that's only ten percent of the time."

"Sounds great. Have you been at it a long time?"

"Maybe too long—my whole career. Nearly twenty-seven years," he says with a sense of resignation. For the first time, he deflates a bit.

"I'd like to know more, but I've got to go now and study for next week."

"Do you have time for some golf this weekend? I've got a tee time tomorrow at Army-Navy Country Club, and my foursome bugged out at the last minute."

"There's always time for golf. I haven't played there yet, but I'd like to. I hear it's a good track."

"Yes, being a private club, they take very good care of it. It's not very long—about sixty-two hundred yards from the championship tees. The fairways are Bermuda and, unless we have a very dry period, are in good shape. The bent-grass greens are absolutely beautiful. The rough can be ruthless, although you probably won't find it very often. Can you meet me there at eight o'clock? That'll give us time to check in and hit a few balls before my nine o'clock tee time. I'll buy you lunch when we finish, if you have time."

"That's very good of you. I'll be there."

The next morning, Mike's up early, looking forward to playing at Army-Navy. Although it's a private club, nonmembers can play it with a member. At 0800 he's standing by the pro shop when the fellow shows up with a big smile on his face. He's beautifully dressed and hauling a red-and-white tour-quality bag with his name stitched on it. "Good morning. I apologize for not introducing myself. My name's Frank Thomson."

"It's my fault. I'm Mike Holmes."

"Well, let's go, Mr. Holmes. We've got a beautiful day to play."

The club offers fifty-four holes of golf. The clubhouse is perched high on the hills of Arlington and Fairfax with good views of DC. The course is fairly tight. It's not difficult, but there are a few challenging holes. No one joins them, so Frank and Mike have an enjoyable, relaxing time. At the end of the round, Frank buys drinks and asks if Mike would like to have dinner with him. He says his wife is visiting family, and he seems lonely, so Mike agrees. That night they have a fun time together swapping stories. They agree to play again the next Saturday. This becomes a regular Saturday event. Frank never mentions his work again until finally Mike asks him about it.

"What can you tell me about your work, Frank? I imagine much of it is classified."

"Yes, it is, but frankly a lot of it is BS. The whole intell game is eighty percent BS. The Soviets probably know just about everything I do, including my office and employee number. Remember, when Roosevelt died in 1945, Joe Stalin knew more about our atom-bomb research than did vice president Harry Truman."

"Yes, I've heard that, but today things must be more controlled."

"There are more systems in place, but technology overcomes them. There are also more agents in the field on all sides. You'll learn a lot about intelligence operations at NIS, but don't accept it all at face value. There are many people passing classified information from both sides every day."

"What? Do you mean that spying is going on all the time? You're kidding me, aren't you?"

"Hell, no. Look at me. I'm fifty years old. I have no children and a wife who thinks I'm a failure because I'm only a team leader. I know all kinds of things that I could pass on to the other side if I wanted to. And I know there are a lot of guys like me," he says with a wry smile. Suddenly, he seems old and tired.

"That's scary, Frank."

"Mike, I've only known you for a couple of weeks, but I can tell you are a straight shooter. I'll tell you something in confidence that will shock you perhaps. Are you ready for this?"

"I guess so. Fire away."

"I know there are a couple foreign agents in our section right now."

"How do you know that?"

"They're a little careless. I've seen things that clearly show they are passing classified data."

"If you're certain, why don't you turn them in?"

"What for? What difference would it make? They're just two of probably thousands of men and women around DC who're doing it."

"What will stop me from turning you in?"

"Frankly, I don't care if you do. As I said, my wife thinks I'm a failure and spends more time in a bottle than with me. I have no kids or real home life. All I have to show for twenty-seven years of work are a couple of plaques and a ten-by-twelve office looking out at other buildings with ten-by-twelve offices. If I did get busted, at least someone would know my name—would know what I've contributed. Mike, I've got an IQ of 175. I graduated summa cum laude with a master's degree in mathematics at age twenty. I go to meetings with people at NSA who are crazy smart and wish I could work with them. I'm as smart as them, but they have a purpose. I have a job. My life sucks."

Mike's heart goes out to this fine man who has spent his working life in service to his country, yet now with the end in sight, feels that somehow he's wasted his life. "Frank, I don't know what to say."

"Neither do I. I should keep my mouth shut. No one cares about me or what I do, and I'm getting to the point that I don't either. What have I got to look forward to—another ten to fifteen years of the same and then retirement?

If I weren't a coward, I would probably shoot myself." His earlier movie-star persona is gone. He's slumped in his chair with a silly "what the hell" look on his face.

"If you go around telling this story to strangers like me, you're going to get into big trouble."

"Hell, Mike, I'm in big trouble. Haven't you been paying attention?"

"Yes, I have but I'm not certain what to do with this information."

"Hey, I've got an idea." He sits up. "Why don't you and I get together and carry out a bit of counterintelligence. It will be good for your career and give me something interesting to do for a change."

"What are you talking about?"

"I'll bet, if I put my head to it, I could ID a number of agents working in our company. There might even be a commie cell. It would be a ball doing it. In the end we could go to your contacts at ONI and turn them in. Then, someone would know that I matter, that I'm not just another smart guy stuck in a ten-by-twelve office in the bowels of a defense contractor."

"That's a pretty big idea, not to mention the risk. I suggest you think it over, Frank. Let's talk about it next week."

On the following Saturday, they're again playing alone and have time to talk as they play. "So, what do you think Frank? Have you given up on the counterintel idea? You're really not going to go through with it?"

"I've been thinking a lot about it. I've already picked out at least four or five fellows that I believe are foreign agents. I'm going to start watching them and talking to them. I'll plant a couple ideas and see if they bite."

"Be very careful, Frank, very careful. You could blow your career and get into something bigger than you. You're smart, but the game you're talking about playing is zero sum. If you lose, it could mean your life. Their retirement program is quick and final. No gold watch."

In midweek Frank calls and says, "Hey, Mike, this is easier than I thought. I've already confirmed two people. These guys are really stupid. They're even going to introduce me to their handlers. They think I'm ready to go over. We're on our way, buddy. I'll see you on Saturday."

Now Mike has to decide what he's going to do if Frank actually delivers information on a communist cell working inside a defense contractor. This is no small matter. Imagine what it will set off. This is well above Mike's pay grade, but he doesn't know who he can take this to if Frank delivers.

Over the next two weeks, they meet each Saturday for golf. Frank is increasingly excited. At last he has something to do that is interesting and potentially rewarding. In the end, he'll be a hero. Maybe his wife will give up the idea that he's a failure. He seldom speaks of friends. This lonely, unappreciated, depressed man finally has his chance at immortality. He'll be remembered, he hopes.

It's now late October, and the course will be closed in a week. There is a chill in the air, the grass is going brown, clouds darken the sky, and the trees are naked, their leaves tumbling freely across the fairways. All the signs are that winter isn't far away. This is their last round together. As they play, Frank tells Mike of his progress, but the joy of the hunt isn't in his voice anymore. When they finish, he says, "Mike, I've made a decision, and I want to share it with you. Can you come over to my house this afternoon? We'll get a pizza and have an early dinner. My wife is visiting her mother and won't be home until Sunday or Monday."

He gives Mike his address in Arlington. After Mike goes home to clean up, he drives over to the address Frank gave him in Arlington. It's a typical colonial-style brick house in a modest community with white trim and a broad green lawn with flowering hedges leading up to the entrance. It's one of a thousand in similar East Coast upper-middle-class cities. As Mike gets out of the car, it starts to rain, and he sprints up to the house. Frank's waiting for him.

"Come in, buddy. Get out of the rain. Let's have a drink. I'll call for pizza in a bit."

"It sure looks like winter is just around the corner. I hate cold weather," says Mike. "Ever since I left North Dakota, I've been able to live in a warm climate. I looks like my streak is over, and I don't like it."

Frank smiles, "Relax buddy. How about a wee dram of Macallan's and a Montecristo? That should set you right."

"Thank you. You've chosen the correct remedy. I just don't have anything to bitch about, so I pick the weather." Mike lights up, blows a smoke ring and asks, "So, what's the big news you have for me?"

"I've come to a conclusion. I've changed my mind. Mike, I'm not going to turn in the spy operation. I've met two handlers. One is Russian, and the other is Chinese. They've both offered me a huge amount of money to turn over data on our latest coding system. I'm talking *big* money. The numbers have lots of zeroes behind. I'll be richer than I ever thought I could be. Besides, if I continue to support them, I'm looking at really huge numbers. I can't pass it up."

This hits Mike hard. He can't believe it. He takes a slow swallow of the Macallans. Then he stands up and steps toward Frank. "Frank, are you crazy? You're no spy. You're a loyal American, using your gifts to fight the enemies of our country. You have to turn these guys in."

"What good would it do to the big picture? The whole intell game is a trade-off. We win one; they win one. In the end, nothing really changes until someone drops the big bomb, and now that's not going to happen. They set me straight. It's all about maintaining balance so that no one side feels it has to drop the bomb. Don't you see? In the end it really doesn't matter what a little guy like me does. It won't change anything. If I don't do it, someone else will. For all I know, someone else is doing the same thing in a different area already. It's an endless, mindless game, Mikey—an endless game that we're all caught up in. I might as well make something out of it for myself."

Mike's stunned. He never saw this coming. Sure, Frank is feeling sorry for himself. He's depressed, but not enough to throw away everything for money, even if it's a lot of money. "Frank, get a grip. You know you can't be a traitor. That's what you're talking about doing: treason, betraying the United States for money. You can't even spend it, Frank. What happens if all of a sudden you start driving a Ferrari or move to a big house? What will your wife think?"

"Well, at least she won't think I'm a failure."

"How will you explain it to her? How will you explain it to yourself?"

"I don't give a damn. At least I'll have done something meaningful. I won't be just a cypher in the great coding machine of life. I'll have made a mark.

In a year I'll have peddled enough data to retire to some warm spot and play golf every day. Hell, I might even dump my wife and find me a hot chick that knows what a man needs and is more than willing to give it to him."

"Frank, my friend, now you're really in fantasy land. You know you're not that kind of jerk. Besides, you've already made a mark. If you feel you're going nowhere in your job, change it. You told me a month ago how much you'd like to work at NSA. Go ahead. Talk to people there. They'd love to have a guy with your knowledge and smarts."

"I already did that. About five years ago, I talked to them, and they turned me down. They've got hundreds of guys like me, crazy smart, trained in their system. They don't need me. My own company doesn't need me. There are dozens of people who do what I do who can walk into my office tomorrow, and the company won't skip a beat. If I don't do it, where am I? Almost thirty years, and I'm nothing. I'm going to do it, Mike. Even if I never spend the money, I'll be able to say to myself, at least I rose above the crowd. Even if I got caught, it would be better than what I have to look forward to. In a few months, you, my only true friend, will be gone, and nothing will change. I'll still be buried in the same old hole. I'm going to do it, Mike. If you want to turn me in or not, that's on your conscience. I'm going to do it, buddy, and you can't stop me."

"Oh, Frank, I beg you to think it over. Talk to someone who can give you another view—your pastor, a friend, someone you know and respect. I'm too young to give you an alternative to finding meaning in your life."

"No, my young friend, you've shown me what it's like to have meaning in your life. You are what I was twenty years ago. I had my vision, but over the decades, the light has gone out. It's too late for me to change anything. This way, I get something out of twenty-seven years of anonymous toil. I'm Charlie Chaplin in *Modern Times*. I'm just stuck in the gears of the big machine. This is the only way out. If I turn in those agents and their handlers, a week later, I'm still stuck in the gears, and someone at CIA or FBI is getting credit for what I've done. A few weeks ago, I was thinking that was my gift to you. But you're too far down in the system. Some big shot will grab this, and no one will remember it was you that brought it in. You see, Mike, even you're caught in the gears."

"Frank. You're right; I'm part of the machine. So are you and two hundred million other Americans. It's called life. Fame is an fleeting goal. At best, it's momentary in the big journey of our lives. The only lasting thing, the only true glory that as human beings we can achieve, is to live a good life, make the best contribution we are able to make, and, if we're lucky, find someone to love us, and then move on. There really isn't anything beyond that. It certainly isn't about money or our picture in the paper. I beg you, my good buddy. Think it over. Talk to someone smarter than me."

On Monday morning, Mike picks up the *Washington Post* and reads that Frank Thomson, an engineer at one of the defense contractors, was found dead by his wife when she returned on Sunday from a visit to her mother. His death was from a self-inflicted gunshot. Mike turns on the morning news, and there it is. A thirty-second story covering a man's fifty years.

In the end, Frank was right. A small notice in the second page of the newspaper sums up his life as the world knows it. Mike's devastated. He feels like he failed Frank. "I didn't feel his hopelessness enough to stop him from destroying himself. I wonder, twenty-five years from now, will I feel the same hopelessness? Right now, at this point in my life, I've accomplished nothing. I don't even have someone who loves me to mourn when I'm gone."

Mike calls in sick and sits in his room trying to find wisdom in a bottle of Macallan's. On the TV nine out of ten stories are bad news: fire, murder, rape, war, fraud, embezzlement, and one suicide that's covered in thirty seconds.

Then, he remembers an old rodeo cowboy he met on the train when he was headed to college. The bent bronc buster said, "It's better gettin' throwed off an ornery bronc or being kicked by a bull now and then 'stead of settin' on the porch watchin' the world go by."

By evening Mike's determined that he won't be another Frank. "I'm going to make a contribution somehow, and I hope—I pray—that I find someone to love me before it's all over."

For the rest of the academic year, he's focused and committed to excelling in school. With Grace in mind all the time, he doesn't feel any value in being with another woman. He manages to handle both the academic and physical challenges. For the first time, he finishes number one in the class.

It's been almost three months since he left Hawaii, and he hasn't heard from Grace. What can that mean? Then, the last week of school, a letter arrives. He thinks, "I hope it doesn't start with 'Dear John.'"

December 9, 1967

Dear Sherlock,

I apologize for taking so long to respond to your note. I started many times and never could express myself adequately. I hope you haven't given up on me. You've been popping in and out of my thoughts constantly ever since Maili. Whenever my mind isn't focused on some task, your face shows up. I like it, but it's maddening. My feelings haven't changed. I believe that sooner or later, somehow, this situation will sort itself out; I pray it will. Until then I would like to keep in touch. Please write again and let me know what you're doing and how you're feeling.

I'm having a good time volunteering at the Chinese Cultural Center. We have an active program for senior citizens on one side along with Chinese art and language programs for children on the other. The old people have stories to tell about their lives in China. The kids are so full of spirit that they're infectious. I feel happy when I'm around them. Jerry will be back soon. I'm a little anxious about his return given what has happened.

Nevertheless, please keep those cards and letters coming, Sherlock. This will work out. I trust the fates to guide us.

Affectionately,

C.J.

Chapter 4

Course Change

February 1968
Washington, DC

Now that NIS is finished, Mike expects to return to CINCPAC at Pearl Harbor and then be assigned somewhere in WestPac. But of course, the navy has a different idea. Instead, he receives orders to report to the newly formed Office for Defense Investigative Services, DC. On Mike's arrival, the XO, Commander Robinson, calls him into his office. He has a type-A personality with a very short military haircut and perfectly pressed uniform. It looks as if he stood up, he would crack. His office appears as though he's expecting the president to visit—not a piece of paper or a paper clip in sight. Mike wonders if Robinson has everything memorized. He doesn't waste time on pleasantries.

Abruptly he says, "Holmes, recently, we've been given a new form of intelligence work: criminal investigation. The program is different than the standard curriculum that you've just completed at NIS. While that was focused on intelligence, this is aimed at combating criminal activity. Naturally, we expect that it will be confined to national-defense cases. You won't be a reincarnation of your cousin Sherlock Holmes," he says with a wry smile. "The course will cover overt criminal acts, criminal intelligence, forensic sciences, information systems, and computer crimes. There are both naval officers and civilians in the class. This training will enhance your inherent investigative talents and what you just went through at NIS. Report to Commander Richard Coon in room 139 for your materials and schedule. You and your classmates are helping us develop this into a very valuable ongoing service. Good luck. Dismissed."

This is a surprising and intriguing development. Mike has heard of the DIS but doesn't know much about it. It could be a great opportunity to learn more about solving complex situations. The next morning he finds a different set of characters than he's been used to in the navy. There are a number of people with law enforcement backgrounds: police officers, lawyers, military police, state troopers, and a couple accountants for tax fraud, he supposes—they're a tough bunch. It's apparent that this is a very serious program, but he's puzzled at its function. Is it a duplicate FBI or CIA operation? He's wondering about his place in it. What does this mean to his naval career? Do they think he's actually a relative of Sherlock and should spend his career on criminal investigations? When he gets a minute, he pens a short note to Grace.

> February 15, 1968
> Dear C. J.,
> Bad news. I expected to return to Pearl after NIS. Now I learn that I'm to attend Defense Investigative Services School.
> The good part about it is that it only lasts about two months.
> I should be back sometime in late May or early June. Miss you.
> Keep the faith.
> Sherlock

Over the following months, the class is put through an intense course in criminology. The law enforcement veterans plow straight ahead. But for Mike, it's a bit of a struggle until he catches on to the new jargon. At NIS he learned about interrogation and information technology, but forensic science is an entirely new world. A great deal of time is directed toward investigative procedures—building a case through interviewing, following clues, developing sources, and working undercover. The use of firearms is touched on, but most of the students have some weapons experience. By the end of the program, his mind is awhirl. He understands the material but will have to learn how to apply it in the field. His hope is that on his first assignment, there'll be experienced people to help him get acclimated.

No such luck. Right out of the box, he's ordered to report to ONI for special assignment. When Mike arrives, he's ushered into the office of the deputy director, Captain McKay. This is unusual. Mike smells a skunk in the woodpile.

They immediately engage in what he calls a listen-and-nod exercise: McKay talks; Mike listens and nods. "Lieutenant, there is a major problem in San Diego that you will solve. Someone at NAS North Island is going around shooting at people. He, presumably a man, is not trying to kill anyone. He just wants to wound them and always in the leg. He must be some type of sociopath. To date, he has taken his shots about once a month. This is now heading into its fourth month, and it's still a total mystery. Your job is to find him and bring him in."

Mike thinks, "This is strange on so many different levels. I've never heard of a serial shooter just trying to wound people. And I don't know why they picked me for this serious assignment. I'm a naval intelligence officer, but my investigative experience is almost zero. All the smart boys must be on assignments elsewhere. It could be that they expect the FBI or CIA will solve the case, and I'm just there to get forensic experience. No matter it's my case now."

The boss continues. "You're going in undercover as a public-relations man. The cover story is that the chief of staff is angry over the way military personnel are being treated because of their service in Vietnam. He wants to put out a favorable story about the navy and its personnel. Your apparent job is to tour the base looking for positive stories. You'll have an assistant, a lieutenant (jg) who's an expert photographer. She'll meet you at the BOQ in San Diego. After you introduce yourselves to Captain McMurray, the CO of North Island, you're on your own. Your orders are waiting for you on my assistant's desk outside. You're to report no later than the twenty-fifth of March. If there are no questions, you'd better get started."

⟡

When Mike arrives in San Diego, he has some time to update Grace with a short note to tell her where he is.

April 27, 1968
Dear C. J.,
    After NIS I expected to be shipped back to WestPac, but the navy had other ideas. I told you in my last short note that I was being sent to a new school, Defense Investigative Services.
    This is a new field for me, difficult but quite interesting. When I finished a week ago, again, I expected to go back to Pearl, but once again the navy surprised me. It seems determined to keep us apart. I'm heading across country to San Diego. Now I'm the real Sherlock Holmes. In this assignment at NAS North Island, I'm to find an unknown sniper who has been shooting people in the leg.
    I say, my dear, most unusual. I must terminate this missive now and have a go at apprehending the miscreant. I shall keep you informed as to the outcome. In the interim, If you are so inclined, you may reach me at the BOQ at NAS North Island for at least a fortnight, more probably somewhat longer.
    Still miss you a lot. Please take good care of yourself,
Sherlock

San Diego is a gorgeous place. It offers ideal weather, a casual yet cosmopolitan atmosphere, and access to Mexico just thirty minutes south. NAS North Island is the largest naval air base on the West Coast. The total on-base population is over twenty thousand military and civilian personnel. Although he's anxious about tackling such an important job, it's exciting to be working at North Island and to be back among operating units. The evening of his arrival, he puts in a call to his new partner, Lt. (jg) Jenae Hendry. She's also quartered in the BOQ. They agree to meet in the dining area for breakfast at 0800.

In the dining room, there are a small number of people still having breakfast. He looks around for female officers. They see each other simultaneously. She stands up and greets him with, "Good morning, sir. I'm Lieutenant (jg) Jenae Hendry. Everyone calls me Jenny." She's about five-foot-eight with an energetic, athletic presence. As he eases himself into the chair across from her, he asks, "Did you arrive yesterday?"

"No, I came in two days ago. I finished my last assignment and had nowhere to go, so I decided to come here and relax in the sun. I was a communications officer at NAS Whidbey Island for the last year. It's a bit damp there, so I'm drying out."

"Is it as wet as Seattle?"

"A bit more. They're just coming into the major rainy season, which will last about four or five months. The weather isn't so bad, but there isn't much entertainment there for a single person."

"I just arrived from DC last night. There's plenty to do there and a large single population."

"From what I gather about this assignment, there probably won't be much time for recreation."

"You could be right. What have you been told about what's going on here?"

Jenny reiterates the story, almost word for word, that Mike was given.

"It looks like after we report to the base commander, we're pretty much on our own—that is, unless he wants to muck about in the case."

"Have you handled cases like this before? I certainly have not. I'm here supposedly as a photographer. I went through AIO School in DC. Do I understand that you went to NIS and then DIS?"

"That's correct."

"I think they gave me this job because they believe a woman is not as threatening and won't arouse suspicion if she goes around poking her nose into other people's business."

He notes that she researched his background for this assignment. That's a good trait; being prepared. But he's thinking, "Michael, she's aggressive. Better watch that, and keep it focused, since she doesn't have any investigative experience."

"That's correct, but this is my first assignment since DIS. We'll have to start by familiarizing ourselves with the base and its operations. I'll be very surprised if the FBI and maybe CIA are not already here stirring up the pot. Do you have experience as a photographer?"

"Some, sir. I'm an amateur, but I've been at it since high school. I've had photos published in magazines and won a few local and regional photo awards. I believe I can handle it. Where do we start, sir?"

"We start with an appointment to talk to the base commander. Undoubtedly, he knows we're coming. I'd like to know what ONI told him about our purpose. I'll call his office this morning, and we'll go from there. If you stay in your room, I'll call and let you know the answer."

"Aye, aye, sir," she says respectfully but with a smile.

"I like this officer. Although this is a new world for her, she moves like she knows where she's going. She seems fearless, which she'll need to be before this very sensitive affair is finished. She's also quite attractive."

Mike goes back to his room, calls the CO's office, and requests a meeting at his convenience. An hour later there's a call back, and he's told to be in Captain McMurray's office at 1300. He lets Jenny know to meet him in the BOQ lobby at 1230.

Promptly at 1245 they walk into the captain's anteroom and give their names to the receptionist. In a command as big as this, the CO has a number of sections under him and several persons on his immediate office staff.

Exactly at 1300 they're escorted into the boss's office and stand at attention five feet from his desk.

He's hung his jacket in the corner, and his eagle is clearly showing on his shirt collar. He has an aura of stern authority about him. The desk has a couple of neat stacks of papers and documents seemingly organized by some system. Nothing random here. He sizes them up with a scowl for a moment and then says, "At ease."

They assume the parade rest position.

"I've been informed that you two are here to work undercover on the shooting case we have. I presume you've looked at the file."

"No, sir. Neither of us has been privileged to see the file as yet. We have sealed orders and a packet of documents with orders not to open them until we see you."

He looks amazed, pauses, and says, "I hope you're a quick study. I'm tired of having interlopers from Washington poking around here. The rumor mill is operating at flank speed, and my people are very nervous. The worst fear is fear of the unknown, and that's where we are. We haven't a clue as to who this idiot is, what he's planning, or why.

"So far the shootings have been irregular and confined to North Island. Hopefully, they won't spread southward. I've arranged an office for you in this building on Level One. I suggest you get down there immediately and respond according to your orders. I want to know everything you find and know it before anyone else does. Do you understand? This shooter is already making my security people look bad. They've been instructed to let you have the run of the base, provided you don't get in the way of operations. They believe that you're here to write some positive stories about the base. My security chief, Steve Prince, knows the real story, but he won't share it with anyone. We'll keep it at that. If you have problems with anyone, let me know. Report to me once a week with a one-page confidential memo until you find out who's doing this. I expect that won't take too long. Dismissed."

With that, they're given maps by the receptionist to find their office and a packet to learn about the base. Once they settle in their office, they open their orders. The case is this: Three months ago, someone shot a petty officer in the leg. No one could tell where the shot came from, but the slug was from a .22-caliber target pistol. This is the first clue. He's using a target pistol because of its accuracy of up to one hundred yards or more. Neither base security nor the local police have been able to come up with a motive or any clues beyond the bullet. Given that it was fired from a pistol, the shooter was either fairly close to the victim or an excellent marksman. With planes taking off and landing all the time, the jet noise could muffle the sound of a small-caliber weapon. Since then, there have been three more attacks. The most recent was three weeks ago. Given the pattern, that suggests that there may be another incident soon.

The first stop is with the head of security, Lieutenant Commander Steven Prince. Prince is what you would expect from a professional security type: large, friendly, but brusque and to the point. The shooter is making big problems for him. If the fellow isn't caught very soon, he'll look very bad.

Prince starts giving out his thoughts. "I believe that it's an outsider. We have many people coming and going through here. Someone with a grudge against the military could get a kick out of playing this game with us. The strange thing is that he shoots people only in the leg, nowhere else."

"The incidents always take place during the workday. Anyone could fire a weapon in midday without someone hearing it because of flight operations. Also, it's windy here, so he can't get too far from his victim and still be accurate.

"He could have a suppressor on it that would muffle the sound and cover most of the muzzle flash. Distance is a good question. He'd have to be firing from a stable platform to be as accurate as he's been."

"I think your suspicion of an outsider gives us someplace to start," Mike offers. "Are there people other than employees who come and go and a regular basis?"

"Sure, vendors. We have suppliers going to the warehouses and commissary with everything from munitions to skateboards to food. There are maintenance crews from the utility and telephone companies. There are delivery people like FedEx and UPS. The list is pretty long."

"Do you check them through the gate?"

"Of course. We usually know they're coming, and we log them in—but not out."

"You don't log the drivers, do you?"

"No, just the company. The company would know who the driver was on a given delivery day if we need to know that."

"This seems like a good place to start. If your office can get the company driver records on the days of the shooting, it might provide some leads. Some vendors probably come only on specific days and go to specific sites. Others, like FedEx or UPS, may make several stops at the base mail center, HQ, or other points. Once we have the list of potential suspects, the vendors must let us know when those individuals will be coming in again. This will make stake-outs more efficient and hopefully more productive. I know it's a big haystack, but we have to find the needle, and do it quickly."

"Consider it done. We'll push the vendors to cooperate and do it quickly and discreetly."

Mike and Jenny catch the shuttle bus back to their office to develop a plan. They agree that obtaining driver records on the day of the shootings might give them a manageable list of suspects to start with. Then, they can go to the places where those identified drivers made stops—for instance, the commissary—and stake them out while doing their cover-story interviews. Due to the urgency of solving this case, they'll have to separate and cover two sites at the same time. Mike says he'll ask Prince to get them a vehicle so they can get around this large base without waiting for the shuttle.

Jenny suggests that Prince might be able to release a man or two to help them cover the ground. "He's on the hot seat big time, and I think he'll coop-erate as much as he can without giving away our cover."

That afternoon Mike and Jenny review the list of vendors with Prince. It seems thorough and includes the names and times of entry. They spend several hours going over and over the list and together develop a schedule of stakeouts for the first four days. At that point they'll get together again and review their progress.

Every morning Mike and Jenny make it a point to rendezvous for breakfast in the BOQ dining room at 0730 to review progress and plan the day. In a couple of days, they've established a productive and pleasant routine. One morning Jenny asks, "Can you tell me about your background, sir? I see by your ring finger that you're not married. Where are you from originally?"

Mike's a bit taken aback because up to now, their time together has not included any personal information. There has been no reason to avoid it. They've simply been too focused on the case to talk about anything else. He answers, "I grew up in North Dakota. I have one younger brother. After college, I was a Rhodes Scholar at Oxford, and then I joined the navy, and that is about it. What about you?"

"I was born in New York but spent most of my life in Colorado after my parents separated when I was three. I don't have any siblings. I left home to go to college and never went back. After graduating, I went to work and studied law at night. When I finished law school four years later, I went directly into OCS in Newport. I had a short tour in DC at JAG but asked to be sent into the fleet. That's how I got to Whidbey Island."

"Sounds like a lot of hard work."

"It was, but I had nothing to go back to, so I just kept charging ahead. I learned, for me at least, that some problems can only be solved by hard work. You can't sit there and complain about how bad your life is or how cruel the world is. The world can be cruel, but it is also filled with opportunity. You just have to make a decision on how to handle it."

"I agree. Hard work is a great palliative. But you do feel alone at times, don't you?"

"Sure, it gets a bit lonely at times. I would like to find someone, but in this business, who has time for romance or family?"

"Along the way, didn't you ever meet someone special?"

"Yes, in my senior year in college, I met a young man who was a petroleum engineer. I was crazy about him. He loved the oil business. His company sent him to work their oil patch near Lake Maracaibo in Venezuela. It's pretty wild country, and I couldn't go with him. After a year of letter writing, it was clear that he loved oil more than me. That realization broke my heart. It drove me to stop waiting for Prince Charming and to make my own way. That's when I decided on law school. I liked the investigative side of the law business. It's what made this assignment so intriguing for me."

"I understand."

"When we finish here, where do you think you'll go next?"

"I expect I'll be sent somewhere in WestPac, given my language ability and interests over there."

"What language do you speak?"

"I studied Chinese when I was at Oxford."

"Wow. I'm impressed."

"I also was introduced to Edwardian English. That, madam, is indeed a superb means through which to surprise, entertain, or befuddle people."

After a second to catch on, she sits back in her chair and laughs.

After three weeks of fruitless stakeouts they're very frustrated. Then, late one afternoon, Jenny and Mike decide to go for a random drive around the base to see if anything speaks to them. They're talking about what to do next when they have to stop at a corner to wait for a large garbage truck to pass. Suddenly, he realizes they've not considered the trash people who roam the base every day picking up waste material. When they get back to their office, he calls Prince. "Steve, we've missed the trash company."

"My god, you're right. I'll get on that immediately."

Over the next week, while they're waiting for the waste-management info, they go over records of all the vendor drivers once more to see if they can find anything suspicious. There's nothing much there—petty indiscretions, mostly kid stuff. No reason to closely check on any of them. Mike files his weekly confidential report with the CO and hopes to stay away from him. He thinks, "I'm not solving his case, and I know he's getting upset by it."

Then, they receive the waste-management company's data. There is so much trash that the company has three trucks working full time to keep the base clean. There are four regular drivers and one young relief driver. The first thing that hits Mike is that the relief man was on the base on every shooting day. Two days later, the man drives into the base, and they're ready to follow him. There is nothing suspicious about his behavior except that he spends a lot of time talking to people on his stops. When Prince's men follow up, the people tell them that he asks a lot of questions about the base and the way it operates—more than one would expect. Prince calls the trash company and tells them he's going to detain the man for questioning. Naturally, they're concerned and insist that Mike wait until their lawyer and human-resources person arrive. The fellow's name is Manuel Torres. He's twenty years old and has been working for the company for almost two years, right out of high school. While they wait, they get him a cold drink and make small talk. He tells them he's working to save money to go to college. He wants to be a detective someday. That's why he's always asking questions. Soon the lawyer and human-resources officer arrive.

Prince tells Manuel that this is a random search. They picked him up to learn if he has heard anything back at the company that might relate to the shootings. "Maybe, Manuel," Mike suggests, "one of the drivers has made negative remarks about the navy, the military, or our country."

"No, sir," he replies. "All of the men seem to be proud to be working here."

Just then Prince is called out of the room. They wait, and one minute later he comes back in with a pistol in his hand. He says, "Manuel, is this yours? What's this doing in your truck?"

He begins to deny it but quickly see's he's caught and admits it's his. "I can explain, man. Where I live, you have to be prepared to defend yourself day or night, man. Two of my friends were kilt last month when someone thought they were in a rival gang. They weren't. They weren't gangbangers, but they got shot anyway. I carry it on my way to work and way home for pertection."

Prince asks him very threateningly, "Don't you know it's a federal offense to carry a gun onto a military base?"

"No, man. I din't know. I'm jist tryin' to pertect myself, man."

The lawyer says, "Manuel, don't say another word." Then, he turns to Prince and Mike and asks, "Can we talk in private?"

They go into a room next door, and the lawyer opens up with, "Do you really think he's the shooter, or is this just a cheap trick to scare the kid?"

Prince replies, "One of my men found it in a small gym bag under the seat."

"Does it match the type of gun that the shooter used?"

"It's a .22 caliber. We'll have to have ballistics check it. In the meantime I'm going to hold him."

"You're wasting your time. I can have him out of here in an hour. Let's be smart about this. I want you to catch the shooter too. But I'm sure, and I think you are too, that this is not your man."

"Maybe not, but I can't tell the boss I let a suspect go before I had a chance to run the gun. I'll hold him overnight and get SDPD ballistics to do a rush test. He may not be the man, but we've checked almost every vendor who came on the base during the shootings, and he was here every time. Besides, we have four more of your men to check, and after a night in the brig, he might remember something he overheard or saw."

"Let him go, and I'll ensure he shows up tomorrow."

"Not a chance. You go find a judge who will release a suspect we haven't had time to interrogate. I don't think you can do it in an hour or eight hours. If he's clean in the morning, you can have him."

Back in the interrogation room, the lawyer explains to Manuel that he has to be held until ballistics checks the gun. He nods and says they'll find it isn't the gun that shot anyone.

The next morning they talk to Manuel again while they wait for the ballistics report. After an hour, it's clear that he hasn't heard or seen anything that would be helpful. In the afternoon, the report shows this is not the shooter's gun. Manuel is released to the lawyer while the navy decides whether or not to press charges for bringing the gun on base.

Next, they turn their attention to the other four drivers. Three of them were on base the days of the shootings. The fourth was on sick leave during one of the incidents. They run the three men's records through the FBI. When the reports come in, Mike and Jenny go to security to look at the reports. The first two don't reveal any past problems. The third, a man named Paul Trammel, is a surprise.

Prince says, "I've heard about this man. He was a hero in Vietnam. The story I heard is that he was a gunnery sergeant, E-7, in a company of marines deployed north of Khe Sanh. The North Vietnamese launched an attack in his area, and the company took heavy losses. The platoon leader was wounded, and Trammel took over the platoon and led a counterattack. I don't know all the details, but apparently he singlehandedly wiped out a large number of the enemy, also captured a large number, and led the platoon to safety. Then he went back and personally carried out a number of wounded. He was badly wounded in his legs and, by the end of the encounter, could barely stumble, much less walk. He was given the Navy Cross, our highest award next to the Medal of Honor. After he recovered from his leg wounds, it was confirmed that he could no longer perform the full duties of an active marine. He was discharged with honors. I remember stories of his prodigious strength. He's a big guy. His nickname is Bull."

Mike says, "I don't think this man could be the shooter, but I'd like to meet him and thank him for this service if nothing else."

Jenny and Steve agree, so they jump into Steve's patrol car and head out in search of Bull. They have his scheduled stops. It's midafternoon when they see his truck just pulling into a pickup station. Steve stops in front of the truck—must be instinct—and they get out. Trammel turns to see them and has a quizzical look on his face. Steve starts. "Good afternoon, Mr. Trammel. How's it going?"

Trammel nods and answers, "Never better. What can I do for you?"

"We've heard about your service in Vietnam and wanted to shake the hand of a true hero."

Trammel replies, "Thanks, but that's past history."

Mike offers his hand and pulls it back, checking for broken fingers. Jenny shakes his hand, and he is gentle with her.

"Mr. Trammel, do you mind if we ask you a few questions about the shootings that have taken place here the past couple months? You get around the base and may have seen something."

"No problem."

"According to your company's records, you were on base the day of every incident. Do you recall anything, anything at all, that might shed some light on this? Did you see or hear anything that might help?"

"I don't remember anything out of the ordinary, if that's what you mean. There's always lots of noise of planes taking off and landing. Sometimes I can't even hear myself think. It reminds me of Nam."

Pointing to the truck, Jenny asks, "These things have always fascinated me, so big and powerful. Would you mind if I got in the cab to see what it's like?"

"I don't mind, but it's against company policy for anyone to get into the truck except the driver. We don't want anyone to get hurt."

Steve speaks up. "We'll take responsibility for anything Lieutenant Hendry might do. Go ahead, Lieutenant; have a look."

Trammel starts to protest but sees it's useless. He's continually shifting his weight back and forth from one leg to another with a small grimace.

Mike asks him, "I heard that you received serious wounds in your legs in Nam. Do they still bother you?"

"Not much. I can still do a job, even though the marines didn't think so."

"Did they discharge you for being unfit for duty?"

"Yes, that was their so-called reason, and it's ridiculous. I can do anything any man can do and do it better and faster except for running. I can bench-press a locomotive. Did the record show that I was the best marksman the marines ever had? I blew the top of the chart off with every hand gun, rifle, and machine gun." At this he checks himself; he realizes it wasn't a good thing to mention.

To make him think Mike missed the implication and can understand his resentment, he asks, "Was the discharge all because you can't run?"

"I can run a little—not enough for combat."

"That doesn't seem to me to make you unfit for duty."

"You're damned right, sir."

Jenny calls down from the cab, "Mr. Trammel, what is this tripod behind the seat for?"

He hesitates for just a second and then replies, "I'm a photography bug. I keep it handy in case I see something I want to shoot—I mean photograph. Little slip of the tongue," he says and laughs.

Steve and Mike laugh with him. "Yes, not a good word to use around here these days."

Jenny calls down, "I love photography too. Where is your camera?"

"I forgot it this morning."

"What do you have?"

"Ah, a Leica."

"Is it an SLR?"

"A what?"

"Single-lens reflex."

"Oh, yes. It only has one lens."

A few minutes later, Jenny has gotten out of the truck and come over to Mike. She looks at him and hesitates until Steve takes Trammel around the truck asking about the lift mechanism. "Sir," she says softly, "he doesn't know what a SLR is. He's no photography fan. Everyone knows what a SLR is. There's something wrong here."

"I agree. Let's let him talk. As my Sioux grandmother once told me, 'My son, you will learn more if you close your mouth and open your ears.' He's quite nervous—and he's angry with the navy for ruling him unfit for duty. He might get excited and blurt out something we can go on. Take my handkerchief, and wipe down the tripod and both windowsills. We might find gunpowder residue."

She looks a little hurt but doesn't say anything as she steps back up into the cab.

Shortly, Trammel and Prince come around to the front of the truck. After the wipe down, Jenny talks to Trammel about photography. Steve and Mike go back around the truck to talk out of earshot. "Steve, we've got a circumstantial case, at least. Do you want to detain him like we did with Torres?"

"Definitely. I'll have the office call the company and tell them we're holding him. They can send someone to pick up the truck and continue the route. I'll tell him we want to take him in for questioning. I don't think he'll fight it. If he does, it'll make him look guilty."

At first Trammel is angry. "What's this? I'm just here doing my job. Why do you want to hassle me? What are you going to do with my truck?"

Prince and Trammell face each other like two bulls who are about to butt heads. But being a marine—once a marine, always a marine—he knows about authority and taking orders. So Trammel pulls the truck out of the way and shuts the motor off. Then he gets into Prince's car in the backseat with Mike.

Of course, the company sends the same lawyer again. "What wild goose chase are you people on this time? Just because we collect your trash doesn't mean our people are felons."

During the questioning, Trammel is composed although clearly angry under the surface. He admits he has guns and regularly goes to a shooting range. He denies that his guns match the shooter's weapon. Mike tries to catch him by asking how he knows that when he doesn't know what kind of gun fired the bullets found in the victims. He's not stupid because he replies, "It doesn't matter what type of gun fired the bullets. It wasn't one of mine."

The questions go on for the next hour with no progress. Prince asks Trammel if they can do a search of his apartment. He agrees. They call JAG to enlist someone to accompany them, but it's now after six o'clock, and there is only a recording. So, in the company of this lawyer, they drive to his place in Chula Vista about twenty minutes south. He lives in a one-bedroom apartment alone. There is no sign of a girlfriend or wife but plenty of evidence that Trammel likes guns. He has magazines and photos and a framed copy of his membership in the National Rifle Association. There are also many photographs of kids' football and basketball teams posing with him. A framed thank-you from the Chula Vista Boys Club hangs in his bedroom. Two hours of turning things over, and they find nothing that links him to the shooting.

Finally, his lawyer says, "Mr. Trammel has cooperated fully, and this meeting is concluded. I'll take responsibility for Mr. Trammel if you release him to me. I'll drive him back to the company to get his car." Prince agrees, and they leave. On the way back to the base, Prince, Mike, and Jenny go over what they have beyond circumstantial evidence. The answer is not much. Still, they believe there is sufficient information to involve someone from JAG.

Late the next morning, they're in Prince's office when a lieutenant from JAG arrives. His name is Lambert. He's a feisty little guy who introduces himself with, "Criminal law is my specialty. If this fellow is anywhere near the crime, I'll nail him."

Mike explains to this modest chap what has happened to date.

He goes off. "Why didn't you involve me before you went to his apartment? You could have contaminated the scene."

"We called JAG yesterday, and no one answered. We know very well what we're doing."

"That's impossible that no one answered. We're open twenty-four-seven just for things like this."

Prince jumps on him and tells him to check for messages because they left one that no one answered. Seeing that he's lost this round, Lambert shifts quickly to the main topic. The group goes through everything from the minute they met Trammel at the truck until his lawyer insisted the meeting was over. After repeated probes, Lambert finally accepts reluctantly that all they have is a thin circumstantial case. Nevertheless, he thinks they should arrest and prosecute. They contact Trammell's lawyer and ask for him and Trammel to come back for a conference. Mike and Prince strongly believe that they have found the shooter. Jenny concurs that her intuition is that he's the man. Still, the case is very weak.

When Trammel and the attorney arrive, Mike goes right to the point, describing all the circumstantial evidence and asking Trammel how the shootings could have happened in his opinion. Despite his lawyer's objections, he describes the hypothetical example. "It's a relatively easy thing to do for a person who knows how to handle guns. It's probably a case of someone on the base being the shooter. Here's the best way to do it. It's just like being a sharpshooter in war. Pick a time and a place, and wait for a victim to appear. Have a stable firing platform."

Jenny interjects, "Like a tripod?"

He pauses. "A tripod could be used. So could any other stable base. If you're shooting a long distance, stability is obviously critical. You also have to have a plan and a reason. You can't just go around firing like a madman. After that it's only a matter of waiting in a place where you can't be seen."

Then Mike asks, "Like a truck?"

"The problem with a truck is its vibrating. You'd have to shut off the motor before attempting a shot. Then, you have to restart it, which could attract attention. That's all there is to it. It's not something that a lot of people couldn't do, especially here where there are thousands of professionals who know how to handle a weapon."

"But how do you explain the gunpowder residue in the truck and on the tripod?"

"I use the tripod sometimes at the shooting range. As for the truck, it's like I said, five people drive that truck. Also, maintenance personnel are in it for test drives, and the residue could have landed there any day, anytime, anywhere."

"But you drove it the day of each shooting."

"That doesn't mean that the shot came from the truck on that day."

For the moment there is silence. Then his lawyer speaks up. "Commander, this is getting redundant and tiring. I think we both realize that there is no way you could convict Mr. Trammel of shooting one, much less three or four, people. All you know is that like hundreds of other people, he was on base on the days of the incidents. There is gunpowder residue in a truck that is driven by all the drivers at the company, and it could have happened at any time over the two months since these incidents occurred. You have no weapon. It seems to me that you have three choices. One, you give up and leave it as an unsolved crime. Two, you continue your investigation of other suspects without bothering my client again. Or three, you offer some way to resolve this in a way that is satisfactory to Mr. Trammel."

Prince strikes back. "We could shadow Mr. Trammel and make his life miserable with further investigation. His attitude toward the Marine Corps is well known. Some people would even empathize with his taking revenge, and that would stigmatize him for life. We can talk to people in Chula Vista about his activity there, and you know how that raises suspicion, even when someone is totally innocent. How do those choices strike you?"

"Yes, you could be total assholes—excuse me, ma'am—harassing a Navy Cross hero and a respected and involved member of his community. But I don't think the navy needs any more negative publicity, do you? Can you visualize people at the gate of the base with protest signs and press coverage? Come on. Be reasonable. Make us a proposal that we can consider."

Prince, Lambert, Jenny, and Mike have prepared for just this scenario and have formulated a deal. As the lead officer in this investigation, Mike states that if Trammel admits to one charge of simple assault, he'll recommend clemency, recognizing prior service; probation in consideration of his wounds; community service; and psychiatric help. It would be up to the judge to set the limits.

The big man jumps to his feet and explodes. "You bastards don't have anything on me, and you know it. But now you want to mark me as a felon for the rest of my life. First the marines screwed me over and now you want to do this to me. I fought in Nam for this country, gave my legs for this country and now you want to make a criminal out of me. You can go fuck yourselves. Excuse me mam."

Mike counters, "Trammell, you know damned well you did it and we've got a strong circumstantial case, strong enough to get you convicted. If we look hard enough and talk to enough people in town and at work, we're bound to find someone who remembers something you said that will incriminate you. Even if you just got drunk and were spouting off, it will sound bad for you. Besides, do you want to spend the next year with this hanging over your head and going to court? Isn't it better to take a small punishment for what you know you did? When we link you to one shooting it will be easy to put the other shootings on you too. Then, you'll go away for a long time."

Trammel looks at his attorney. He's sweating profusely. The attorney says, "We need to talk." They go into the next room to discuss the offer. It's fifteen minutes of yelling that can be heard through the walls. When they come back, Trammel grudgingly agrees that they've reached a solution, but he still doesn't like it. Mike thinks, this will save the navy bad publicity and is fair to Trammel. The deal is done and Trammel is released to his attorney. The marine is an honorable man whose anger took him over the edge. With some counseling and maybe a short sentence hopefully he will be able to get on with his life. By the time Mike and Jenny get back to the BOQ, it's too late for dinner. They stop in the O Club for a drink and a couple of sandwiches and then call it a day. They've solved the problem, but neither of them feels good about Trammel.

Mike thinks to himself, "Actually, I'm greatly relieved. I wasn't prepared for this job. Yet, through luck and help from Prince and Jenny, we pulled it off. I did get a kick out of the chase though.

After Mike and Jenny make their final report to McMurray and to McKay, that officially wraps their assignment. They clean out their office and decide to go to a celebratory dinner. Mike tells Jenny that he's heard of nice place in La Jolla right on the beach. He says, "In fact, it's so close to the water that at high tide, the spray hits the windows." He makes a reservation for 1900. Out of courtesy and gratitude, they invite Prince to come along, but he says he wants to get back to his family, something they can appreciate.

Once we're at their table by the window, he asks Jenny, "What would you like to do next? Would you like to go to NIS?"

"That would be good, but I think I'd prefer DIS. I'm a lawyer, and that would be more interesting than working in JAG, I think. From what I can see, DIS would be largely field investigative work, which I like a whole lot better than writing briefs."

"For what it's worth, I'll make a recommendation to that effect."

"Well, what about you? Where do you expect they will send you?"

"My guess is WestPac. Something unexpected always seems to come out of the blue. I can't plan from one assignment to the next."

The following day they each have envelopes delivered detailing their next duty stations.. Jenny is ordered to DC to await the next DIS class. The good news for Mike is that he's ordered to report to the CINCPAC Intell section at Pearl. Immediately, he fires off a letter to Grace.

June 1, 1968
Dear C.J.
    The job is done, mission completed. We found the shooter and no one got shot in the process. This being my first criminal case, it was potentially dangerous since we didn't know the mentality of

the shooter. I was admittedly nervous going in. I was in over my head with no prior experience to go on. But in the end it worked out and I learned a lot. Now I'm confident that I can handle any unexpected situation.

The good news is that I'll truly be coming back to Pearl. No more surprise last minute changes. I'm really looking forward to seeing you and learning where, if anywhere, we go from here.
Sincerely,
Sherlock

Chapter 5

Good and Bad News

June 1968
Honolulu

Midmorning of 8 June, Mike lands on Oahu. The magical flowery scent of the islands overwhelms even the smell of jet fuel at the airport. It's so good to be back in Paradise. The best part, of course, is that he'll be able to see Grace again. It's been almost nine months. In an hour, he's through the airport, past the flower stands along the roadside, and into the Pearl Harbor BOQ. At the desk, he asks if any mail has been forwarded. There is a copy of the *Stars and Stripes*, some Pearl Harbor base activities notices, and one envelope. He can see it's from Grace. As soon as he gets into room, he drops his B-4 bag and tears open the letter.

May 25, 1968

Dear Sherlock,

Jerry is back from WestPac. We're having a difficult time. He's become exceedingly focused on partying. He stays sober enough to fly, but his attitude is anything but great. I don't know what he wants from me. I don't think he has sensed anything about my feelings for him since you've come into my life. We not as touchy feely as we were when we were first married, but that is nothing new. He likes to flirt with all the women, but I don't think he goes any further.

He's just so committed to flying and partying that I doubt he has time for any other women. Maybe I'm the fool, but I'm not going to take this forever.

Obviously, Grace hadn't received Mike's letter when she wrote to him. He wonders if his letter has arrived at her mother's house yet. Does she know he is in town? This isn't the reception he was imagining or hoping for. He'll just have to call Mrs. Liu to let her know he is in town. She probably won't be happy to hear that either. What a dilemma.

Mike's orders are to report to HQ, CINCPAC at 1000 for assignment. When he checks in later that morning, he learns that he will be assigned to the intelligence function reporting to Captain Knowles. Intelligence is divided into strategic, operational, and tactical. If he gets strategic, he'll probably stay at HQ in Pearl. The intelligence mission is to provide CINCPAC with information needed to plan and carry out both defensive and offensive operations across the Asia Pacific Theater. As America becomes increasingly involved in Vietnam, there is pressure put on the intell function to ensure that US forces are properly positioned and equipped for their mission there.

At 0945 Mike reports to Captain Knowles's office. The receptionist gives him a packet and tells him to read it quickly and then report to Commander Minton at 1130, two doors down; he'll be Mike's new boss.

Mike crams the material and knocks on Minton's door at 1125. The receptionist tells him to sit down. Minton will see him in a few minutes. Promptly at 1130, he's ushered in. He stands at attention in front of the desk. "Lieutenant Holmes reporting as ordered, sir."

Minton is a rangy build, probably well over six feet. He has an easygoing, cowboy style that sometimes that sometimes creeps out from under the disciplined demeanor of a senior officer. He looks up, smiles and says, "At ease, Holmes. I'm glad you're finally here; we need you on station ASAP."

Whoa. Mike wonders what "on station" means in this case.

"It's no secret that the Tet Offensive last January caught us by surprise. A lot of people died because we didn't see it coming. Obviously, we need to increase the intell presence there. You'll leave tomorrow and report to the intell officer on the USS *Ranger*, CV-61, off the east coast of Nam. My yeoman has your orders. You'd better get going. If you have anything to take care of here, get to it. Good luck."

The yeoman in the front office hands Mike another envelope with his travel orders. She volunteers, "Lieutenant Holmes, You're expected in the Nam office ASAP for a briefing today. Then, tomorrow you've got a seat on the plane out of Hickam to Manila departing at 0700. There you will transfer to a plane to Tan San Nhut. In Nam, Repo Depo will get you transport to the *Ranger*."

Just like that, he's in and out. Mike goes back to his room and sits on his bed for a few minutes to catch up on what just happened. Then, he picks up Grace's letter and looks at Mrs. Liu's phone number. Lifting the receiver, he dials. Grace answers the phone. With a lump in his throat, barely able to speak, he says, "Good morning; it's Sherlock."

"Oh, Michael, it's so good to hear your voice. Your letter just came yesterday. Nine months is a very long time when you miss someone. Did you get my letter? I'm sorry that I laid my problem on you. Do you remember what I look like? I'm the short, red-haired Irish girl. How are you? I need to see you."

"Up to ten seconds ago, I was tired. Now I feel great. It's Kathleen, isn't it?"

"Yes, yes. That's me. Kathleen O'Reilly Dong. Tell me what's happening with you. Are you being assigned to CINCPAC HQ?"

"The bad news is that I'm in briefings today. I leave tomorrow for Vietnam. I'm assigned to a ship off the coast of Vietnam."

"Oh, no. Don't you dare tell me I won't get to see you? How about tonight? Can you come to my mother's house? We'll fix a great Chinese meal for you."

"Yes. Of course, madam. I shan't miss the opportunity to visit you again. I trust that you have not aged significantly over the course of the past year. I shall go to the taxi rank and engage a vehicle. I have the address. Would the six o'clock hour be satisfactory?"

"Well, Mr. Smartass Holmes, we'll see who has aged and who is still gorgeous. Just get your butt over here. And be on time. I've got a hug for you that will pop your eyes out."

By 1800 he's walking up the steps to Mrs. Liu's house in Nuuanu Valley. No sooner does he put a foot on the porch than Grace bursts through the door and jumps into his arms. The hug is so tight that they nearly smother each other. Ignoring that a neighbor might be looking, she relaxes her grip and gives him a deep, soft, warm kiss, which he returns with feeling. They step back, still holding hands, and look at each other. She's beautifully dressed. He's only seen her in a muumuu and beachwear. Now she's has pearl earrings, a pearl necklace, deep-blue silk top with a Chinese flower motif, beautifully fitted white capri pants, and white-silk flats. It's a picture he'll never forget.

"Well, Mr. Smartass, how do I look?"

"Even better than I remember," he says reluctant to let her go.

"Come inside and meet my mother. She doesn't believe that you are as good as I've described you. Also, she isn't keen about this relationship. But since I feel so strongly about you, she is going along with it, hoping that somehow I don't get hurt."

They walk hand in hand through the living and dining room. Mrs. Liu comes out of the kitchen, wiping her hands on a dish towel. She's bigger than he imagined she'd be; maybe five foot five. But she's a bit stooped and pale. Her hand shakes when she reaches out to touch his. He says in Chinese that he's very happy to meet her.

She looks at him with a small, polite grimace that shows she's not that happy meeting him. Speaking to Grace in Chinese, she says, "At least he's handsome, but is he kind? He looks like a Mongolian."

Grace says, "He speaks Mandarin, Mother."

The lady looks at Mike and blushes. Then she welcomes him in Chinese and tells them to have a seat in the living room while she finishes making dinner.

Grace and Mike take a seat on the sofa in the living room. They hold hands and grin like a couple of teenagers. "Tell me all about your time at NIS, and what is this defense service thing? Are you switching careers?"

"No, DIS is a study of criminology, but it's simply an added capability. I'm still a line officer, and naval intelligence is my designator. DIS is just another school like Nuclear Weapons Defense, Radio Technology, or some other course.

"NIS was very interesting. Now I know how to pick locks, interrogate prisoners, cultivate assets—that's people I'm trying to recruit to spy for us—or build a library of intelligence that will probably never be used. There was also a special section on how to avoid being seduced by beautiful enemy agents. I flunked that."

"Well, see if you can flunk this, sailor boy," she says wrapping her arms around him and kissing him sweetly.

"I think I need a remedial class. Could you give me that again?"

She does.

"Now I think I've got it." The warmth pours through his body. "My god," he thinks, "how I miss this." He says, "So what have you been doing while I was away keeping the world safe for democracy?"

"Unfortunately, nothing too interesting. But I feel that I'm wasting my life and my education just being a housewife. Besides the problem I told you about in my letter, I'm keeping busy volunteering at the cultural center. I really enjoy it, but I would like to do something more, you know, be something more. I'm thinking of going back to school and finishing my M.A.

I'm here helping Mom. She's not well, and I'm very worried about her. As I mentioned in the letter Jerry is back and doing his two favorite things: flying and partying. Mom has never liked his lighthearted attitude. He doesn't take anything seriously, including our marriage."

Mrs. Liu comes in and tells them to come to dinner. In the dining room, the table is covered with a fine linen cloth, heavily embroidered in Asian motifs and supporting an array of exquisite chinaware. This probably came with them from China. He's never seen such beautiful place settings, plates, bowls, and platters. The knives, forks, and serving utensils are gold plated. Even the glassware is highly decorated with Chinese symbols. To top it off there is a set of engraved porcelain chopsticks by each plate.

Mike pulls her chair out and helps her be seated. Grace looks at him and smiles. "Mrs. Liu," he starts in Mandarin, "I've never seen anything so beautiful, including your lovely daughter, who is a tribute to you. You must tell me about your table. What do all the embroidered figures mean? Is there a story?"

The old lady looks up at him, and for the first time, he feels she doesn't resent him. Then, she proceeds to relate the tale of the tablecloth. The cloth pictures an ancient Chinese myth about a family of great wealth and honor. It shows the parents, grandparents, and children. It's covered with buildings, trees, flowers, birds, and several small mammals, like cats and rabbits. She goes on in great length, clearly enjoying teaching him some of the fine points of her culture. After about ten minutes, Grace interrupts to note that the food is getting cold. Mr. Liu stops and, with a big, energetic smile, begins to pass the plates and bowls. Now she's relaxed and happy.

The food is not the typical Chinese most American restaurants serve. The textures and flavors are exquisite. Dinner finishes with delicious small cookies and sweet tea. It's been going on for almost two hours before he sees Mrs. Liu beginning to slow down and look tired. At that point, he says, "Madam Liu, your table is exquisite, and the flavors of the food are something that I've never had the pleasure to taste before. This has been an extraordinary experience for me. I am so profoundly happy to have learned so much about your homeland. These are the things they didn't teach me in Chinese class. When I come back from WestPac, I hope you will invite me again."

She nods, and he can see that she appreciates his interest. She says in Mandarin that she is happy he enjoyed it and will be welcome to come back any time. At this point she gives a small glance to Grace. As she struggles to push her chair back, Mike gets up and helps her stand. He gives her a little hug. She looks at Grace and whispers nearly inaudibly, "He is a nice man— better than the other. I'm tired and need to go to bed."

Grace gives her a very warm thank-you hug and says to her, "We'll clean up, Mother."

Turning to Mike, the tired old lady nods and heads out of the room.

Once she's gone, Grace steps into his arms. With a sigh of relief, she says, "It was very good of you to talk about the table and the food. Jerry never says anything except thank you. You've won her over."

Slowly they work together on the dishes until everything is clean and put away. Grace looks at him, and her eyes begin to tear. It's nearly ten o'clock, and both of them have to leave. Grace stops for a minute at her mom's room to check on her. She comes back with a nod. Without a word they pick up their things and head out to her car.

The drive back to Pearl is silent. Mike holds her free hand. They're both too emotional to talk much. When they pull up to the BOQ, she stops the motor. Turning to him and taking both his hands, she asks, "When do you think you'll be back?"

"It's hard to tell. The *Ranger* has been on station for over a year. In another few months, it might be due for repairs and upgrades. I hope that will bring her back to Pearl, but it could be done in the Philippines at Subic Bay. We'll just have to wait and see. As soon as I know, you'll know. We can write. You just address it to me care of the APO. I'm really going to miss you. Tonight was bittersweet. It was a picture of what I hope our life could be. We just have to keep the faith and see what fate has in store for us."

I hope so. I don't know how much longer I can stay in this situation. Mom insists that my duty is here. But my heart is with you. I'm being torn apart.

Chapter 6

Shipping Out

June 1968
Aboard the *Ranger*

The *Ranger* is a Forrestal class ship. The Forrestal class is the first super carriers in the navy. They're called that because of their extraordinarily high tonnage, full integration of the angled deck, and extremely strong air wing, capable of handling eighty to a hundred aircraft. The Forrestals have a stable and comfortable aircraft platform even in very rough weather.

At Tan Son Nhut, Mike has to wait a couple of days before getting a ride on an SNB mail plane to the *Ranger*. After checking in with the Officer of the Deck he reports to Lieutenant Commander Cedric Johnson, CO of the intelligence function. It's a small unit. In addition to Johnson, they have two noncom translators, who speak Vietnamese and Chinese. Mike's the only one on board who has been through Intell school. Johnson is a nervous man who's misassigned. How he got this job, only the navy knows. He realizes he's in over his head. He's constantly changing orders, so they don't know what to expect minute to minute. He jumps at the least movement. When Captain Skovill, commanding officer of the ship, wants to talk to Johnson or Mike, Johnson almost pees in his skivvies. About once a week, he orders his staff to go through a field day drill. Instead of monitoring radio communications between VCs and Chinese, they are devoting precious time to housekeeping.

Johnson doesn't like Mike because he's better trained and better suited for this mission. Whenever possible, he overrides Mike's recommendations or takes them to the XO, indicating that he had provided guidance and oversight to the report. In truth, he only knows what Mike chooses to let him know. Conversely, Mike has a career to think of, so he has to do what he can to make his tour successful. The two NCOs see that Mike's a buffer between them and Johnson and wholeheartedly support him. Whenever he has time, Mike studies Vietnamese with the NCO interpreter. He won't be fluent, but it may come in handy while he's still in this area.

Mike's letters to Grace are quite simple. He can't say anything about what they're doing here. Basically, they provide air support for the troops in the field. They also conduct bombing missions to soften targets for them.

After two months, Mike receives Grace's first letter. She tells him that Jerry has been transferred to Moffett Field on the San Francisco peninsula. Also, she tells him her mother's health is failing. No other words about Jerry except that she periodically has to go back to Moffett for a while to be with him. She notes, "I'm not sure that he really misses me. He's the life of the party and loves flirting with anything in a skirt. A girl has to have a strong self-image to put up with this."

The first six months aboard the *Ranger* are devoted to picking up intelligence from radio intercepts, overflights, damage photography, and reports from men in the field. Michael had read that the reason for the increased intell action is that on 30 January 1968, the Viet Cong, a South Vietnamese guerilla force, and the North Vietnamese Army launched an attack with eighty thousand troops striking more than one hundred towns and cities, South Vietnam. The initial attacks stun the country. Quickly American and ARVN (Army of the Republic of Vietnam) troops regrouped, and inflicted massive casualties on VC/NVA forces. But the offensive had a profound effect on the United States and South Vietnam. This was a massive failure on the part of the intell community that cannot happen again.

Mike can see they're wasting their time and adding little value here. He informs Johnson that the two interpreters and Mike will monitor VC/NVA radios 24/7. There are teams, often led by warrant officers with the appropriate ethnic backgrounds, who go behind enemy lines and bring out pieces of electronic equipment to be analyzed in one of the labs in Hawaii or Washington, DC. Through these means, the US military learns what radio frequencies their crystals were set for so they can be monitored.

Johnson is uncertain about this arrangement. He really doesn't understand this game. Mike feels a bit sorry for him, being placed in a position he wasn't trained for. Their mission description is so broad that they could do almost anything. Johnson is afraid to tip his hand by asking the CO what his needs or expectations are. Johnson is further concerned when Mike tells him he'll take the midnight to 0800 watch because, knowing the Chinese habits, that's the time during which they are most likely to pass critical information. Johnson likes to spend hours talking to Mike and "briefing him" on what intelligence is all about. This is his way to pick Mike's brain. He asks what Mike thinks about something and then agrees with him, adding some superfluous point or useless opinion. The midnight shift gives Mike an excuse not to have to deal with him until Mike awakes after noon.

Throughout CINCPAC, there is great concern that the Communists will try another attack around the Tet anniversary since the first one had been so successful. In January 1969, the unit is on full alert 24/7 to make sure they don't miss anything. The Vietnamese surprise them by not attacking on Tet but waiting until it's passed and the US forces have presumably relaxed. Four nights later, on 2 February, about 0200, Mike's monitoring several frequencies switching back and forth as the light board picks up any signals. When one lights up, he tunes it in and hears an animated conversation just starting. He knows it is only beginning because they're using standard greetings. It's between a Chinese man and a Viet-speaking Chinese man.

Mike rouses his Vietnamese-speaking NCO who would have the 0800 to 1600 shift. Mike doesn't know how long this will last, but it sounds very intense, and they may resort to Vietnamese at any time. Although the NCO has been teaching Mike Vietnamese, Mike is certainly not fluent enough for this. The NCO stumbles in five minutes later and puts on his headphones. Mike tells him, "If they start speaking Vietnamese, it will be up to you to tape record and translate."

Turning back to the Chinese conversation, it's clear that this is an important issue. The speakers switch back and forth between conversational and military jargon. In time it starts to make sense. They are discussing a plan to move an unusually large component of munitions and troops into Vietnam from China to support the NVA. There is a long border between the two countries, and the shipment can come across anywhere. Movement will be tomorrow night starting at midnight, twenty-two hours from now. The unanswered central question is, where will it take place?

They've obviously spent a long time planning the transfer, so they don't have to talk about the route. Just as clearly, they have staged the munitions inside the Chinese border and are making preparations on the VC side. They don't want to take chances that it will be discovered. With the US and the South Vietnamese flying recon constantly, the danger of discovery is substantial. Then, Mike and the NCO work up a detailed report of what they heard. At 0700 Mike leaves the watch to the NCO and wakes up Johnson. "Sir, this is a transcription that we intercepted early this morning. I believe it is very important and needs to go topside ASAP."

Johnson can hardly believe what Mike hands him. He seems frightened by the gravity of the intelligence that he holds in his hand. It's a career-determining moment. Mike tries to not only reassure him of its truth and gravity but urges him to take it immediately to the XO.

He says, "I'll look this over. If it's warranted, I'll take it topside. In the meantime, you get some sleep."

Johnson doesn't have a clue about the implications of what Mike's shown him. Mike knows his game. He'll take the report to the executive officer, possibly with some inconsequential changes he'll throw in. But Mike also knows Johnson can't answer any questions that the CO or XO might have, and they're sure to have a lot of them. Clearly, this information needs to be acted on immediately. There are only sixteen hours before the munitions and troops start to cross the border. If they make it uncontested, many South Vietnamese and American troops will suffer. The Vietnam-China border is several hundred miles long. The report gives a list of possible transfer coordinates as best it could without any local knowledge support. So, not having any choice, Mike takes Johnson's order and goes to his room. He lies on the bunk fully clothed. Mike knows that once the captain sees the report and discovers that Johnson is unclear about the details, he will be called to his quarters near the bridge.

Sure enough, at 0830, Johnson gets up his nerve to deliver the report. Shortly thereafter, Mike's summoned to the Combat Information Center (CIC). When he arrives, Johnson starts to explain how they put the report together, but Captain Skovill cuts him off and focuses his steel-blue eyes on Mike. His questions are pointed and rapid. "Are you the one who personally heard the conversation? How clear was the transmission? Are you certain of the details? Specifically, where do you believe the move will take place? The most critical questions are, when and where? It must be precise."

Mike has a good answer for each, one including the time, but admittedly has some uncertainty about the place. Here they need someone with local ground knowledge of the border area. Something this heavy will have to have a significant well-paved road to travel. There are a couple of possibilities. The captain turns to his XO and tells him to find someone, somehow, who Mike can talk with to pinpoint the move. Then he asks both Johnson and Mike what they recommend. Out of courtesy to rank, Mike lets Johnson go first. He has no ideas and mumbles some vague generalities, so the captain turns to Mike to go over the key points in the report that indicated the possible transfer points. After some hard grilling, he dismisses them and tells Mike that as soon as they find the person with local knowledge, he wants to see him back in CIC. He doesn't say anything to Johnson.

Johnson and Mike leave, and as soon as they're out of sight and hearing, Johnson starts to chew out Mike for insubordination. "I ought to have you keelhauled. You made me look like a fool in there."

Mike has to take it because no matter what Johnson says, Mike's already won the day.

"Return to your quarters and stay there until I summon you."

Once again, Mike lies down on his bunk still fully clothed. He's in the middle between being exhausted and wanting to know what the captain will do with the intell. Within an hour, the level of activity on the ship picks up. It's humming, almost throbbing. You can just feel the intensity, energy, and urgency rolling throughout the ship. The Ranger It is several hundred miles south of the latitude of the shipment. The ship shudders and leans to port as the captain turns the great ship around and starts steaming north at flank speed. By now it is coming up on 1300. Communications are streaming out to the strategic commander of the South Vietnamese command in Saigon. This will lead to a squadron of fighter bombers preparing to strike the point Mike claims is the target. If he's proven to be wrong, the United States will have spent millions on a false alarm, and Mike's career will be over. Johnson knows that his will be also. He's in his room probably in a catatonic state or else bouncing off the walls like a handball.

About 1500 Mike's called by the XO to report to CIC. When he arrives, Johnson is standing at the big planning table making more unfounded suggestions. The XO says he has a local expert on a secure frequency ashore ready to discuss the terrain and roads. The XO motions Mike to the table and tells Johnson to step back. Mike goes over the key elements with the local expert. He repeats the magnitude of what is going to cross the border. At the end of the discussion, they decide that the enemy most likely will split the move into two parts for safety and speed. The part with the munitions will take the well-paved eastern highway that can handle the weight because they need to get the arms undercover ASAP. The other part will come down the western road, which is smaller but will be easy for the lighter troop trucks to navigate. Mike and the local man select the two points on the map where they believe the transfer will take place. He passes their decision to the XO. After a long pause, the XO steps back, looks very hard at Mike, and asks, "Are you absolutely positive that this information is accurate, son?"

"Sir, the info is accurate, and the only risk is that it's a set-up. If we have time, we can do a high altitude recon to find evidence of the buildup. However, throughout the discussion I overheard last night, the tone and words being used suggests it's genuine. I feel extremely confident that it's not a ruse."

The XO says that he has run the intell through MAC in Saigon, and the consensus is that it's legit. The only question is where it will happen. "Okay, Lieutenant," he says, "We're committing a large portion of our firepower to this based on your word. You damn well better be right. Dismissed!"

Mike returns to his quarters and lies down once more. This time exhaustion takes over, and he fall asleep. Six hours later he wakes with a start as the ship lurches. They are launching aircraft, probably reconnaissance to look for any evidence of a buildup in the target area to confirm the report. Mike checks with the two men in the intell center. They're very excited and more than a little apprehensive. They understand the magnitude of the operation. They also hear an increase in traffic indicating that something is happening on shore. Mike goes to take a shower and then to the officer's wardroom. He's not eaten for about twenty hours. The ship is buzzing. Preparations are underway for a launch of fighter bombers.

Of course Chinese radar will pick up the planes coming north and east from the carrier. They probably will scramble MIG-21s from the closest VN and Chinese air fields. So long as the planes don't act hostile or get too close to the border, the Chinese most likely will not fire on them. The plan is to let the transfer start unimpeded to ensure that everything is across the border and into Vietnamese territory. This will avoid a provocation with China. Low-level fighters will drop napalm and flares that will light up the place. Then, fighter bombers will saturate the target area with high explosives followed by strafing runs from both types of aircraft. It occurs to Mike that if anything goes wrong, and China retaliates, he might be responsible for starting World War III.

About 0400, the XO calls Mike to CIC. He's there with Captain Skovill, and they're weary but smiling. Everything turned out just as Mike had predicted. They wiped out the shipment. "Well done," says the captain. "This won't hurt your career." Mike shakes hands with them as well as with the ops officer. He also learns that on the way north, a flight of six air force fighters saw several MIG-17s taking off from a previously unknown air strip. It's probably a maintenance base. Three of the fighters peeled off and attacked the MIGs as they begin to climb out. The score was four MIGs bagged and one base damaged without so much as a single bullet hole in our side. Now the air force is happy too.

It's nearly a month later when the *Ranger* heads back to port in South Vietnam for refueling and rearming. The XO calls Mike to his quarters.

Doctor Jac

"Lieutenant, I've received orders for you that on our arriving in port you're to brief the joint command in Saigon. Immediately afterward, you're to fly to Hong Kong and brief our consul general and the British naval command there. Well done."

Chapter 7

Kidnapped

February 1969
Hong Kong

When the ship docks, Mike gathers his gear and disembarks. He catches a ride to the BOQ in Saigon. After reporting to HQ, he's told they'll call him when the briefing is set up. Until then he's on his own to wander the city but not leave it.

Even though it is the dry season in Saigon, February is still hot and muggy. The average winter temperature here is about eighty degrees Fahrenheit. He spends the first day strolling about the city. Frankly, it stinks. Quickly he loses interest in seeing any more. He just wants to get the hell out of there. This is a good time to write to Grace.

February 27, 1969
Dear C. J.,

I've just landed in Saigon. When the Ranger docked, I was told to report to HQ here and brief them on the raid I helped set up while on board ship.

One night I intercepted a radio communication between the Chinese and VNs. To make a long story short, it led to our destroying a major munitions reinforcement from China into northern VN. I shouldn't be telling you this, so <u>don't share it</u>.

> Now I'm here to brief HQ on the raid. Then, I'm going to Hong Kong to brief the US Consul General and the British naval command. As you know, the Brits still control HK, and they like to think the South China Sea is theirs as well.
>
> After I finish that, I'll be assigned a new duty station. I'm hoping they send me back to Pearl. I really miss you. In transit,
> Sherlock
> P. S.
> Give your mom a hug for me. Tell her I can still taste her wonderful dinner.

By the time she gets that letter, Mike thinks he should be finished with Hong Kong and headed for his next assignment. After five days, finally, the high command has time for the briefing. It's a very long two-day ordeal. The political arguing among the services at this level is disheartening. He thought they were all here to win this war together. It's like a basketball team where everyone just grabs the ball and shoots with little playmaking and teamwork.

On 3 March Mike takes off for Hong Kong. The flight takes about two hours. Once aboard the plane, he opens his orders that confirm he's to provide a complete briefing to the Hong Kong consul general. It states that Hong Kong is part of the British Commonwealth, which he already knew. He's also to brief the CO and staff of the Royal Navy on the events leading up to the raid as well as the intelligence they have on the result to date.

The landing in HK is an adventure. Kai Tak airport in the Kowloon peninsula opposite Hong Kong island is one of the scariest airports to land in anywhere in the world. This is especially true if the northeast wind is blowing at forty-five degrees to the final leg flight path. Runway 13 requires some white-knuckle flying. It starts with a steep descent heading northeast over Victoria Harbor and then very low over very densely populated western Kowloon. Just two nautical miles from touchdown, the pilot must make a forty-seven-degree right turn to line up with the runway. With the often low clouds, this is close to impossible since there is no instrument guidance system at this time. Typically the plane will go into the turn at a height of about 650 feet and exit it at a height of 140 feet. "Are you kidding me? One hundred and forty feet is half the length of a football field. We're coming in so low that I can see the figures on the television sets in the tenement living rooms below. The nearest housing can't be more than a couple hundred yards from touchdown. So, this is what they call the Kai Tak Heart Attack?"

After they land and he gets his breath back, Mike heads to the Hong Kong island side and goes directly to the US Consulate on Garden Road. There he'll be assigned quarters and prepare to debrief the consul general and staff. The next morning he's on site early working with the AV staff to set up the graphics. They make a few changes from the ones he employed in the joint-command briefing in Saigon. Mike learns what they want to see and how they want to hear it. The interrogations are long and sometimes confrontational, especially with the economic attaché, who's clearly a CIA agent.

After two days of grilling and discussion, Mike makes an appointment to sing the same song to the Royal Navy command. He finishes that grueling examination in one day. At this time, since the United Kingdom still controls Hong Kong, it likes to think it also controls the waters in that part of the world. The atmosphere clears somewhat as they realize the Americans have no intent of upstaging them. Being essentially good fellows, the Brits invite Mike for drinks at the Royal Navy Fleet Club. There he can practice his Edwardian English and get some pointers.

The next night Mike has off, so he decides to treat himself to dinner at the Mandarin Oriental Hotel on Connaught Road. He's feeling pretty full of himself. How many lieutenants provide the intell to launch a massive strike and then brief the high commands? After dinner he goes for a walk, hoping to locate a tobacco shop that sells good cigars. It's unlikely that he'll find a shop on this main street, since this is the area of high-end stores. In a couple of blocks, he looks down a side street and sees a small tobacco shop wedged in between a sushi restaurant and a brightly lit record store. As he pushes open the door, he leaves the street noise behind and encounters the odor of decades of tobacco and smoke. This would knock a nonsmoker out. But for him it's delicious. The shop walls seem to shine with the oils of the tobacco. In one corner are two easy chairs and a small elephant-base table with an ashtray. There's a yellowish light that illuminates an elderly Chinese man in a smock standing with his hands on the counter facing Mike. His fingers are stained from years of handling and smoking tobacco products. Although Mike speaks Mandarin, this man probably speaks Cantonese. So Mike tries English. Being citizens of a crown colony of the British Commonwealth, all educated people speak English. "Good evening, sir."

He replies in kind and, with a slight bow, asks how he is this beautiful evening. "How may I help you?" he asks.

"I'm looking for a good cigar to celebrate an event."

"Wonderful, sir. Do you have a favorite brand?"

"I'd like Montecristo, if you have it."

"Of course, sir—it's one of the best cigars in the world. They're over here. How many would you like?"

Mike knows enough to ask the price before purchasing. If an American asks about the cost, the shopkeepers don't think you have a lot of money and may state a lower price than if you don't ask.

"What is the price?"

"Fifteen US dollars. Seventy-nine Hong Kong dollars."

"I'll take two."

"Very good, sir. May I show you a recent arrival of a new cigar?"

"Certainly."

"Do you like a mild cigar or a full-bodied one?"

"I prefer mild."

He moves to the right side of the counter and reaches in to pull out a box. "These are a new brand. They are very mild—handmade of course. The maker has given us a very good introductory price. Here. You can smell the mildness. They are from the Philippines. The filler and binder are grown in Tagaytay on the slopes of the old volcano at two thousand feet above sea level and overlooking Lake Taal. They use only long seco fillers for light, smooth, consistent burning. It has a beautiful ash also."

Machine-made cigars take chopped up tobacco leaves, sometimes including stems, and wrap them in paper made from tobacco leaves. Aficionados call these, derisively, "sweepings." Machine-made cigars are cheaper and sometimes burn unevenly or have plugs through which the smoke can't travel.

He continues, "The tobacco farm is not very large, so the production is limited at this time. The wrapper is shade grown in Baguio. Because Baguio is at five thousand feet elevation, the temperature is relatively cool. This makes the wrapper very mild." He hands Mike a cigar. "What do you think of the aroma?"

Mike picks up the cigar. It's a corona about five and a half inches long and two-thirds of an inch in width, the most common size. Thickness is determined by what is called ring gauge. In this case, the cigar is a 42 ring gauge. "It's slightly sweet and very light, with some sense of leather and toast," Mike says.

"Would you like to try one? They are only five US dollars because of the introductory offer. That is thirty-five HKD. You can take it with you or smoke it here." He gestures toward the two easy chairs.

"Yes, it sounds interesting. I'll try it here. If I like it, I'll take a few with me."

The old tobacconist gives Mike the cigar and a box of wooden matches. Mike relaxes into the easy chair, lights up, and begins to enjoy a truly mild but flavorful smoke. The shop is quiet due to the late hour, so the old man lights one and joins Mike. The cigar burns evenly but quickly. Mike tells the old man that he speaks Mandarin. This immediately changes the relationship, although Mike can't understand his Cantonese, and the man speaks only a bit of Mandarin. They chat in English about how business is in Hong Kong, what the influence of the PRC is here, and what he thinks the long term holds for the region. In about thirty minutes, Mike finishes the cigar. There is a lingering aroma of cherry and coffee. There is no heavy aftertaste. Actually, there is a very slight, pleasant sweetness. It might be too light for people who like full-bodied maduros, but it's very good for Mike's taste. He buys three of the Filipinos.

Once he steps back onto the side street, the spring air is refreshing. Suddenly something hits his head very hard from behind. He goes down and then senses that he's being picked up and tossed into something hard. He drifts in and out of consciousness, feeling that he's being roughly handled. The next thing he's aware of is that he's in a dimly lit room, tied to a chair, stripped to his underwear, blindfolded, and surrounded by what sounds like three or four Chinese men and, he thinks, one woman. There is a strong odor that he recognizes but can't put a finger on. The room is very stuffy, and the odor almost makes him vomit. He can't tell exactly how many people there are because of the blindfold. Someone grabs his hair and starts asking questions about US strategy, plans, and arms level in Vietnam. The bastard is smoking one of Mike's cigars and blowing smoke in his face. He is too stupid to pick the Montecristo. He's puffing on the Filipino.

"You picked the wrong man to kidnap. I'm just a lieutenant. They don't share plans with me. I just do as I'm ordered."

A stinging slap in the face almost knocks Mike off the chair. There is something about a slap that makes him very angry. It's a personal insult. "You coward, you wouldn't have the courage to do that if I wasn't tied down."

Then he does it again harder, and Mike's on the floor. "You tell us, Lieutenan, or we make you very hurt," he says as they set his chair and him back up.

Mike repeats, "I don't have that type of information, and if I did, I sure wouldn't tell you. So fuck off."

Once more, he's treated to two slaps, one on the right followed quickly by one on the left side of his face. He can taste blood where his teeth have cut his cheek. This goes on for he guesses a half hour: them screaming at him, threatening him, and him repeating only name, rank, and serial number. Despite his resistance, inside he's scared. These idiots could really hurt him or even kill him, but he figures the best defense is a strong offense and tells them to shove it. In the background, he hears a man repeatedly cursing at him with what must be his favorite expression: *"Ngo dill kau kui, ngo dill kui lo mo."* It is an expression regarding one's mother that is too filthy to render in English.

Then, things quiet down for a few minutes as they huddle and discuss what to do now. Clearly, they are amateurs. In one way that is worse than if they were professionals. These idiots may run out of options soon, panic and just decide to dump him in the Harbor.

The next move is the woman. She uses a cool, wet cloth to wipe Mike's face. She says, "We sorry we hurt you, Lieutenan', but we need to know these things, you unnerstan'? If you just answer questions, we take you back, and you no more get hurt."

He smiles to himself. Does she really think this is going to work? He responds with name, rank, and seri…when he's interrupted by two hard blows with something heavy that feels like a cricket bat on each of his knee caps. The pain shoots up his legs into his groin and stomach. Their question is repeated, and so is his gasping answer. Then, he's dumped forward out of the chair and makes a three-point landing on his knees and nose. His bladder opens from the shock, and he urinates. Someone once told him that the knees are a very sensitive part of the body. They're right. He passes out from the pain. He doesn't know how long they leave him on the floor. When he comes to, they yank him back into the chair and threaten to kill him if he doesn't talk. His mumbled answers don't change. Someone is alternatively punching him in the stomach and banging on his sore legs. By now, he's so sore all over that he hardly responds. Fortunately, they soon tire of that. There is another break as they yell at each other. There is no progress. It's evident that they're not professionals at interrogation, thank god. If they were, they could make it much more painful. They're very frustrated and seemingly tired of this game. They break off the grilling and gag him so that he can't make any sounds. For a while he doesn't hear anything, so he guesses they're on a break. He's still tied to the chair, blindfolded, and sitting in his urine. Although he's exhausted, the pain won't let him sleep.

Mike's in a twilight zone. Periodically, he fades in and out. When he comes to again, there's still no one in the room. He has no sense of time passing. The blindfold doesn't let him see even a sliver of light. It seems like time is suspended. The ropes are very tight. He can't work them loose. After what seems like forever, the faint sounds from the street die away. It must be very late.

Eventually, they return. He hears them talking about food, so he guesses it's morning. The process starts again. Their breath is foul. He tries to show no reaction to their blows. Finally, someone loses his patience. When Mike doesn't reply to his questions, Mike is punched in the mouth. He feels his jawbone break, and blood pours out of his mouth. Then, someone yells in Chinese, "You fool; now he can't talk."

Just as he expected, it's panic time. This is the most dangerous stage. Not many choices. They have to get rid of him in a way that can't be traced back to them. After much heated arguing and yelling back and forth, Mike thinks he hears them deciding to move him, but they don't want to do it in daylight. They leave him to sit through the day, still bound and leaking urine. There's no sense in putting the gag back on. He couldn't yell if he wanted to. They're waiting for nightfall before they dispose of him. That's an ugly word, dispose, when applied to oneself.

When it's apparently dark, they come back. Still blindfolded, they untie him and dress him roughly. Two men grab him under each arm and drag him down some stairs. His knees are throbbing as they bang on the steps. His legs won't hold him. On the first floor, the uniquely foul smell that he thinks is cooking durian almost makes him vomit. He can tell its dark out again, so he's been in their custody for about twenty-four hours. Since this is a weekend, no one knows he's missing. If anyone noticed that he'd not returned to his room last night, they might guess that he's running around with one of the nightclub girls.

Once on the street, they throw him into a car. They drive around, making lots of turns so he won't be able to lead anyone back to their building. The cursing man pokes him painfully on his knees and laughs in a high-pitched, hyena-like howl, continually repeating his obscene mantra in Mike's face with his foul-smelling breath. Finally, they stop the car. Now what? Quickly and roughly they toss him out into an alley, still blindfolded, and quickly drive away. The good news they're gone and he's still alive.

In just a few seconds, he's surrounded by a group of people who are remarking on how badly he looks. At first they think he's drunk. Then they see the blindfold now down around his neck. He points to his broken jaw. He tries to tell them through his shattered teeth to get the police. Soon the police and an ambulance arrive and take him to a hospital. He relaxes and falls asleep. It's sometime midday when he wakes up. He's in considerable pain. Several MDs and nurses are around the bed talking and gesturing vigorously. After the chair above the durian restaurant, the fresh, cool bed feels great, and the hospital smell is a relief. They've given him a sponge bath, so he doesn't stink any more. The terrible odor of the restaurant and the grilling room is gone. The lights are bright and the conversation animated.

Mike doesn't understand most of their Cantonese and doesn't get most of the medical terms either. With all these people talking and pointing, he feels like a sideshow freak. There's more than enough pain in his legs and mouth. He's really not ready for a chat but gestures that he's in pain. They add more painkillers to his IV and, since he won't be dancing tonight, he decides to let go and go back to sleep.

The next time he wakes up, a nurse notices and gets up. She's tall and slender, and, for a split second, he instinctively thinks, "Grace." She looks at him, doesn't say a word, and leaves the room. Shortly thereafter, she returns with two doctors. They introduce themselves in English. With a conversation in medical Chinglish, they say he has a broken nose, which they have already repaired. They inform him that the patellar bones on both knees have vertical fractures, and there are some small tears in the ligaments. The patella, or kneecap, is the flat bone in front of the knee joint. It's there to protect the knee. The ligaments around it connect the bones and muscles up and down the leg. Surgery is necessary, and it will take about six weeks to heal. "Heal" means being able to stand and wobble. Even then full use will require a period in physical and cardio therapy. The final note is he can expect to have arthritis in both knees the rest of his life. Mike asks the docs to keep that news to themselves. If the navy finds out, his career might be over, like Trammels. Then, they offer more good news. The jaw is broken, and a couple teeth are missing. Next comes the really good news. Through the hole where the broken teeth were removed, Mike can be fed liquids while his jaw is wired shut. After the jaw heals, a dentist will build a bridge to fill the open space. Thanks for small favors. After all that, he takes a little liquid nourishment, although he's too sore to be hungry. After "dinner," they boost the IV with more painkillers, and he's out again.

The next day, the US delegation is in attendance, peopled by the consul general and a couple of the so-called political and economic attaches. After the CG asks Mike how he's feeling, he says that within a week or so, they'll evacuate him to Letterman Army Medical Center in San Francisco. Then, the officers jump in and start pumping for information about the experience. Mike tells them about the odor and the fellow who kept yelling those swear words. He remembers that he had a high-pitched voice as well. In time, they run out of questions as Mike runs out of energy.

Four days later, Mike's feeling reasonably well. Now they come back with questions and suggestions regarding the smell and the cursing man. They offer a number of odors until Mike identifies one. There is no question about it—this is the smell. It's durian, a large fruit grown in this part of the world. The odor is from a shop that processes it. Durian has a distinctive smell that foreigners find unpleasant. It has been described in many foul terms, such as garbage, dirty socks, rotten onions, turpentine, and raw sewage. Perhaps one of the least offensive ones is, "It smells like hell but tastes like heaven." The restaurant must specialize in cooking durian dishes for the smell to be that pervasive. This narrows the search considerably because there are only a couple of restaurants and food stands that specialize in it.

The police choose two restaurants and stake them out. Surveillance reveals an unusually large number of men repeatedly coming and going up the stairs above the durian restaurant on the east side of town near the harbor. A raid uncovers Communist documents and captures several men with previous arrest records for petty crimes. After some interrogation, they tell Mike they believe the cursing high-pitched-hyena man is a US consular employee. The police ask if they can bring him to the room so he can positively ID him by sound. Mike's more than happy to find the bastard who did this to him, but he's never seen him. They devise a plan where they will cover Mike's eyes and bring in two men. As they talk, he's to let them know if one of them is the man. In the morning the nurse wraps a gauze bandage around Mike's head. The suspects think he can't talk due to the broken jaw. The plan is that the cops will get a conversation going with one man on each side of bed.

In they come. They tell the suspects Mike's not able to talk much because of his jaw. They can see it's wired shut, and one of the mugs snickers. The dialogue starts, and the cops make prejudicial remarks about white men to get the men agitated. In a few seconds, one of them responds with an oath that is not the one Mike heard but is definitely the man who he heard. He talks some more. Mike opens his eyes slightly as though he's still in a daze. One of the men is surprised and then smiles wickedly. He's the one with the same voice. Through clenched teeth, in Chinese, Mike tells him he is an asshole, and when he gets out of the hospital, he is going to beat the shit out of him. That does it. He lets loose a string of curses with *"Ngo dill kau kui"* being the leading epithet. That completes the ID, and he's hauled off, very angry that he's been spotted.

When the gang is captured the woman testifies that Mike would not reveal anything despite the torture. As a result he is put in for a heroism medal: the Navy and Marine Corps medal. This is the highest level award for noncombat heroism. It depends on the actual level of personal "life threatening" risk experienced by the awardee. Mike certainly qualifies.

Back at the consulate, the staff verifies that when he's upset, his favorite curse words are *"Ngo dill kau kui."* After some additional work on him and testimony from consulate people, it turns out that he is a Communist agent put in the consulate to spy.

As he rests in the hospital the next several days, an old letter from Grace finally catches up with him.

September 18, 1968

Dear Sherlock,

After you left I decided to stop feeling sorry for myself and do something useful. I enrolled at UH-Manoa to work on my M.A. Like you, I'm in Asian Studies. It's going to be really good to get back to studying again. I've missed the intellectual challenge the past several years.

This will bring back many memories of growing up in China and later in Taiwan. I think then at least subconsciously I learned a lot about the intrigues of the world. I remember my father talking to mon about his experiences with Chiang. I was too young to understand, but now those times are making sense for me. I hope one day I will be able to share that with you. Given what you are going through it would make a lot of sense for you.

I even fantasize of maybe one day writing a memoir about my experiences growing up in the middle of the civil war. That was an important time both for China and the world as the communists under Mao took over.

Please write when you have time.

Studiously,

C.J.

After another month in the hospital the docs declare him fit for travel and he's evacuated to the States.

Chapter 8

Beached

December 1969
San Francisco

I t's a very long flight from Hong Kong to Travis Air Force Base outside of Sacramento, California. There's a refueling stop along the way. Needless to say, Mike can't get off and walk around. He can't tell which tropical paradise they land at since there are no windows in this no-class section. In place of a mai tai he gets a pain pill. Sleep seems the best way to get through this. Hours later he feels the bump as the plane hits the runway. At last, back home in America. Travis is the main port of entry for injured or wounded military personnel. From there he's driven with two others in an ambulance to Letterman Hospital in San Francisco.

The hospital is in the middle of San Francisco at the west end of Lombard Street. It looks out toward the Golden Gate Bridge. Letterman handles major acute cases. The staff of highly skilled surgeons work wonders on the horrible wounds of US warriors.

If you're lucky, you get a bed in the tower with a view of the bay and the Bridge. If not, on the east side, you have a view of Lombard and Union Streets populated with small shops and restaurants. On the south and west sides, you look into a conifer forest. All the Letterman staff are first class. They've treated just about every wound or injury there is. Mike's knees and jaw present no problems for them.

The ENT specialist inspects the work on the nose and jaw. "First-class work," she says. "It should heal nicely in about four weeks."

The orthopedist and rheumatologist have a different story. The x-rays show the full extent of the damage. They take turns explaining it. "Both patellas have small fractures. They're not as bad as we'd been led to believe," the orthopedist states, "The ligaments aren't ruptured, and the meniscus isn't torn. There is fluid buildup that I know is painful and will get worse, so we'll put a drain in each leg. The prognosis in Hong Kong is correct. You won't be playing volleyball for several months."

The rheumatologist continues, "Normal healing time is five to six weeks. That will be followed by physical therapy to help the leg muscles function again after a long rest in a cast. That is just to get you to a walking state. One thing you can count on for sure is that you'll have arthritis in both knees the rest of your life. Don't plan on running any marathons."

His larger concern is whether or not the navy will find him unfit for duty like the marines did with Trammel. He asks in very strong language that they downplay his long-term prognosis.

Once he's settled, finally he has the energy and time to write to Grace.

January 8, 1970
Dear C. J.,
    While I was in HK giving the briefings, I was detained, shall we say, by some unfriendly folk who wanted information that I wouldn't give them. They took out their displeasure on my knees and jaw. As a result I'll be laid up for a couple months recuperating at Letterman Hospital in San Francisco.
    I sure could use a little TLC about now. Your letter from September '68 finally caught up with me in Hong Kong. You might have figured I was a lost cause because of the mail delays.
    In any event, I pray you are well. How is your mom? Give her a hug for me. Limply yours,
Sherlock

After a couple weeks, he's still not heard from Grace. He hopes it's just that the mail is chasing him. Still, he's getting worried. His letter must have gotten to her mother's house by now, and she would know where he is.

Mike's imagination wants to run wild. He has to keep it reined in. "Come on, Michael; you know she loves you, so be cool. You know how the navy works; Jerry might have been transferred to Greenland suddenly, and she had to go along. Maybe she's still in Honolulu taking care of her mother. The old lady didn't look well. Hell, anything could be blocking her from writing. Just keep the faith."

It's Monday morning, 26 January. The bay area's rainy season is in full force. The cold North Pacific wind howls through the Golden Gate and spins around the Presidio forest. The trees sway and try to shake off with their watery burden. Occasionally, a large, water-logged branch becomes too heavy and a eucalyptus lets it go crashing onto the waterlogged forest floor. Although the hospital is warm, the feeling of the storm sends a cold pulse through him. He's always hated cold weather since he was growing up in North Dakota. Wasn't it Mark Twain who said the coldest winter he ever spent was a summer in San Francisco? Well, the winter in SF is no treat either.

There's a small knock on the doorjamb of the room. No one knocks on the door here. They just come in. He's reading the paper, and as he looks up, he refocuses his eyes. There's a woman standing there, and it isn't a nurse with a needle.

"Hi, sailor, wanna have some fun?" It's Grace. She takes several quick steps to his bed and gives him a warm but short kiss. Stepping back, she glances at the door to see if anyone is there. "I'd like to jump in there with you, but I don't think that would be acceptable hospital protocol, do you?"

"What the heck are you doing here? How did you get here? Where have you been the last couple months? I haven't heard from you. I was worried that you might have been hurt or transferred to Greenland or something."

"Slow down, Sherlock. I'll tell you everything. A couple weeks after you left, Jerry received orders to Moffett Field, just a half hour south of here on the Peninsula. I've been there ever since, except for a week early in January, when I had to go back to Honolulu to help Mom. I'm a volunteer with a navy wives' club. We take turns coming up here to visit the patients. We read to some of them, help them write letters, even play cards—anything to make their time here a little less painful and boring.

"I found your last letter when I was home a week ago. I've written to you a couple times since you left on the *Ranger*. I guess my letters haven't caught up to you yet. Mom's not doing well. I'm going back again in a week to relieve the nurse I've hired to care for her.

"But how are you? When will your jaw heal so you can kiss me again? How about your legs? Do they hurt much? I hope the knees aren't permanently damaged…are they?"

The next two hours they don't leave a nanosecond of silence. Mike describes the raid at the *Ranger* and his briefings in Saigon and Hong Kong. When he comes to the kidnapping, he leaves out the graphic part and just describes the wounds.

"My god, Michael, I've missed you so much. Mom has asked about you several times. She wants to know what you say in your letters. She smiles when I read your references to her. It is so wonderful to see you again," she says, holding his hand. "How long will you be here? Do you know if you'll go back to CINCPAC?"

"I've got about a month maximum; that will lead into rehab for a few weeks. In the long term, I think the knees will be okay but probably a bit tender for some time. After that I expect to come back to CINCPAC, but you never can tell with the navy. A military career is a series of disconnected assignments anywhere in the world. How are you doing with Jerry? Has he calmed down at all?"

"No. it's status quo. I wrote about it in my last letter to you. I've decided that I'm not going to put up with this for the rest of my life. Even if you weren't here I have to leave him eventually. I doubt that he cares. The only thing holding me back is mom. She's quite sick and I don't want to add this upset to her. Oh, my god, I have to go. I'm riding with three other wives, and we agreed to meet in the lobby fifteen minutes ago. I guess their patients weren't as interesting as mine. Sweetheart, I promise to write to you whenever I'm at Mom's. Please keep those cards and letters coming, Sherlock. They mean more than you can imagine to me." Grace leans over and gives him a very soft kiss hoping it won't hurt his jaw. Then, she stands up, and, with tears beginning to show in her eyes, she turns and hurries out.

A week after Grace left for Honolulu, Mike's feeling sorry for himself. It was so wonderful to be with her even for a couple of hours. One afternoon, Miss Bassett comes into the room and says, "Well, when are you going to get off you lazy butt? Volleyball practice is this afternoon. Are you going to be there?" Bassett is a tough old gal who has worked with thousands of wounded service people. Under her hard shell is an extremely caring woman. She works somewhere in the admin side of Letterman.

"Absolutely, just get my sneakers ready. What time?"

"Actually, we're going to have to move you. Letterman is an acute care and trauma center. We don't have the space for malingerers like you. We need your bed, so you have to go."

"That's too bad. I was just getting used to what your staff calls food. Do you serve rejected K rations?"

"If you don't appreciate our haute cuisine, we could stop feeding you. Unfortunately, we'll never know if that works because we're shipping your worthless butt out to a rehab and convalescent center. They're better equipped to deal with slackers and to put you through your paces so you can learn to walk again. Perhaps then the navy will get some value out of you."

"And where might the new torture chamber be located?"

"We had two choices. One was the Presidio at Monterey. They have a good record for stimulating the quick recovery of the sick, lame, and lazy. But it's too close to the Pebble Beach Golf Course. You might be tempted to make a career there. Since you're attached to CINCPAC, we decided to ship your useless carcass to Tripler."

He can't believe his ears. Tripler Army Hospital is located on Moanalua Ridge above Honolulu overlooking Waikiki Beach. That's blessing number one. Blessing number two is that Grace has returned to Honolulu. One plus one equals halleluiah.

Within five days Mike's been discharged from Letterman and flown to Tripler. As soon as he's settled, he calls Mrs. Liu's number.

"Hello; Mrs. Liu's residence."

"Hi, cutie, guess where I am?"

"Michael, what are you doing? I didn't expect to hear from you so soon. Are you okay? They haven't amputated any vital parts, have they?"

"No, my love. I've been transferred to Tripler for rehab and convalescence. I'll be here until I'm released to return to active duty at Pearl."

"Tripler? Do you mean Tripler Hospital up on the hill?"

"Yes, mam. That's the one. I'll finish my rehab and convalesce right in your backyard. God is truly on our side at last. When do you have to go back to Moffett?"

"Oh my god, that's fantastic. Can you have visitors? Of course you can. I'll be there if I have to scale the wall."

"I have to have a day or two to get into the routine here. I'll call just as soon as I'm free. How's Mom?"

"She's so-so, just old and very frail."

"The knees still hurt, but they're slowly getting less sensitive. When you come, we can move out to the lanai area and get away from the ward."

"I'll ask the lady next door to come over. She and another lady like to come here and play mahjong with Mom. I'll be able to spend the afternoon with you. This is wonderful. Now I know that fate is on our side. See you soon. Don't make me wait too long. I might get a better offer from one of the bruddas down on Waikiki."

⚜

Rehab is like a junior hospital without so many people in great pain. Paradoxically, as the initial pain lessens, rehabilitation brings up a new level of discomfort. Mike can't feel sorry for himself when he sees some of the terrible injuries to others. Young men stumble about on crutches or in wheelchairs, mostly cheerful through the soreness of rehab exercises. One fellow is wrapped in some strange body braces. He jerks along, trying to get his balance and move with some semblance of normalcy. Others are not as lucky. They've lost limbs or have been horribly burned or disfigured, and some are even blind.

After a couple of days of resettling and monitoring vital signs to ensure that fundamentally all is well, one morning a tiny, young physical therapist comes in at 0730 and introduces herself as Sandy Hong. "It's time to get up, lazybones. We have a lot of work to do with you."

Mike replies, "No therapy before 0900."

"Our routine starts at 0730. You can't lie in bed all day and expect to walk again."

"Madam, I respect your professional skills and experience. In addition, I appreciate that this emporium of pain has a routine that should be followed in order to sustain efficiency. That notwithstanding, in spite of the aforesaid, I cannot function with any degree of productivity at such an absurd hour as 0730."

"Oh, my, aren't you the one? Well, we'll just change everything to suit you," she says with a dour little smile. After debating opposing points of view, Sandy leaves to treat another patient and return at 0900. She's a real doll. Her attitude and approach are very refreshing. It almost makes him want to get into therapy. When she returns, the first thing she does is pull the sheets off and start massaging his thighs and calves. For a ninety-pound wonder, she's very strong. The massage begins with firm, deep, but not too painful pressure on both sides of the knee running from midthigh to midshin. No twisting, just up and down, deep and deeper. The discomfort is almost sensual. After the muscles are warmed up a bit, she wants to teach him how to get out of bed. This is no small accomplishment with stiff, sore knees. Besides the pain of moving, there is the fear of falling. Sandy assures him that she will not let him lose his balance and crash. "First, you let your legs droop over the side of the bed as you sit up. I know your legs won't straighten out now, but they will in time. Next, you grab the handlebars on this walker. Lean forward as far as you can, and slowly push up. When you get your chest upright, your hips will drop your legs to the floor."

"Easier said than done."

"Come on; don't be a sissy." Sandy prods until she gets him upright, and then she and another therapist manhandle him from the walker into a wheelchair. There is considerable pain despite the medication. They wheel him into the hallway and head for a therapy room. He's quite a sight going down the hall with two nearly ramrod-straight legs leading the way. Within a week, a routine has been established, and he's allowed to have afternoon and evening visitors.

Grace's visits are welcome breaks from the exercises. They go to the lanai or the cafeteria, mostly with the aid of a wheelchair at first. Later, he'll graduate to a walker and then crutches and finally a cane. By then he'll probably be ready to return to active duty. The physical-therapy regimen is designed to build up the muscles that begin to atrophy as early as two weeks in casts. Most importantly, he has to regain balance. Tossing stiff legs around requires good balance to keep from meeting the floor face first. They start by learning how to stand up. Even that is a challenge. Over the next few weeks, he graduates to moving awkwardly, slowly, and very painfully with a walker.

Lying in bed most of the day causes him to sleep several hours when they're not taking daily blood samples at 0700 or giving shots for various purposes. In all, he counts forty punctures including IVs and blood samplings during the first two weeks after arriving in Letterman. When they came by to check vital signs or stab him, they always ask what the pain level is on a scale of one to ten. He learns that any point up to and including a seven does not earn painkillers. Accordingly, his pain level increases to eight or nine.

At Tripler there is only a weekly blood sample to make sure that there are no infections. The therapy continues now with stretching and practicing standing up, turning, and shifting weight from side to side. It's just like a baby learning to walk, except for the pain. The legs prefer to remain straight. Stretching, resistance, massaging, and hobbling on a walker, crutches, and then canes manage to keep the pain level up. The goal is to walk around the corridors of the rehab center first without a walker, then without crutches, and then with two canes. Each day Sandy says, "Very good. Tomorrow we'll add another loop."

Walking with or without assistance maintains chronic soreness, but it must be attempted. No matter what, standing compresses everything in the knee joint that was traumatized by the blows to the patellas that they find later also tore the edge of the meniscus in one knee. Any little twist shoots a reminder up his thighs that all is not well yet. By the end of the third week, Mike's tottering along with a minimum of discomfort but is by no means stable. He shuffles along more than walks. Sliding the feet rather than picking them up helps keep the pain down but doesn't help the rehab. Quick turns result in wobbles, staggers, and occasional falls if the therapist is not close by. It's embarrassing to lie on the floor and not be able to get up unassisted. Still, he can't complain because his wounds are nothing compared to men back from Vietnam who will never be able to function like they did when they first headed west across the Pacific.

The physical therapy takes about a month in all. Then, he's also introduced to occupational therapy. This is self-help practice. It covers his ability to take care of himself at home. He has to demonstrate that he can make a simple meal, wash the dishes, take a shower, go to the bathroom, and dress himself. Since arriving at Tripler, he's only had sponge baths. His first shower thanks to OT is one of the greatest feelings ever. The nurse's assistant who helps him shower is a stocky, middle-aged Filipino lady, Angelica Flores. As he's rubbing the dead skin off his abdomen and thighs, she says, "Don't forget the balloons." He laughs so hard he has to sit down again. She's a doll, and they become good friends.

Most of the staff are challenging yet very sensitive to his struggle to walk unaided again. They do have a mean streak, though. They deliberately drop things on the floor to see if he can pick them up. There are little therapeutic games they play to test coordination, strength, comprehension, and other motor skills. Tasks he's taken for granted since he was six years old have to be relearned. The last check is to determine if the blows to his jaw and head caused any permanent brain damage. There are tests of comprehension, expression, hand-eye coordination, and speech. These he passes with no problems. He's on his way to being ambulatory again. He just needs to build up some strength.

His jaw has been wired shut for weeks, and meals come through a straw. This makes it hard to ingest enough calories to put back some of the weight he's lost or to build stamina. By the time the jaw is healed and the teeth replaced, Mike will have dropped about twenty pounds.

After she left the hospital and was driving back to Moffett, Grace was troubled. Of course, her feminine side felt sorry for him. She wants to take care of him. On the other hand, she asks herself, "How would I feel about Michael if he was never fully functional again. What if he would always need crutches or canes to get around? What if he couldn't go to the beach with me and play in the surf? How would I feel if I became a caretaker the rest of my life? Do I love him enough to take on that responsibility?"

For the next week the thoughts continue to bother her. She has some time while caring for her mother to examine her deepest, most honest feelings for Mike. When she first saw him at Letterman, she was stunned. Both his legs were in casts. His jaw was wired. His broken nose was not fully healed, and he still had signs of bruises on his face. She didn't notice that he was lying on his right side until a nurse and an orderly came in and painfully turned him on his other side. They said they had to do this hourly, twenty-four hours a day, because the skin on his thighs, buttocks, and back was raw from abrasions he'd suffered in the chair while he was being tortured. She could see it was very painful to move him because they took a great deal of care and time to turn him. He grunted several times during the procedure, and when it was over, he was sweating and breathing very deeply as if to breathe away the pain.

After she went back to Honolulu to care for her mother, Mike called to say he'd been transferred for rehab to Tripler. At first she was overjoyed. Then, she felt guilty for her earlier feelings. They had some good times together for the two weeks she was in Honolulu. They went on short fun excursions around the island. Nevertheless, when she had to go back to Moffett, she still felt guilty about her initial shock and feelings. Still, she really didn't know what she would do if faced with a caretaking life. The key question is, "If I let him go because of a disability, and later I saw him with another woman, how would I feel? The answer is, it would bother me."

Chapter 9

Mission Irregular

April 1970
Honolulu

After Mike's released from Tripler, he's given another two weeks leave to get his feet back on the ground, so to speak. He and Grace have a couple days before she has to go back to Moffett. One afternoon they make a picnic lunch and drive out to Maili Beach. They need some quiet time together to discuss their future.

"Grace, I don't know what I have to offer you given my life in the navy. You know from Jerry's experience what it's like to be married to a naval officer. Do you want that for the rest of your life?"

"That's a good question sweetheart. It is difficult, the separations, not knowing if your husband is safe, not knowing what or where the next assignment will be. When I married Jerry I didn't realize what it would be like. I was young, not thinking too far ahead. I should have known, having grown up in a military family. My father even warned me about what kind of man Jerry was, but I was too naïve."

"I understand the stress military wives must be under," he says. "If I were a woman I don't know that I would opt for it."

"Now that I'm a little older and wiser I think it comes down to one basic issue. How much do you love the man? Are you willing to put up with all that just to be with him and share the adventures, good and bad?"

"I'm afraid to ask you that question. When you stop and think hard about it, are you willing to deal with all that to be with me?"

Grace looks at Mike and her smile answers the question. "Life is difficult no matter what path one chooses. If you find someone who has your heart you have to go with him. Does that answer your question?"

When his leave is up, Mike's directed to report at 0900 on Monday to the new intell boss, a Captain Bradley. When Mike enters his office, the yeoman receptionist directs him to a conference room. In ten minutes, a captain he assumes is Bradley and two other commanders enter the room. What could this mean?

The captain opens with, "Lieutenant Holmes, you performance on the Ranger and later in Hong Kong was in the highest levels of naval service. You're a marked man in this outfit. You've performed admirably in all assignments to date. As you have been told, you have been awarded the Navy and Marine Corps Medal for your courage in withstanding torture without divulging important information to the enemy in Hong Kong and then later identifying the torturers. Also, it is my pleasure to award you the Navy Commendation medal for your part in exposing the Chinese reinforcement plan while on the Ranger." The captain pins both medals on Mike's jacket. Congratulations. The young boy from Dakota has proven himself and been recognized just as his dad promised.

"Now to the business of the day. You've demonstrated your resourcefulness and courage. We have an extraordinary mission for you. We expect it could take as much as a year, perhaps more, and it is top secret. You cannot tell anyone where you're going, what you're doing, or what the objective is. Is that clear?"

"Yes, sir." What the hell could this be, he wonders?

"We've learned that the Chinese are planning to build some new type of ship that will be the most sophisticated small vessel on the seas. I say small not knowing precisely what that means. The best intell we have indicates it will be something the size of a destroyer or perhaps a bit smaller, such as a destroyer escort. This is a surprise in that the Chinese have not previously built DEs. We need to know what they plan to do with these ships and what their capability will be so we can counteract it. You're going to find out for us."

"Just how do they expect me to accomplish this?" Mike asks himself. "I say, Michael, you're good, but this escapade stretches one's imagination. It will certainly tax even your notable capabilities. One might rightfully list it at the top of surreal challenges. Do they expect you to walk into the Chinese Admiralty Building and request the specifications and mission of these new ships, thank you very much, old chap?"

The captain continues, "To date, our undercover CIA agent in Shanghai has not been able to find out the planned size and use of these vessels. My guess is that this is part of a new coastal expansion plan. The Chinese are probably going to extend their reach beyond the standard two-hundred-mile limit and take a strong position in the South China Sea. I'm certain that they want to be right in the middle of the shipping lanes that run from Japan to Singapore."

"Sir," Mike replies, "With all due respect, how do you envision me accomplishing this mission? Granted, I speak Chinese, but no one can mistake me for a Chinese man."

"Of course not, Holmes. There is a quite detailed plan for how you're going to do this. Commanders Hannon and Minton will describe it. You'd better take notes. It's rather complex."

Commander Hannon starts. "First, we've created a new identity for you since you are going to be living in Shanghai."

That's a great opener.

"Henceforth, Lieutenant Holmes will be out of touch for the next year or so. You will take on the identity of Miguel Cesar Hernandez, a Panamanian native. The name was chosen on purpose. First, since your name is Michael, someone might have called you Miguel jokingly in the past. If they do it now, you'll respond reflexively. If we named you Jose, for example, you might not. Second, the initials MCH are the same as your real name. Again, if someone asks you to initial a document and you're distracted and write MCH, that won't create a problem."

Pretty clever.

Commander Minton picks up the story. "To begin, you'll be sequestered here for as long as it takes you to grow a beard and longer hair, probably less than a month. When you leave here, you'll be flown secretly to Panama City and take residence there as M. C. Hernandez in an apartment and an office that we will prepare for you. The only contact you'll have, at least initially, is the two agents in your office, who are going to immerse you in Spanish-language lessons. Since the United States still controls the canal zone, we have ways to make things happen, such as creating a false set of records of Miguel Hernandez's life. You'll have to memorize your past before you arrive in Panama. We've made it easy for you. You are a foundling raised by nuns in Panama City. This way you don't have to memorize family data, and you will never run into someone who knows one of your relatives. With your beard, longer hair, and your slightly dark complexion, you should be able to pass for a Panamanian after you've mastered Panamanian Spanish.

You'll be the Directora de Operaciones de Mercantil S. A., a Panamanian company. Like many Panamanian operations that are merely fronts for various and often nefarious activities, Mercantil S. A. is just a name. Mercantil S. A., through you, is going to put out an urgent request for proposal for the construction of a small, high-speed boat. The boat's design and exact specifications will be worked out before you send the RFP. The point of this is simply to give you a seemingly legitimate reason to be in Shanghai. Unknown to the China State Shipbuilding Corporation (CSSC), they'll be the only RFP recipient. They'll be given the contract, and we expect the construction will take place at the Shanghai Shipyards on the Yangtze or Huangpu Rivers in the same area as the new secret ships. CSSC was founded just six years ago and is eager to win foreign shipbuilding contracts. After CSSC replies to the RFP, assuming they do, you'll go to Shanghai to finalize negotiations of the contract—with our approval of course. We'll provide more data for you to study over the time it takes to be fluent in Spanish. Finally, you're going to move to a special area here at Pearl, where your only contact will be the housekeeping and kitchen staff. We call it Hotel Solitary. Remember, you cannot tell anyone what's happening. It's good that you don't have a wife and children at this time. You can take the rest of the day in your room to begin to study this packet. Be ready tonight at 0200. We'll send an escort who will take you to your new quarters. I'll be in touch with you to go over the plan again before you leave."

The captain asks, "Is the plan clear, basically?"

"Yes, sir. But I have one question. How will I communicate with you once I'm on the ground in Shanghai?"

Minton replies, "You can send coded messages by cable to Mercantil in Panama. The agent there, Rosa, will relay them to us through Starcom. If nothing else works, we'll connect you with a local agent who can send and receive for you. But that is only a last resort. One can never tell when an agent changes sides and double-crosses you."

The captain finishes with, "If that's clear, and I don't see you again before you leave, let me impress on you the criticality of this mission. Failure to learn China's plan could cost us greatly in many ways. I have total faith in you based on what you've shown so far. Don't let me down. Good luck. Dismissed."

Mike has just enough time to write one heartrending letter to Grace. It's very difficult, given what they said at Maili, to now tell her he will be gone for a year, with no opportunity to stay in contact. This will really put her to the test. She might decide it's just too much and he wouldn't blame her if she dumped him.

April 13, 1970
Pearl Harbor
Dear CJ
I've just been given one of the most difficult assignments imaginable.
For the next year I will be incommunicado. I won't be able to write to you and you won't know where am. I'm so sorry to put you through this, but I have no choice.
All I can tell you, and maybe I shouldn't, is that it is not a combat situation. I will miss you terribly sweetheart. Please take good care of yourself. I'll be back just as soon as I can.
I love you.
Sherlock

"What a great way to start," Mike thinks. "Whoever thought up this caper has a fantastic imagination. The chance of this working out and us coming up with China's new ship plan is probably one in a hundred, maybe one in a thousand. It's freaking hard to believe that a sane person would think that this will work. There are so many ways that it can go wrong I don't even want to count them.

"On top of this, what about Grace? I haven't heard from her for a month. I'm not going to hear from her for at least a year. I can't write to her. But I'm going to leave a message at her mother's house that I will be gone for about a year. Mikey, the odds of this relationship enduring are about the same as the mission succeeding. You've facing a double whammy. Shit, shit, shit."

The next month should be a lot of fun. Basically, Mike will be in solitary confinement just watching his beard grow and reading about this crazy plan. Being part Sioux Indian, he doesn't have a heavy beard, but he does have a bit of the Indian stoicism. It should be enough, along with the long hair, to change his attitude along with his appearance. He has to make a plan for how he's going to pull this off. It will be another character test, one he can't afford to fail.

Back in his room Mike boxes up his gear for storage and spends the rest of the day and night running scenarios of what might work. It's idle-mind chatter until he has more info on Shanghai and the shipyards. The mission packet is stuffed with information on Panama, Panama City, the Canal Zone, and Shanghai living conditions, climate, current political status, CSSC background, and of course the RFP specs. There is also a Spanish-language set of discs and workbooks. He'll have plenty of time over the next couple of weeks to start the language study. Finally, there is sketchy data on Mercantil S. A. That's not unusual for these kinds of organizations.

Mike pulls the basic specifications on the vessel that the navy wants the Chinese to build. The RFP reads as follows:

Length: 20 meters (66 feet)
Beam: 4 meters (13.2 feet)

Draft: 2 meters (6.5 feet)
Hull: Deep V hull (designed for comparatively soft ride in moderate
seas at high speed
Speed: 40 knots (1knot/hour = 1.6 mph; 64 mph)
Twin engines capable of propelling the boat at 40 knots
Distance: 400 nautical miles at 12 kt/h
Bullet-proof wheelhouse
Night-vision devices
Radar and Long-range acoustic devices to detect aircraft and vessels
Two 50-caliber machineguns below decks that can be raised fore and
aft electrically

Suddenly Mike realizes that this is a smuggler's boat! He suspects the coast guard and navy would like to add it to their fleet. They would use it as an interceptor for illegal activities around America's coastline. "The United States could easily build this vessel, but we probably want to see what the Chinese come up with. They'll also probably build it more cheaply than we can. Looking ahead, once the contract is in negotiation, I expect I'll make my first trip to Shanghai to conclude the deal and get the project underway. I don't know how long it will take them to build the vessel, but that is really not the point. It could be that as soon as I know China's secret ship plan, my job is finished, and I can disappear from Shanghai. The alternative could be that I stay until the boat's structure is completed, and we load it aboard a cargo ship bound for Panama. Uncle Sam would undoubtedly want to look over the Chinese workmanship."

Still, images of Grace keep interrupting his thoughts. Over the past year, he's fantasized how one day they might be together long enough to develop their relationship. "Wishful ruminations, old chap. The lady is committed to another lad. Although she's shown interest in you, that does not mean she is prepared to change her life to be with you. Stiffen up. It's time to set aside weak hopes and move on with your life, old boy."

Promptly at 0200, there's a knock on the door. Two marines salute and announce that they have come to escort Mike to his new quarters. They pick up the gear that had been provided for the mission and head out of this building. It's a walk of a hundred yards or so to another building. One of them unlocks the door and leads the way with Mike and the other marine following. This building is quite similar to what they just left except that the only exit is in the rear to a yard that can be used for relaxation or exercise. He wonders if this single exit would pass the fire code. The lead marine opens the door to Mike's room and motions him inside. He feels like a prisoner. They put his gear down and hand him a key. He's told that he can order breakfast over the phone. There is a menu and dialing instructions next to the phone. With that, they salute and leave. Mike calls in a breakfast order and gets ready for bed. He's hyped, and it's hard to get to sleep. This has been the first of what he expects will be many interesting days to come in Hotel Solitary.

In the morning he showers and dresses casually in shorts and a T-shirt. The phone rings, and a voice says, "Good morning, Senor Hernandez."

He hesitates and almost says, "You have the wrong number." Instead, after a short pause he answers, "Yes." Should he have said, "Si?" The voice asks if he would like to eat in his room or in the yard in back. He chooses door number two. After breakfast he goes back to his cell—that is to say, room—and starts to organize the project material. There are actually two rooms, one for sleeping and one for living, if that is what you want to call it. There is a large table to lay out work material. He decides on a routine. Since he's physically rather inactive, he'll restrict himself to two meals a day, breakfast around 0930 and dinner about 1700. In between, he'll have some of Hawaii's delicious fresh fruits in midday. Farther down the passageway, there is a small gallery. It has a coffee pot, soft-drink machine, fruit bowl, and a hotplate to make a cup of tea. There doesn't seem to be anyone else in the building. The first night, dinner consists of a Caesar salad, a nice piece of mahi mahi on a bed of jasmine rice, a fresh fruit medley, a glass of pinot grigio, and a macadamia nut cookie. At least the prisoner is well fed.

Along with the mission material is the Spanish-language course booklet and a set of audio discs. He decides he needs a work schedule so he doesn't just sit here watching TV. After breakfast he'll study Spanish for two to three hours, break for some fruit, study the material on Panama and Shanghai for two hours, and then exercise in the backyard. Finally, he'll take another pass at the Spanish vocabulary cards. That will take him to about 1700, and he can have dinner. After that, he'll go out back, use the exercise equipment, and walk the track around the inside of the yard. The rest of the evening until bedtime, he'll read one of the books or magazines on the shelves or the *Honolulu Star Bulletin* newspaper that is dropped off each day. With this routine, by the time he leaves for Panama, he should have the basic grammar and some vocabulary. This will give him a head start into the immersion program there. In the end, his Spanish might be good enough to fool most people. He just hopes he doesn't meet many people in Shanghai who speak Spanish. It's difficult to fool a native when you are a second-language speaker.

Mike's letter is waiting for Grace when she returns from Moffett two weeks later. It is devastating. She had committed herself at Maili and now this. In addition to the letter, her mother is sinking fast. Within a month the frail old lady dies. Grace has no one to console her.

Chapter 10

Panama Schooling

June 1970
Panama City

In three weeks Mike's beard has sprouted enough to cover his cheeks and chin. It's decided that he should ship out. The same marines pick him up and take him to the flight line at NAS Pearl Harbor. The base is a joint operation of the navy and the air force's Hickam AFB. There is a Gulfstream II ready to go when he arrives. There are only three other passengers. The hatch is closed. They roll out and take off for San Diego. Five hours and twenty-three hundred nautical miles later, they land at NAS North Island. It was about forty months since he was here working on the sniper case with Jenny. In an hour, the plane is refueled with extra tanks and flight checked, and a new crew is on board. This leg has only one other passenger, who sits down and goes to sleep before they take off. In about eight hours and something over three thousand nautical miles, they're coming into Aeropuerto Tocumen, Panama, west and north of the city. Now it's almost midnight. The air is humid, and it's quite warm. He's passed through customs as a diplomatic officer in about two minutes. The customs agent asks, in Spanish naturally, if this is his first time in Panama, and he just nods affirmatively rather than chance his Spanish. A man in plainclothes picks Mike up and deposits him at his apartment with hardly a word. His only chance to practice Spanish is a short "Muchas gracias."

When he opens the door to the new place, it smells like no one has been there for some time. Despite the outside humidity, he throws open the sliding door that leads onto a small balcony. The apartment is simple: one bedroom, a combination living and dining room, a kitchen, and a bathroom. Inside the front door, there is a tall, traditional, mahogany hall tree holding two raincoats and umbrellas. There is what looks like fresh food in the refrigerator and sundries filling the cabinets. On the bed Mike finds an envelope. Inside a note in Spanish reads, he thinks, "I'll call you in the morning about 9:00 a.m." It's signed "Alfonso." He has to credit whoever organized this. They don't seem to have missed a step. It takes him a couple of hours to settle, shower, and lie in bed hoping to go to sleep. At 0910 the phone rings. He answers. *"Hola, bueno."*

"Buenos dias, Senor Hernandez. Soy Alfonso. Como esta?"

"Muy bien, actualmente mejor que nunca, gracias" (Actually, never better).

"Oh ho, very good, senor. Did you sleep well?"

"Yes—oh, *si, gracias.*"

"If you can be ready to go to the office, I will pick you up in front of your building at eleven in the morning. *Está bueno?*"

"Si. Está bueno."

At 1100 Mike's standing in the shade outside the entrance to the building. He judges the temperature to be in the high eighties and humid. There are heavy clouds threatening to explode with rain. The question he asks Alfonso after the usual *buenos dias* exchanges is, "What is the average temperature here?"

"It's typically in the nineties year round. There is a rainy season that starts in May with about four inches a month and builds up through October with thirteen inches and rain almost every day. By November it's back down to ten inches as it tapers off to one or two inches in January."

Just his luck, it's mid-June. It's only a few blocks from the apartment to the office. By the time they reach the office building, it's started to rain. They park underneath the building and take a small elevator up to the fourth floor. On a door numbered 4D, there is a sign reading Mercantil S. A. Alfonso ushers Mike in, and he's greeted by a lady in her midforties who introduces herself.

"Buenos dias. Mucho gusto, Senor Hernandez. Mi nombre es Rosarita. Llámeme Rosa." (Nice to meet you. My name is Rosarita, call me Rosa). Before

he can reply, she says, "*Que sólo hablamos español en la oficina*" (We speak only Spanish in the office).

Rosa is a short, plump, high-energy lady with a big smile and a clear image of a person in charge. He's to learn that she is way ahead of the game. She takes care of everything before he even thinks to ask for it. Her organizational skills are beyond the call of duty. Mike quickly learns he can trust her with anything. Alfonso, on the other hand, while seemingly intelligent, is not so energetic. As they talk he says, "*Yo creo* life is about fun more than work" (I believe).

The office is about four hundred square feet, just large enough to house three desks, a large conference table, and several chairs. There's a slide projector and a video projector on the table aimed at a screen on the wall. On the table there are a number of study booklets, cards, and guides to help Mike learn. The starkness is relieved by a number of tropical plants in the corners.

Reality smacks him in the face. This is going to be an interesting couple of months. Alfonso and Rosa go on to tell him that immersion means they speak Spanish exclusively. When they hit something that they just can't get around, such as explaining the complicated origin of some slang, he must find a way in Spanish to ask the question. As Rosa says, "*Muchas verbos en Englese y en Español son simular o lo mismo* (Many words are similar or the same). We try to eliminate English so that you begin to think in Spanish. They say that once you dream in Spanish, you have made the transition."

Panama City houses about seven hundred thousand people on the Pacific Coast, the western terminus of the canal. It's on a broad, flat plain leading up to the jungled mountains north and east of the city. From the office he can look out through the rain at a sea of mostly residential and small office buildings. The main part of town, San Miguelito, is several blocks southwest of here.

"*Mis amigos*, I need to speak a little English now just to understand how we will proceed. As you must know, I will have to send a document to Shanghai soon, and I need to know how we will prepare and mail that. I assume it will go by some international courier such as DHL. Will you be taking care of those matters as well as teaching me Spanish? Are there any other employees involved in this project?"

Rosa tells Mike that she and Alfonso are the only people involved and are prepared to carry out all necessary logistical tasks as well as teach him Spanish. Mike will communicate from Shanghai by cable with them, sometimes in code, and they in turn will relay information back and forth with Commander Minton at CINCPAC via the Starcom facility the United States maintains there. With that, they set out a schedule of study that will include applications for shopping, eating at restaurants, attending sporting events, and visiting museums and festivals. Being an international terminus city, there are restaurants of all types. Everything from Peruvian to French, Thai, Greek, Italian, and American seems to thrive. These trips are helpful in two ways. One, it is an opportunity to practice the language in everyday situations. He has to learn how uncommon words like "anchovies" come out in Spanish. (It's *anchoas*, by the way.) The other value is to have personal experience with the city in the event that he meets someone in China who has been to Panama City. He'll need to be familiar with life here. Alfonso drives while Rosa describes the city in detail. They mix study with the familiarization tour. As a sidebar, it helps to break up the stress of constant study. Within a month he can answer Rosa's quiz about Panama, Panama City, the canal, and the surrounding areas.

Everything proceeds according to plan. Having previously studied Chinese, one of the most difficult languages, learning Spanish is a breeze since it is one of the easiest languages for an English speaker.

After a month to get his feet on the ground, Mike focuses on the RFP to be sent to China. Although he's supposed to be a Spanish speaker, the RFP is written in English, the common language of most business documents. The specifications are clear and complete. All he needs to do is review and sign the prepared document and cover letter and have Rosa send it via DHL to the head of sales at China State Shipbuilding Corporation. Mike unseals the original and checks it to ensure there are no errors or no damage to it since he received it at Pearl. It passes. The only thing that must be added is a response deadline. This could not have been in the original because the navy did not know how long it would take him to be ready to deal with a CSSC response. Mike adds the note that all bids must be received no later than August 15, 1970, in order to be eligible for consideration. Furthermore, the contract will be awarded within thirty days of approval of the winning bid. Then he signs the cover letter and completes the packet. The packet is put into another padded envelope, and Rosa calls DHL for pickup. It is Monday, July 1, 1970. Rosa sends a message on Starcom to Commander Minton to let them know the packet was sent.

Mike waited this long to send the RFP in the event that should the Chinese respond quickly to Sr. Hernandez, he had better be ready with his new identity and language skill. For the next weeks, they make a strong push on the Spanish studies. On the 10th of July, they receive a cable acknowledging receipt of the RFP. In it CSSC's sales manager, Mr. Zhang Wei, thanks Mercantil S. A. for including them as a prospective vendor. He goes on to state that they are interested in bidding and will be able to meet the 15 August date. Rosa passes that information on to Minton. Now they have nothing to do but study and wait for their reply.

The next several weeks pass uneventfully as the three of them continue to work on Spanish fluency, and Mike studies Shanghai and the Chinese shipbuilding industry. The language goes very well. He's able to converse easily with waiters in restaurants and clerks in stores. At one restaurant on Calle 52 featuring Lebanese cuisine, the three are having dinner when a friend of Rosa's stops at their table. Rosa introduces Mike and invites the lady to join them. This ups the blood pressure. Mike goes through the next hour with no problems. As the lady stands up to leave, she tells him how much she enjoyed her time and invites Rosa, Alfonso, and Mike to a fiesta at her house next month. How's that for a passing grade?

Later, there are two things Mike most remembers from Panama. Number one was the constant attempt to assimilate Panamanian Spanish idioms. Number two was the luscious ladies of this steaming city. Panamanian women are the most naturally provocative you'll see anywhere. Skintight short skirts, deep cleavage, fantastic hairdos, and makeup that call out, "Bite this." A neighbor lady, Luciana, was one of the wildest. When she said, "*Buenos dias chico,*" you knew it was going to be a *very good* day—topping, one might say. Going all the way with her was like diving into a boiling whirlpool. Stretching your imagination to the extreme limits fails to complete the picture.

On August 13 the office receives a DHL package. It contains the bid from CSSC. They can't judge the cost they quote, but the date of completion looks good. Their bid states that they will complete the structure within eight months of the signing of the contact and a down payment of 10 percent. They don't mention whether the construction will be aluminum, fiberglass, or laminated wood. Obviously steel would be too heavy given the draft requirements. He'll have to clarify this later. The guess is they're quoting laminated wood similar to the WWII PT boats. Those boats were not actually plywood as many believe. They were made of diagonally layered one-inch-thick mahogany planks with a glue-impregnated layer of canvas in between. Holding all this together were thousands of bronze screws and copper rivets. The bid asks for progress payments based on successfully completing checkpoints every thirty days. Should Mercantil S. A. want CSSC to do the fitting out, that will take another sixty days at a cost stated in the bid. Mike repackages the documents, and Rosa sends them out to Commander Minton the next day. He adds a letter stating he's prepared to go to Shanghai to meet the CSSC reps and inspect the shipyard where the keel will be laid.

Ten days later, Mike takes a call from Minton. "Commander, I feel prepared to be Sr. Hernandez in Shanghai as soon as necessary."

"Holmes, the CSSC bid looks workable, at least good enough to enter into negotiations. You need to schedule a meeting there. After you meet with them, if the project looks feasible, get in touch with me through Starcom. If the captain agrees, we will have you go ahead to negotiate the final contract terms. Once we all agree, Mercantil S. A. will then award the contract to

CSSC, and a tentative letter of credit for the full amount will be prepared by Banco Nacional de Panama based on our instructions. If all goes well, CSSC can then draw progress payments from the bank per the terms of the contract."

Mike waits two weeks before contacting CSSC. The RFP stated that the award would be made within thirty days of August 15. On September 13, he sends a cable to CSSC suggesting that they are the lead bidder and that he would like to come to Shanghai to finalize the project. When Mike hears back from them three days later, suggesting they meet on September 22, if he's available, he has Rosa book a commercial flight to Shanghai on September 19, as well as a hotel room. This will give Mike time to arrive and decompress from the jet lag before the meeting. Once Rosa has confirmed the travel arrangements, the last step at this point is to cable back that Mike agrees to meet at their address on the morning of the 22nd, and would they please confirm and leave directions at the hotel the Waldorf Astoria Bund. Again they notify Minton of the plan.

Over the next week they clean up the office and his apartment preparatory to his departure. Over the length of the project, although it's a great distance, he may move back and forth between Shanghai and Panama. They need CSSC to believe that Mercantil S. A. is a real company with various business interests. It's going to be a tightrope walk. The office and apartment will be kept until the project is completed.

Now that the initial tension has eased and everything is in place for China, Mike has time to relax and reflect for a few days. Naturally, his thoughts go back to Grace. He decides to write her a letter, but it's a letter he can never mail.

September 16, 1970
My dear C. J.,
    The mission is on track. So far everything has gone as planned.
    I wish I could share it with you, but no one can know who I am, where I am or what I'm doing.

Basically, I've disappeared from the face of the earth. I have a few days with little to do except travel to the place that I've been training for since I left Hawaii.

The next phase will be the most intense and critical of the mission. It will take several months, perhaps a bit more. There is much danger in that my true identity can never be revealed. If I'm exposed it could be fatal, or worse.

Nevertheless, my dear, since the concatenation of circumstances impedes the development of our relationship; I must carry on in the best tradition of our naval service. Pray be of good spirits, madam, for as they say, the darkest hour immediately precedes the dawn. (Couldn't resist it.)

What's happening with you? Are you well and happy? I was sorry to hear your mother is failing. Do you have any other family or close friends in the area to help you cope? I hope that Jerry is supporting you through this difficult time. Hopefully, she will recover and live a long time.

Even though we're not together and maybe never will be, I'm still happy that I met you. That one evening in Hawaii, our time at Tripler, and our talk at Maili, will be with me the rest of my life. Thank you.
Love,
Sherlock

Chapter 11

Into the Tiger's Mouth

September 1970
Shanghai

On 19 September, Mike boards a flight at Tocumen bound for LAX and on to Shanghai's Hongqiao airport, SHA. He leaves behind the constant humidity of Panama for the more unpredictable weather of Shanghai. He arrives after what seems like two days but is only about twenty-four hours considering stopover time in LAX.

International travel is a beastly way to spend one's time. There isn't much good one can say about squandering a day packed into a pressurized metal tube with more than two hundred strangers, many of whom have failed to adopt suitable hygienic rituals. The only available pastimes are cinematic efforts of little interest, boring tomes that promote eye strain and food that should pass without comment in polite conversation.

SHA is about eight miles from downtown Shanghai and is adjacent to the Hongqiao railway station. Since Mike's new here, he decides to take a taxi into town. Traffic is heavy, and it takes over half an hour to reach city center.

Shanghai is an energetic city. Being a port, it has elements of San Francisco, Amsterdam, and Hong Kong. The promenade along the Huangpu River reminds him of the Seine in Paris. The city is a treasure. Mike has to remind himself why he's there. He can't get caught up in the exuberance of this stirring city teeming with over eleven million people.

His hotel is the venerable Waldorf Astoria Bund Hotel. This place is a landmark building on Shanghai's Bund, the elegant center of town. Its famous

Long Bar is about thirty-four meters of carved mahogany opposite plush leather chairs and booths. The lobby is exquisitely furnished with antique Chinese pieces. There are fresh flowers along the pathways between the old and the new building. The WA has the charm of the past and the comfort of modern times. Breakfast is served in a sunken garden-like area under a high ceiling with a colored glass opening to the gallery above. The staff, while accommodating, have much to learn from the Asian Indians about customer service.

Mike's first step outside is the Bund Promenade. It is also referred to as Zhongshan Dong Yi Lu (East Zhongshan First). The word "bund" means "embankment." This elegant fifty-foot-wide walk runs along the northwest side of the Huangpu for a mile just as it turns east toward the coast. On it are located the banks, hotels, and headquarters of government and international organizations. There is an array of over twenty major buildings that have changed little since the 1930s. All were constructed in Western-inspired, often art deco styles. A half-hour walk in the humid air is enough to let him decompress and send him back to the hotel for a shower and a nap. He has the next day off to relax and continue to recover.

In the morning he places a call to CSSC to Mr. Zhang Wei. "Mr. Zhang, this is Miguel Hernandez. I arrived yesterday and am staying at the Waldorf Astoria Bund." After the usual pleasantries, they agree to meet in the WA's Long Bar at 1800 for a get-acquainted drink. Mike wants to gain a sense of the man and the way he works with foreigners and learn who will be at the meeting on the 22nd.

Zhang arrives promptly at six. He's a short stout man, maybe five foot six and 180 pounds, with a large smile showing off a couple gold-capped teeth. Mike estimates his age at sixty. His left arm is bent. Although Mike tries not to notice, Zhang offers, "My arm is a souvenir of the war with the Japanese during their occupation of China. I was a young naval officer. We attacked one of their gunboats on the Yangtze River, and I was hit by machinegun fire. It knocked me overboard. I was fortunate that one of the sailors leaped into the water with a line. They pulled us back on board, and we steamed off with severe damage to our boat."

"That must have been frightening, to fall overboard and not be able to swim with an injured arm. I've never been in combat. It would be terrifying." Mike can't tell him about Vietnam and Hong Kong because that was Michael Holmes's, not Miguel Hernandez's.

Mike has many questions to ask about the bid and their ability to build the boat. He has the sense that the man likes to talk; typical of a salesman. "Mr. Zhang, if we award the contract to CSSC, where would you lay the keel? You have a number of shipyards in the greater Shanghai region. What types of ships are you building near here now?"

"We've not decided yet, but it would probably be one of the yards close to the city. It's a small boat, and we don't need a large dock for it. Rather than lay the keel in one of the large yards along the Yangtze, we have yards on the Huangpu that can handle it. When we build small boats, we use one of the facilities on the river. There are several to choose from. It will not be a problem to select the most efficient one. For larger vessels, we usually select a yard on the coast. For example, we've just laid the keel on a three-hundred-foot ship in a yard across from the end of the Huangpu where it meets the Yangtze."

"I'm certain that you can find a suitable site. But keep in mind that although our boat is small, it will have to be loaded onto a cargo vessel for transport to Panama. So you may have to build it farther downstream, where it will be a short tow and easy load to a large ship."

He replies with a slight frown. "It will not be a problem to handle a boat of this size. Our dock along the Huangpu can handle up to thirty-five thousand dwt. That is much more than your little boat's size."

Mike sees that Zhang does not like to be contradicted. After a few more feeler questions like that, they conclude because Zhang claims to have a dinner meeting to attend. He confirms the 9:00 a.m. meeting tomorrow and stands up to leave. When Mike asks for directions, he says, "It will be too confusing for your first time, and I don't want the taxi to get lost. I will send a car to collect you at 8:30 a.m. Our office is just a mile downriver. But the entrance is a bit unclear. I'll see you then."

Well, this is a less-than-exciting start. If they build the boat somewhere along the river, Mike will have a difficult time finding a reason to visit the target yard out on the coast. "Okay, Holmes, put your thinking cap on. You've just encountered your first problem, and it is a large one. You have to find another way to get yourself out to the shipyards where the new ships are being built."

At 0830 Mike's sitting in a large, red-leather wingback chair in the lobby of the hotel waiting for the driver. The space is old-world rococo. It has loads of marble, high ceilings, polished desks, flowers, and a cross-section of local and foreign travelers. He sees every conceivable costume from native Chinese jackets to Middle Eastern robes and Western suits. This is truly a long way from North Dakota. After waiting for a while, Mike takes a step outside to gauge the weather: hot and humid. The temperature is in the high eighties and the humidity about 80 percent. Just like his arrival in Panama City. Statistics show September experiences about five inches of rain. Shanghai weather varies from hot and humid in the summer to cool and humid in the winter. He learns later that September is the last of the hot months. From then through January, the temperature will cool gradually until reaches the midfifties and then starts back up. Everything seems to have a moist sheen on it. Mike decides to retreat to the cool of the lobby to wait for his ride.

Presently, a tall, thin man in what must be a driver's outfit comes through the swinging doors and looks around. Mike suspects this is his man. He sees Mike and apparently comes to the same conclusion. "Mr. Hernandez?" he manages to get out through a thick Chinese accent. Mike nods and gets up. He motions Mike toward the door. On the curb is a black, late-model Mercedes waiting. In fifteen minutes of plowing through heavy traffic, they're at the entrance to CSSC headquarters. It's a large building. Although there seems to be an attempt to impress, there is a worn look that takes away from its prominence. There is a man with a broom moving around sweeping and wiping the brass doorframe and handles. It's not an AAA entrance.

Inside the lobby is spacious with a large black-marble reception desk guarding it. On the sides are two armed, uniformed soldiers. At the desk are several ladies—receptionists and an apparent supervisor. Mike's greeted by name. Obviously, Zhang gave them a description. After he signs in, the supervisor says with a smile, "Mr. Hernandez, Mr. Zhang is expecting you. Please follow this lady. She will take you to his office."

Zhang's anteroom is a bit less than one would expect in such a place. A sofa, two chairs, brightly upholstered in red Chinese scenes with black-varnished mahogany arms, and a matching coffee table make up the room. The furniture shows a little wear. There are pictures of ships on the walls and literature on the table, in Chinese and English. When they come through the door, another receptionist stands up and bows slightly. "Good morning, sir. Welcome to CSSC. Mr. Zhang is waiting for you. Please come in." Inside is a second room, not his office. Another older, very proper woman stands up and greets him also.

"Good morning, sir. I am Mrs. Lao, Mr. Zhang's executive assistant. Mr. Zhang is waiting for you." She steps to the door on her right and opens it. Looking inside, in Chinese, she says, "Mr. Hernandez is here, sir."

Zhang comes around his desk and greets Mike. "*Zǎoshang hǎo*," he says, "We will meet in my conference room next door. Mr. Li, Mr. Yang, and Mr. Zhao are waiting for us."

The conference room is typical, including the usual large portrait of Mao Zedong at the head of the room flanked by flags of the People's Republic, CSSC, and the Shanghai Municipality. Mike's introduced to the three gentlemen. First, Mr. Li is managing director of CSSC. He is here just for a few minutes to welcome Mike. Then, Mr. Yang, who is a senior executive in operations, and Mr. Zhao, in a similar position in engineering, come around the table to shake Mike's hand. Both have rather limp grips. After initial pleasantries and an offer of tea, Mr. Li leaves, and they get down to business. Copies of the bid, which have been translated into Chinese, are in front of each man.

Zhang says that CSSC is honored to have been selected for this project and assures Mike that the boat will meet all expectations. Mike replies that Mercantil has not officially given CSSC the award yet, and this visit is to clarify key points in the bid as well as share with them the overall goal. This stops Zhang for just a second. He glances quickly at Yang and Zhao before smiling at Mike and asking what questions he has.

"Sir, it was unclear in your bid what material you intended to use for the hull and deck."

He nods to Yang, who jumps in quickly saying that since the vessel is relatively small, they thought wood would be suitable—pressure-treated mahogany, specifically.

Mike asks, "Is the bid based on wood?"

He nods a bit sheepishly as though Mike caught him pulling a fast one. Then, Mike asks why they didn't bid it based on aluminum or fiberglass. Both are better suited for saltwater operations.

"Sir, we did not know it was for deep-ocean applications."

That's a very weak reason given the size and speed of the vessel. Mike lets him know that in a nice but clear way. There is a long moment of silence, and he can see that his comment was not unexpected.

Zhao jumps in and says, "Of course, if you insist on either aluminum or fiberglass, the cost will change."

"Can you say at this time how much more it would be?"

"No, sir. We have discussed it but have not worked out the cost."

"Gentlemen, then I suggest we recess until such time as you can rebid the project in either or both of the other materials. We cannot accept a wooden vessel for the conditions wherein this must operate. I think you understand that the vessel must perform under extreme conditions periodically and must be both strong and fast. Can you give me an idea how long this might delay your bid?"

Zhang looks at Yang. Yang and Zhao look at each other and mutter between themselves for about ten seconds. "I can't believe that they didn't see this coming. Did they think that we Latinos are stupid?"

Zhang looks at Mike and says, "We had thought about this, and believe that we can give you a new price within a week. Is that satisfactory?"

Mike knows they expected it and had already worked out at least a rough price. They can't say they can come back in just a day or two because it will expose the fact that they expected to have to bid in another material. Again, it looks like they're a bit embarrassed. He accepts their reply and suggests they set the next meeting for one week from today, September 29, at the same time. They all nod and agree. The meeting is adjourned. Actually, from Mike's standpoint the delay works in his favor. It gives him more time to find a way to the offshore shipyards.

The driver is standing by, and in a few minutes, Mike's back at the WA. Since he must assume that his every move is under surveillance, he needs to send a coded cable to Rosa at Mercantil describing what happened and when the next meeting will be held. She will forward it to Minton via Starcom and get back with Minton's reply.

❦

On Monday the same driver picks Mike up at the hotel and delivers him to CSSC. He's escorted immediately to Zhang's office. Mrs. Lao greets him and opens the door to Zhang's office. He's waiting for Mike with a big smile. "We've been working hard all week and have prepared a new price that I'm certain you will find satisfactory. Yang and Zhao are waiting for us in the conference room."

They stand up when Mike and Zhang enter and have a strange look on their faces. Mike just smiles and greets them, "*Zǎoshang hǎo.*" They're going to have to make the first move.

Yang begins, "We have looked at both aluminum and fiberglass options. Each has its advantages and disadvantages. Although fiberglass would handle seawater slightly better, we believe that building the boat in reinforced aluminum would be faster, and the hull would be very strong, strong enough for any extreme conditions it might encounter. Also, if there is ever extensive damage, it should be easier to repair. So we are bidding to build with aluminum, and this is our revised bid." He slides the new proposal across the table to Mike.

Mike picks up the bid and looks immediately at the price. It's considerably higher than the first bid for a wooden boat. That doesn't surprise him. It could have been their plan all along to bid first in wood without stating it.

They would know he wouldn't accept wood. Then, believing that the project would be theirs, they came back with a high price. It's the old bait and switch game. These guys should sell used cars.

Mike bounces back in his chair as though he's been kicked in the chest. For a second he doesn't say anything. Then, slowly and with great seriousness, he leans forward. "Gentlemen, this is quite a surprise. I'm afraid my associates will never accept this price. We may have to go to the second bidder." Of course, there is no other bidder, but they don't know that.

Now it's their turn to react, and they look at each other without saying a word. The Chinese are master negotiators. He expects they are in for a real tussle. Mike sits back and waits silently with his fingers steepled in front of his mouth. Zhao says something very quietly to Yang, and they look at each other and then at Mike.

Zhang asks if he has a reasonable figure that Mercantil would accept. Mike answers that they were expecting them to come back at about 15 percent less than they did.

The three men recoil, as he expected them to do. Now the negotiation is really underway. After a few seconds, Mr. Zhang says, "That would be very difficult. Can you give us a little time now to discuss a more reasonable counter-price? Perhaps you would like to make a visit to our maritime exhibit on the first floor. Or you might also like some tea in our visitors' lounge?"

Mike leans forward again, and, with his arms on the table, he gives the bid a quick, almost disdainful look. "I believe we are at a critical point in this project, gentlemen. If we can't reach agreement quickly, I will have to return to Panama and start the bidding process again." There is no expression on his face as he delivers this apparent ultimatum. He just makes a matter-of-fact statement.

To himself he says, "If they refuse to drop the price significantly and we can't reach an agreement, the deal is off. Then I have no reason to be in Shanghai. The mission will have failed, and I will be the one who screwed it up."

"Please give us some time now while you are here. I can have my assistant, Mrs. Lao, escort you to the exhibits and then take you to tea, if you like."

Mike hesitates for about five seconds, looking down at the bid on the table again. Then he replies, "That will be suitable. How long do you think it will take for you come back with a more reasonable bid?"

Zhang looks at the other two men and says, "I think we can produce something in about an hour or perhaps a bit more. If you agree to our new price, then we will have to get approval from Mr. Li, of course."

"I understand." They expect he will ask for a small further reduction on their next bid. Then, they will take it to Li, who will come back with another counter and supposedly final price.

Zhang nods and excuses himself for a few minutes. Presently, he returns with Mrs. Lao and says she will be happy to take Mike on the tour.

❦

Mike spends the next hour and a half with Mrs. Lao, a very pleasant, sophisticated lady in her midfifties. After a tour of their exhibits, they sit in the lounge over some fragrant tea and rice cakes. Presently, a young woman comes over to the table. She excuses herself for interrupting us and tells Mrs. Lao quietly that Mr. Zhang is ready for them.

Back in the conference room, the three men are smiling broadly as Mike enters. It is their unspoken signal that they believe they have a bid that he will accept. He nods but keeps a straight face. He wants them to know that he is getting tired of this game and is very serious about the price concession.

Zhang starts. "We have tried very hard to find ways to reduce the price and meet your needs. I'm afraid that we cannot come all the way to the point you suggested. However, we believe that you will find our new proposal reasonable and acceptable." With that, he slides the cover sheet of the proposal with the new price across the table and sits back with a big smile, as do the other two men.

Mike's first reaction to this is going to be important, so he pauses and looks directly at Zhang before pulling the sheet to the space in front of him. This is actually a comedic scene. Again, Mike's thinking, "The final price is not that important. What is important, of course, is that I have reason to be in Shanghai long enough to gather the intelligence about the new ships. Nevertheless, I have to play it straight." Slowly, he disengages his eyes from Zhang and looks down at the sheet. They've cut the price by almost five percent. After a moment, Mike closes his eyes. He wants to give the impression that he's disappointed and yet leave room for more negotiation. He takes a couple of deep breaths, still with his eyes closed. Then, gradually he opens them and looks once more at the sheet and then at the three men.

"Gentlemen, I said I was looking for something like a fifteen percent reduction, and you've come back with less than five percent. There is absolutely no way that my associates and I can accept this price." He stops. There is not a sound in the room. Has he blown it?

For the first time all day, Mr. Zhao speaks up rather nervously. "Sir, we have made reductions across the vessel. Any further cuts might endanger its integrity." I expect that he was given the lead-off spot so that Yang and Zhang could bat clean-up and close the deal with another small reduction.

"There is always room for a lower cost without compromising the vessel through greater efficiency and lower prices of raw material. Surely there is room for another ten percent reduction to reach my cost."

Now it's Yang's turn. They knew Mike would not accept their price, so they have choreographed their response ahead of the meeting. "If you insist, we will have to rebid the material costs and then rethink our processes. That will take time, and you stated that you wanted to move to a conclusion as quickly as possible."

"Yes, time is an issue, but cost is number one. If I give you more time, can you rethink the project and rebid to meet my cost?"

They look at each other back and forth a couple times with a few murmurs that he can't quite make out. They might be falling back on a local dialect that Mike doesn't fully understand. After a few minutes of this, they all nod, and Zhang turns back.

"We are willing to review the project one last time to learn if we can find a price that you will believe is reasonable. However, this will take some time, as we will have to start almost at the beginning. Are you willing to wait for that?"

"How long a delay are you expecting?" Mike uses negative terms when talking about their actions to keep the sense that this is their fault and that they will have to remedy the situation. He wants them to believe that he is truly expecting a much lower price and is disappointed that they bid first in wood, which was not at all a reasonable proposal.

Zhang says, "It will take at least two weeks, maybe more, to review and revise the proposal for a new price." He looks at Mike for a reaction.

"If you believe that you can come back with a price such as I've described without compromising the vessel, I can wait two weeks at most. This will be the last bid. If CSSC cannot perform at that level, I will have to go back to Panama and contact one of the other bidders. We need this vessel and have already taken on a delay. This is your final opportunity. Can we set another final meeting date for two weeks from today at the same time?"

Zhang looks quickly at Yang and Zhao. They nod. He then says, "Very well. Let us plan to meet again two weeks from today, October 13, at nine o'clock in the morning."

Mike has a lot of time on his hands, so he writes letters to C. J. and then tears them up. He feels like a fool, yet while he's writing, he feels good. He'll use the next two weeks continuing to seek out people that might tell him anything from anywhere about the ships. His cover story is that he is looking for other business opportunities for Mercantil in China.

Chapter 12

Moment of Truth

October 1970
Shanghai

It's now clear that he's going to have to stay on site to see this project through as well as fulfill the true mission. It will be prohibitively expensive to stay at the WA. Mike calls Mrs. Lao and asks for her assistance in navigating the local real-estate market. She is immediately helpful. She gives him the name of a reputable realtor as well as information about the better part of the city for apartments. The exercise goes well, and within a week he's found an apartment northeast of the WA and has moved into it.

That out of the way, he spends the next ten days before the CSSC meeting touring every site in and around Shanghai. He continues meeting as many businesspeople as he can, looking for and hoping to find a channel of information about the new ships while he talks about other possible business opportunities. He reads every newspaper and business journal, but there is nothing in them about the ships. This is unusual because the Chinese are working hard at letting the world know how rapidly they are progressing as an industrial power.

His main contact with CSSC has become Mrs. Lao. She has taken him on as a project to become comfortable during his stay in the city. On Wednesday, October 1, she calls him at his new apartment. "Mr. Hernandez, this is Mrs. Lao. How are you today? I hope you are finding your apartment suitable. I have taken the liberty of booking a harbor tour for you on this Sunday morning. It will give you a better idea of the shipbuilding capabilities of Shanghai area."

"Yes. Thank you. I'm certain it will. Shanghai is truly a great port city. I've heard of your shipyards; that is one reason why we invited CSSC to bid on our project. Clearly, you are becoming a world-class shipbuilding center."

"Thank you, sir. You probably know that this Friday is the beginning of the Golden Week Holiday. This is an important time for Chinese people. There will be big celebrations across the country. A dear friend of mine, Madam Liang, is having a large Golden Week Holiday party on Sunday evening. I have told her about you, and she asked me to invite you. You will meet many important people there. Would you like to go with me?"

"That would be splendid. Please tell me how to dress. Shall I bring a gift of some sort? I don't know your social customs very well. I need you to guide me. And can you tell me something about Madam Liang?"

"Very good; I will tell Madam Liang you are coming, and I will help you prepare. Madam Liang is a very important person. She is a longtime friend of Chairman Mao. When he was coming to power, the Liang family supported him. The Liangs are a wealthy merchant family going back to the days of Sun Yat Sen. They own a couple hundred *mou* (one *mou* equals six acres) where they raise livestock and grow rice and barley. When the Cultural Revolution came and many wealthy people were purged, they were protected due to their relationship with the chairman. It is rumored that the chairman receives a piece of the profits from the land. Madam Liang has a lovely country house on the farm and another south of Shanghai on the coast. She lives in a large apartment building that she owns in the Bund. That is where the party will be."

On Sunday afternoon Mrs. Lao and a driver "collect" Mike, as they call it. He's surprised to find a beautiful young lady in the car along with Mrs. Lao. Mrs. Lao introduces her.

"Mr. Hernandez, this is Miss Sun. I hope you don't mind her joining us. She is the daughter of one of my cousins."

"Of course not. Who could not enjoy the company of such a beautiful lady?"

The young woman blushes and bows slightly. Is she shy or just a coquette? "My name is Sun Bo. Please, sir, just call me Bo."

"'Bo' means 'precious.' Wouldn't you agree this is the proper name for her?" inserts Mrs. Lao.

"Yes, without question this is a precious lady," he replies, and once again she blushes. She's quite petite, maybe five feet and one hundred pounds. But she's packed rather tightly. He can feel a cyclone of energy inside that package. There is a mature individual hiding behind the blushes.

Madam Liang's building is just off the corner of Nanjing Road and Jiangxi Road North, near the Metro station. It's a beautiful example of the neoclassical architecture of the early twentieth century that abounds in the Bund. The elevator takes them to the top floor and opens onto a beautiful view of the Bund looking southeast toward the river. A brisk wind has cleared away most of the smog that lingers over the city, and the sight is evocative of European capitals. There is a very spacious, exquisitely appointed room, obviously designed for large parties. Already there are a couple dozen people milling about with drinks in their hands, talking and admiring the view. Mrs. Lao and Bo walk with Mike to a bar, where they're presented with crystal champagne flutes. They're offered champagne, aromatic tea, or a beverage of their choice. Then, they stroll about the room meeting several people whom Mrs. Lao knows. When she introduces Bo, several people note that they have met her previously. Not as fresh as first appeared.

In about an hour, the room suddenly becomes quiet, and he looks around to see a small, elderly woman enter the room from the elevator. She's wrapped in an elaborately embroidered sea-green cheongsam with her thick, iridescent black hair arranged on top of her head, captured by ivory combs. This is Madam Liang. Mrs. Lao said that Madam Liang lives in the floor below this ballroom. Immediately, all eyes are on this little Chinese doll. She is radiant. Her dark eyes dart about the room taking in everything. He can feel her presence although he's at least forty feet from her. They stand and wait as the tiny grand dame floats about the room, momentarily blessing each guest with her presence. Everyone is most courteous, almost reverential in her presence. Eventually, she sees Mrs. Lao standing with the bearded foreigner, and she glides their way.

The two ladies greet each other warmly, clearly dear friends. Then, Mrs. Lao introduces Mike. The lady, only slightly over five feet tall, raises her eyes to Mike and then flinches slightly when she hears his Chinese greeting. He wonders if he's offended her. "Where did you learn to speak Chinese?" she asks.

He's staggered. This is a question he had never expected or was prepared for. "In Panama," he replies.

"Were you taught by an Englishman?"

He stammers, "Yes, how did you know?"

"You speak with an English accent and rhythm. We will have to talk more later Senor Hernandez." she says and looks at him inquisitively as she moves off. She's scary.

The rest of the evening flows uneventfully. He's introduced to a number of people. One that interests him is a stocky fellow, about fifty years old, whose name he doesn't quite catch. This fellow is rather outspoken. He says very proudly that he owns an electronics company that supplies Shanghai's industrial and shipbuilding projects. But before they can get into a serious conversation, without excusing himself, he flits off to talk to another group. Mrs. Lao says his name is Lin. She knows and doesn't like him. "His tongue is bigger and faster than his brain," she claims.

As the evening winds down, Mrs. Lao indicates it's time to leave. As the three of them climb into the car, Mrs. Lao asks, "Since it is still early, would you like to join us for a drink?"

"That would be delightful," Mike answers.

The driver drops them at what appears to be an upscale club. As they enter, she's greeted as a regular customer, and they're led to a booth in a quiet corner. Mrs. Lao says something to a waiter and then turns to Mike and Bo and says, "I hope you don't mind. I've ordered the specialty of the house—a sampling of tea and spirits."

They spend an hour chatting about the party, Madam Liang's exquisite apartment, and general business conditions. It seems that among the Chinese, everyone is involved in business. Miss Sun, now his friend Bo, is an interesting person. Just as he sensed, she's a mature young lady. She has her seductive ways that she is slowly revealing. He finds her very appealing. Again, he thinks, "Why didn't I come across women like this before I met Grace?"

Throughout the Golden Week Holiday, not much work is going on outside of the hospitality business. Mike takes the harbor tour that Mrs. Lao arranged, and it is very enlightening. The Huangpu divides Shanghai. It's quite wide, up to four hundred meters across. It empties into the sea about a mile downstream from the Bund. At that point the tour boat turns left and goes up the coast on the north side of Shanghai before turning northwest into the mouth of the great Yangtze River, the third longest in the world after the Nile and the Amazon. Actually, in China, Yangtze refers only to the lower eighteen hundred miles of the river from its confluence with the Min River in Sichuan Province down to Shanghai. The Chinese name for the whole thirty-nine-hundred-mile river is Chang Jiang, meaning Long River. It flows all the way across the country from the mountain glaciers in the extreme west to the East China Sea at Shanghai. At the confluence of where the river meets the sea, there are large shipbuilding facilities. His bet is this is where the new ships are being built. As they pass, he sneaks a few photos with the mini-camera under his coat. There really is little to see except the tops of the yard's equipment and the masts of ships in dry docks.

Toward the end of the week, Mrs. Lao calls to ask if he would be interested in attending a classical Chinese play at a local theater. Not having anything to do and seeing it as another opportunity to bond with her, he gratefully accepts. She tells him she will collect him on Friday evening at seven o'clock.

Mike's waiting in the lobby when she arrives with the driver and, guess who, Bo, of course. As they leave for the theater, Mrs. Lao notes that she feels she is coming down with something. She starts coughing and, after a few minutes, tells the driver to go to the theater and then take her home. She turns to Mike and explains that she's feeling weak, and would he mind if she left Bo and him to go on together?

Despite her best attempts, she isn't a great actress. Bo expresses her concern as they get out of the car, and he offers to pass on the play, but Mrs. Lao insists they go on together. After the car pulls away, Bo and he look at each other and laugh. This was all a set-up.

"Miss Sun, would you do me the pleasure of attending the theater with me this evening?"

She smiles, going along with the game. She replies, "Thank you so much for asking me, Sr. Hernandez. It will be a pleasure." He offers her his arm, and, taking it tightly, she moves hip to hip with him as they enter the building. Throughout the performance, Bo sits as close as she can. Often she smiles and, during breaks, whispers about something in the play or the people around them. At the end of the evening, she asks if she can show him parts of Shanghai that tourists never see. Of course, he agrees, and they settle on next Tuesday morning. She says she will meet him with a driver at ten.

Tuesday morning it's raining. This isn't a good day for sightseeing. Instead, Bo says, "There is a very nice inn southeast of the city where we could have lunch. It's on the ocean, so we can watch ships go by. It only takes about an hour by car."

"That's a splendid idea. Let's go."

As they work their way out of town, they cross the Huangpu and drive slowly through the rain-inhibited city traffic. Bo says, "If it wasn't raining, we could stop at YuYuann Garden. It's about five hundred years old and beautifully kept now."

Shanghai is a flat alluvial plane only a few meters above sea level. As they slide southeast into the Pudong District, they find more open space. Within an hour they pull up in front of an unpretentious, very old-looking building just a few yards from the East China Sea. It seems to be an inn. On either side of the entrance, there appear to be a few rooms and, in the center, the lobby and probably beyond it a restaurant.

Running to get in out of the rain that is now nearly a monsoon, they find themselves inside a cozy building, reeking of old wood and sea salt and warmed by a blazing fire in a large fieldstone fireplace. The small restaurant is sparsely populated with small tables and frames the view out to sea.

There is no one there. In the distance they can barely see through the rain a freighter headed southward while another passes inbound north toward Shanghai.

"Do you like it?" Bo asks.

"It's gorgeous," he replies.

The host shows them to a table with an unobstructed view. They order tea and some types of *bao*. These are various fist-sized buns. They're stuffed with just about anything you can get dough around. Some are quite spicy, but most are more palatable. The storm is intensifying, accompanied by flashes of lightning. They order a small carafe of some light liqueur to warm themselves. It has a bit of a kick. Now it's clear that they're not going anywhere, so they settle in and acquire a slight buzz from the drink.

After a while Mike notices that it's late afternoon. They've been there for about four hours just chatting and enjoying each other. Bo is more cultured than he would have expected. She attended college in Los Angeles at USC. She's well read, including some of the work of Steinbeck and Hemingway, plus, surprisingly, Octavio Paz and Jorge Luis Borges. Bo has a great sense of humor and laughs easily. It's no surprise that she asks many questions about Mike's background and business in Shanghai. "What is Panama like? Tell me about your family. What does your company do? Why did they choose CSSC as the boat builder?" There is no question in his mind that she is a plant by the two ladies. They figure and are traditionally correct that pretty girls often make men's tongues wag.

Throughout the time, the rain has continued with no breaks. It's almost typhoon strength. Typhoons are possible but unusual in this region. The warmth of the fireplace and the drinks are turning their buzzes into snoozes. It's so relaxing here. It's like a private little world on the edge of the sea. Eventually, the host comes to the table and tells them that the road they came on has a washout. He doesn't know how long it will take to repair it, but most certainly it won't be today. So he asks if they would like a room to spend the night.

He looks at Bo, and she just smiles and shrugs her shoulders. "It can't be helped. The gods have decreed that we must spend this evening together."

"I guess you're right."

Turning to the host, Mike answers in the affirmative. The man smiles and says he will have a room prepared for them. He adds that they have a hot spring and robes if they care to relax. Mike feels like if he gets any more relaxed, he'll fall asleep.

In a few minutes, the man returns with a key and says the room is ready. They have no luggage, just jackets, umbrellas, and Bo's purse. "Let's go see the room," Mike suggests. She agrees.

As they walk down the hallway to an end unit, the man notes it is more private, even though there is no one else in the inn.

Once inside, Bo exclaims, "It's lovely," clapping her hands together. She flops on the low bed that looks like it's not much more than a couple of mattresses piled atop each other. On the west wall is a stone fireplace with a fire laid and burning. Already its heat has taken the damp chill from the room. Mike crosses the room to a large window and pulls the shade aside. He noticed as they walked to the room that they went up several steps. This room is a several feet higher than most of the rest of inn and has a splendid view toward the rain-swept sea. However, visibility is less than fifty yards. There's no sign of it letting up. Mike turns back to the room, and there is Bo looking at him with a big, mischievous smile and her arms reaching out.

Grace, where are you now that I need you? Bo is disappointed that they go to dinner early.

⌘

By now Mike's explored the Shanghai waterfront thoroughly. He sees where CSSC proposes to build the boat. It's along the Huangpu. Early on Friday morning, Mr. Zhang calls him to apologize. He says that due to the slowdown of work during the Golden Week Holiday, they will not have the revised bid ready on Monday the 13th. He claims that some of the suppliers are working short shifts due to the holiday and have not gotten back to him. He asks if they can delay until the 20th. Mike shows disappointment but tells him he understands. They agree to meet on Monday at 9:00 a.m.

An hour later Mrs. Lao calls. Mike wonders if there is a connection. Are they playing ping pong with me he asks himself? Mrs. Lao inquires if he would like to have lunch with her on one of the river cruise boats this afternoon. His bet is that this is to make him feel better after the bad news of the delayed bid. He doesn't have anything better to do, and he enjoys Mrs. Lao's company. They agree to meet at the boat dock that is in walking distance to the south of his apartment. It's a breezy fall day with the temperature around seventy. The first of the dying leaves drop from the tree and are blown around with papers and other flotsam. The humidity is still high, as the rainy season is just ending. As they're enjoying the views along the river, she tells Mike that Madam Liang would like to invite him to a small dinner party at her residence next Thursday, October 16. This is both good and bad news. The lady has great contacts and might introduce him to someone from whom he can gather intelligence on the new ships. However, he thinks that she's suspicious. She's like a cat playing with a mouse. She's the *mao*, and he's the *laoshu*. Still, he can't refuse her invitation.

On Thursday Mrs. Lao and a driver collect him and drive to Madam Liang's building. Bo is not along this time. Her job is probably done. Too bad. They take the elevator up to madam's floor, one level below the ballroom where she held the Golden Week Holiday reception. Mrs. Lao steps out of the elevator first. Mike looks over her shoulder into a splendid lobby. Two large, highly decorated, four-foot-tall Chinese vases flank the entrance to the apartment. The floor is polished white marble flecked with black and gold. The walls are Chinese red. The entry is the typical Chinese arch fronting large, rich reddish-brown Philippine mahogany doors. A servant opens the doors and bows them into the apartment. Another rather tall and thin, elegant woman, probably the head of the household, leads them to the drawing room, where Madam Liang is waiting to receive them. It appears they are the first to arrive.

"Welcome to my humble home," Madam Liang greets them and motions them to a richly embroidered settee on her right. "My other guests will arrive soon, but I especially wanted to speak more with you, Senor Hernandez. You fascinate me. There is an aura about you that I have not penetrated. Usually

I can see quite clearly into the soul of a man. But there is something masking you. Why do you think that is, sir?"

"Madam, I have no idea. I'm simply a businessman from Panama here to oversee the building of a small vessel for our company."

"What kind of company is that, sir?"

"The company name is Mercantil S. A. We're in the trading business. We buy and sell goods wherever there is an opportunity."

"Is there danger in your trading business?"

"No, not typically. However, in some seas, there are sometimes pirates who would like to board us and take our cargo."

"Is that why you have specified machinegun platforms in your vessel?"

Hopefully without betraying his surprise, he replies, "I see Madam has done her homework."

"One must be cautious with whomever she first meets, wouldn't you agree?"

"Yes, mam. The world is a dangerous place. Caution is a very practical trait."

"I have invited some very interesting people this evening. I believe you will enjoy meeting them. There is the sound of the elevator rising. They will be here momentarily. We can talk more later, senor," she says with an emphasis on "senor" while looking intently and directly at Mike.

There are a dozen other guests who arrive quickly one after another. It appears that they were given a different start time about thirty minutes later than his. After an exquisite dinner and elegant desserts, the guests again wander about the dining room or sit on the settees around the edge. Mike learns they are all businesspeople of considerable wealth and presence. The most fascinating man is the Mr. Lin he met briefly last time. Lin states he owns an electronics company that supplies industry and shipbuilding projects. Without appearing to spend too much time with him, Mike finds he is overwhelmed with himself and rather obsequious to the madam. When asked, he takes off with great fervor to explain his business and how important and successful it is. Mike steers their discussion around to shipbuilding, and Lin begins with joyous enthusiasm reciting a number of projects he has supplied. As Mike refrains from showing him that he's impressed, Lin continues to push. At last, he moves close to Mike and says quietly that he is involved with the new destroyers that people are talking about. He claims he knows the project better than most.

"How is that? They are very secretive. Are you directly involved as a supplier?"

"Absolutely—we are providing the infrastructure throughout the ship for the electronics and computer system."

Mike rewards him with raised eyebrows. "That is extraordinary. The builders must have great confidence in your ability to fulfill their requirements."

"They do. They do. Would you like to see what we are doing? No one has seen the plan outside of our company."

"Are you certain that it is allowable for me to see it?"

"No, it isn't. But no one will know. I will take you to my company, and in my office, you will be able to see the plan. If anyone asks, I will tell them you are a consultant assisting me with something else. If you are interested, I will invite you to lunch at my office when I return from my next trip."

Bingo! This is better than Mike had ever hoped for. A front-row seat, and he doesn't have to risk getting shot at. "When you are available for my visit, just call me. Here is my number. I'm most interested in what you are doing."

Before they can go further, there is a signal that the evening is winding down. People start to say good night to the madam and collect their coats. Mrs. Lao signals him to hold back. They are the last to approach the madam, and she touches his sleeve gently. He realizes she wants to talk when the other guests are gone.

As the elevator door closes on the last couple, Madam Liang motions them back to the settee again.

"Did you have an interesting evening, senor?"

"Yes, mam. The guests were quite stimulating."

"I saw that you spent a good deal of time with Mr. Lin. Was he stimulating?"

"He's quite an interesting gentleman with much to talk about."

"He mostly likes to talk about himself, wouldn't you say?"

Mike laughs a little and agrees. "He is quite impressed with himself."

"May I ask what you talked about?"

"It was almost exclusively his business projects. I did inquire about the possibility of Mercantil supplying raw materials for his projects."

"Did he mention his work on the new ships?"

Mike pauses for a second. This is it. This is why he was invited. This old dame is exceedingly clever. She can be very dangerous. "Yes, he did mention that."

"Do you find that especially interesting?"

"Madam Liang, I beg your pardon. I don't mean to offend, but what do you have in mind? It seems there is something going on behind that beautiful face."

"Senor, you are most gracious and very clever. Just who are you? Are you actually a Panamanian? Sir, I am an old lady who has survived many dangerous situations. Please do not insult me. I know when something is other than what it appears to be. But let me put your fears to rest. What you are is of interest to me, but you need not fear me. I will not expose you. If I exposed every pretender or every deceitful person I meet, I would have very little time for anything else. Shanghai, like Panama, is a world center for intrigue. Many things pass quietly, unseen through our city, just as they do yours, if you are actually from Panama. I have not taken the time or effort to trace your background, which I can if I must. But, please just tell me—in confidence, I assure you—who you are, and why you are here."

Now is the moment of truth. Basically, he's been exposed, but not yet fully. Mike hesitates, assembling his thoughts. He glances at Mrs. Lao. If I tell Madam Liang who I am, what about Mrs. Lao and CSSC?

Before he can say anything, Madam Liang sees his glance at Mrs. Lao and turns to him. "Don't be concerned about Mrs. Lao. She is my dearest friend and confidante. We work together and do not share our thoughts with others. Actually, she was the first person to have some doubts. That's why she introduced you to me. But do not worry; she will not compromise your project at CSSC."

Chapter 13

The New Partner

November 1970
Shanghai

Mike has to believe Madam Liang when she claims that she and Mrs. Lao will not bring harm to him. If they wanted to, they could have taken their suspicions to the authorities before this. Clearly, she is a very clever and very resourceful woman. Her mention of the new ships leads him to believe she knows more about them.

With another glance at Mrs. Lao, turning toward Madam Liang, Mike leans forward and speaks softly. He doesn't want any of the staff to hear. "Ladies, I put myself in your hands. It is true that I am not the person I pretend to be. In fact, my name is not Hernandez. It is Holmes. I'm not Panamanian. I'm a US naval intelligence officer. Madam, your ear is extraordinary. I learned Chinese in England while on a Rhodes scholarship at Oxford. That is why you picked up on the English accent. My purpose in being here is to gather as much intelligence as possible about the new warships. That is my interest in talking with Mr. Lin."

"You need not worry about my staff overhearing you. They are all dedicated to me. They know that I have a number of activities that are beyond my apparent business interests. And as I said, Mrs. Lao is my closest associate."

"Thank you, but I have been told that you have a close relationship with Chairman Mao. How is that, if I may ask?"

"It is true that I've known the chairman for many years. In 1949, as he was taking control in China, my family supported him. At one time early on, he wanted to divorce Jiang Qing and marry me. My father would not allow it, thank god. But whenever he needed money or equipment, we took care of him. As a result, he protected us during the Cultural Revolution and still does till today. He has shown himself to be a great revolutionary but not a great statesman. The Cultural Revolution and the Great Leap Forward were disasters for millions of people. He is now an old man, and he is not building a sustainable political leadership. There is much infighting and corruption among the upper levels of government. Many common people are not better off today than when Sun Yat Sen overthrew the monarchy fifty years ago. Chinese people are very resourceful. We look first at preserving our family and then dealing with what the state brings. Actually, Mrs. Lao is my cousin. Her mother was my father's sister. We are protecting our family first and always."

These women are extraordinary. He'll have to work hard to keep up with them. "That is quite a story, madam. I admire how you have been able to survive through all the changes that China has experienced. Is there a way that we can work together that will not violate your ethics or position? My government would make it very much worth your time and effort."

"There are many aspects of life in China that Mrs. Lao and I abhor. We will not do anything that will directly harm the Chinese people. Nevertheless, there may be some small cases where we can work together with the hope of maintaining balance between our two nations so that there is no need to go to war. For instance, in the case of the new warships, these are vessels of destruction. We see value in helping to restrain their uses for promoting conflict. For example, we will not assist you if your intent is to blow up the ships during their construction. But we might help you obtain the intelligence you seek if that would play a role in balancing the military power between our two countries. A reasonable sign of gratitude would be appreciated, of course. Do you understand me?"

"That is a most pragmatic position to take. I admire your ability to sustain such balance. How would you propose to help me fulfill my mission?"

"Assuming that you truly understand us and desire to partner along the broad lines I have just outlined, the first step is for you to follow up with Mr. Lin and learn what you can from him. In the meantime, we will talk with our contacts in the shipyard where they are building the new destroyers. We will learn what we can about the other aspects of the vessels. When you believe you have all you can obtain through Mr. Lin, please let Mrs. Lao know, and we will meet again. In the interim, I warn you to move very cautiously. I'm certain that, while you might not be under constant surveillance, the authorities are aware of you. All foreigners are suspects in China. Be careful where you go and what you do. *Zhù hǎo yùn*" (Good luck).

On Monday the CSSC driver collects Mike and deposits him at the company. Mr. Zhang again greets him with a big smile and takes him into the conference room, where Yang and Zhao are waiting, also with big smiles. After a brief inquiry from Zhang about his sightseeing experiences, they get down to business.

Zhang slides the latest proposal sheet to Mike and says, "We have worked very hard to remove all possible costs. We believe you will find this, our final bid, satisfactory." His emphasis is on the word "final."

Mike looks at him and the other two for a second to get a feel of their resolve as well. Then, he looks down at the bid. They've dropped the price by another 3 percent. That means they've halved the 15 percent that he requested. It is about what he expected. They are not about to lose the project, but on the other hand, they have to save face. So they're splitting the difference. Mike takes a long minute to let everyone settle in. Then, he looks up and says, "I appreciate what you have attempted to do. Has Mr. Li seen and approved this price?"

"Yes, as I said, this is our final price, and Mr. Li has approved it."

"Well, it is not what I had hoped to see. If we agree to this, how soon can you start, and how long will it take to finish?"

"We can start within ten days and finish according to the build time in our original proposal, which will now be March. There will be no further delays if you accept this."

"Very well. I will cable my associates today, and I should have a response within a few days. Thank you for your effort."

When he returns to his apartment, he sends the bid off to Rosa in Panama. She relays it to Minton in Pearl. Mike expects to hear from him, through her, within a week. Minton will probably accept it and add a question about how Mike is enjoying his time in Shanghai. In the improbable event that someone other than Rosa and Minton sees the cable text, they will provide a simple code. If Mike replies somewhat positively, Minton will know that he has not made much progress on the intell mission. If Mike is effusive in his comments about Shanghai, Minton will take it to mean that Mike is making good progress.

Within a week Commander Minton has accepted the CSSC bid, and Rosa has relayed the message. Mike notifies Zhang and makes a date with him early in January and to finalize the launch date for the boat. All Mike has left to do is check back with Mr. Yang about every fortnight for a progress report.

Over the next three months, Mike and Mrs. Lao develop a routine. Approximately twice a month, usually on a Tuesday, they have dinner with a man or a couple that Mrs. Lao invites. The guests are always involved in the shipbuilding business. This is natural since he is in town on a shipbuilding project as well. The conversations are usually interesting but do not always lead to a follow-up meeting. On those that do, he is invited to the man's company to see his work. During the visit, the conversation always manages to touch on the new destroyers. Casual comments slowly add up to intelligence on the ships. Most people do not have much information, but they do know which dry docks the ships are in. On one occasion, Mike's taken across the mouth of the Yangtze to a dry dock where his host's ship is being built. From there he points out the dock where a destroyer is sitting. There is very little to see since the keel has been laid recently, and only the bow and outline of the superstructure are visible. The curvature of the bow is unusual, but Mike can't get a close view of it. At least he knows where to look if he can get back there.

In the middle of December, Mr. Lin calls. "I apologize for the delay. I've been traveling to our projects in the docks at Dalian, Guangzhou, and

Jiangnan. Jiangnan is on Changxing Island, and it's where the new ships are being built."

"I understand and appreciate how busy you must be with your company serving so many projects."

He goes on for the next half hour telling Mike about his projects, and Mike lets him rattle on. It's good for his ego and helps build the relationship. Finally, he says, "I will have some time next month. I would like to have you to my office for lunch. I can show you some interesting projects then." He ends with a small laugh for Mike to hint at what he means.

"That will be splendid. You choose the date. My schedule is quite flexible."

On Tuesday, January 25, Lin sends a car to collect Mike. He arrives at Lin's building just before noon. A young man greets Mike and escorts him to Lin's office. His office is what one would expect of an egotist. It's quite large, very expensively decorated, and has a view out to the east over the river.

His desk is enormous, well beyond any practical need. It is dark mahogany with mother-of-pearl inlays around the rim and down the corners. The edges are richly carved with images that are probably Chinese gods. The top of the desk holds only a couple of sheets of paper. Around the room are various color- ful flags and a large portrait of himself, with Chairman Mao of course. There is a large coffee table covered with picture books of the shipbuilding industry. Surrounding it are several elegant chairs and one large sofa. Everything in the room is bright, lots of red and gold accents everywhere.

Lin comes out from behind the desk and shakes Mike's hand vigorously. "Welcome to Lin Enterprises. I have much to show you that I believe you will find impressive." He goes on for another minute as they stand in the center of the large room on an enormous red-and-yellow antique art deco Chinese car- pet. It must be twelve by ten feet. At last he motions Mike to a chair in front of his desk. He moves behind it and sits down, beaming like the potentate that he obviously believes himself to be. Typically, in a case such as this, they would sit around the coffee table, but it is clear that he wants to impress Mike with himself behind the desk and under the portraits of the chairman and himself side by side. "Would you like something to drink?" he asks.

"A little tea would be very nice."

He reaches to a small console on the top of the desk, presses a button, and says, "Tea." Within sixty seconds, a woman enters from a side door with a small cart carrying a teapot and cups.

"Would you like to see the story of Lin Enterprises?"

"That would be a pleasure, I'm sure."

Again he reaches to the console and pushes another button. To the right on the wall, a panel slides back, revealing a screen. "Which language do you prefer: Chinese, Japanese, Spanish, English, French or German?"

"Spanish would be good; thank you."

With the touch of the console, again the screen lights up, and a movie with a title in Spanish begins. For the next fifteen minutes, Mike's treated to the Lin story. It's actually quite interesting and informative, even if it is a bit overbearing, with his face in almost every scene.

When it ends, Mike turns back to him. "That was most impressive. You have truly built an extraordinary enterprise here. I congratulate you."

He beams and nods. "Now we can have our lunch in the dining room next door." He motions them to the right, and they walk into a room about twelve by fifteen feet. There is a beautifully covered table and embroidered silk chairs. He takes a seat at the head of the table and motions Mike to the chair on his right hand. "This is my small dining room, reserved for special guests," he adds, smiling proudly. "I have taken the liberty of ordering some Chinese delicacies. I hope you will enjoy them."

"I'm certain I will. Thank you." Through lunch they chat about the news of the day in Shanghai, China, and Asia in general. He offers his views on the shipping industry and shipbuilding. When they finish, they return to Lin's office.

"Now, let me show you what is happening with the new ships." Reaching into a drawer on the left of the huge desk, he pulls out several sheets and a roll of paper. "Let me tell you about the overall design first. Then, I'll show you some details of the electronics. These are guided missile destroyers. They will be equipped with multiple sets of new-type weapons. Each vessel will be able to attack surface warships, aircraft, and submarines independently or in an electronically linked attack with other ships of the People's Liberation Navy. They will also possess strong capabilities for conducting long-distance early warnings and detection of the enemy in support of a regional air-defense operation. For example, they'll have the latest X-Band radars, giving it very advanced defense characteristics; cruising speeds of thirty knots; long-range land-attack missiles; medium- and long-range air-defense missiles; and medium-range antisubmarine missiles. In total, they will carry fifty-six such missiles."

He continues with details and then switches to the drawings of the ship's electronics system. Mike is concentrating on the details as Lin rattles on about his part in the project. He does everything Mike could want except give him a copy of the electronics plan. They spend about an hour going over the project. Mike must walk a tightrope. He has to show strong interest but not ask questions that he would like to ask about the weapons, for example. Nevertheless, Lin seems happy to answer and even elaborate on the ships. Then, he looks at his watch and says, "I'm afraid I must end this very interesting discussion. I have a group coming in to talk about a new project. The next time I go to the dock, would you like to go with me and see the progress on the ships?"

"That would be very good, if you don't think it would be a problem taking me. This is a sensitive project, and I don't know that they will like a foreigner around."

"Yes, I know. But I think I can take you. I will think about how to introduce you and let you know if it is possible. It won't be for a few weeks, as I have another trip. Will you still be here for a few more months?"

"Yes, the keel has been laid, and we project a launch in April. I will be here for that."

"Very good; I will call you when I return. *Xīnnián kuàilè*" (Have a happy new year).

Mike's thinking, "This is going to be a very good year if things keep going like this." On returning to apartment, he starts transferring everything he can remember to paper so he won't forget it. The main points are their coordinated-attack capabilities and long-range early-detection equipment.

Chapter 14

Secret Service Interrogation

February 1971
Shanghai

A week after his meeting with Lin, there is a knock on his door at 0830. He opens it to find two very determined-looking men staring at him.

"Mr. Hernandez? My name is Wong, and this is Mr. Guo. May we come in?"

"Who are you, and what do you want?"

"We are from the Ministry of State Security (China's intelligence service). Here are my credentials. We would like you to come to the office to discuss certain matters."

"Am I under arrest?"

"No, sir, but our director, Mr. Zhu, would like to speak with you."

"Just what activities do you want to discuss?"

"Sir, that is for Mr. Zhu to say."

It's clear that these are just the messengers, and they aren't going to go away. Mike has no choice but to comply.

A half hour later, he's ushered into Zhu's office by the two agents. Zhu rises and greets him formally with a nod but no handshake. This is not going to be a party. "Mr. Hernandez, please have a seat. Thank you for coming. I just have a few questions about your activities in Shanghai."

"I'm certain you know who I am and why I'm here. What type of questions do you have?"

"Sir. We have observed that you have spent a good deal of time and many meetings with Mrs. Lao from the CSSC. What is the nature of those meetings?"

"You know that Mrs. Lao is the executive assistant to Mr. Zhang, sales and marketing director of CSSC. We discuss the boat that CSSC is building for my company."

"Why did you meet so many times with her, approximately once a week and not in the CSSC offices?

"There are many details to discuss, and she acts in Mr. Zhang's behalf on those details for which he does not have time. Also, we have become friends and enjoy having lunch or dinner together outside of the formal setting of the office. Is that a crime?"

"Sir, we are not speaking of crimes. We simply want to understand the true nature of your business in Shanghai. Your activities are somewhat unusual for a businessman."

"Why is that? Specifically, what are you referring to? Having lunch with a nice lady who represents the company producing my boat is certainly not unusual."

"We see that you have also visited with Madam Liang several times. What is the nature of that?"

"Actually, by count I have only seen her twice at her residence, as you most certainly know. The first time, her friend, Mrs. Lao, took me to Madam Liang's Golden Week Holiday party. Then about two weeks later, I was invited to Madam Liang's as part of a large dinner party. I've not seen her since that night."

"What did you discuss after the party? You were the last to leave."

"Congratulations; you are quite thorough. We just made small talk. You know, 'How do you like Shanghai? What have you seen? Be sure to go on the river cruise. Don't forget to see YuYuan Gardens.' Things like that."

"Did you talk business with Madam Liang?"

"What business? I have no business with her."

"Are you certain you are not engaged in any business with Madam Liang?"

"I don't know anything about her business interests. I told her that Mercantil is a trading company, but so far as I know, she is simply a charming old lady."

"You must know that the Liang family has multiple interests in China as well as outside the country."

"Do they? We didn't speak of that, although I did offer to find commodities if she knew anyone who needed them. But that was a very small and insignificant part of our conversation."

"Also we noted that you were in Mr. Lin's office this week. You spent almost three hours with him. What was the nature of your business there?"

"I don't believe it is any of your business what Mr. Lin and I talked about."

"Mr. Hernandez, in Shanghai everything is our business. Again, what were the topics you covered with Mr. Ling?"

"Frankly, Mr. Zhu, I don't like your insinuating that I am doing something inappropriate or illegal. What makes you suggest that? Do you have any evidence that I have violated any laws or regulations during my time in Shanghai? If this is the way you treat foreign businesspeople, I will recommend to my associates that in the future we take our business elsewhere. Shanghai is not the only shipbuilding region in the world."

"Just answer my question, Mr. Hernandez," he spits out while leaning forward in a menacing manner.

"If you continue to treat me like a criminal, I will contact our consulate in Beijing and file a formal protest."

"Sir, how will you contact your consulate if I detain you incommunicado until I can investigate your activities more fully? Who will support your intransigence? From what we know, you were not accompanied by anyone from your firm. If I detain you, no one will know your whereabouts for some time."

"You would not dare to detain a citizen of a sovereign nation without cause."

"Mr. Hernandez, I have cause. You are refusing to cooperate on what could be a matter of grave consequence. I suggest you answer my questions now."

"He's getting hot. The last thing I need is to get thrown in jail. I have no choice at this minute," he thinks. "Sir, after I cooperate, and you release me from any unlawful detention, I intend to file a protest with you superiors."

"You may do that, but my superiors will support me fully. Now, answer my question. I ask again, what is the nature of your visit with Mr. Lin, and why did it take three hours?"

Mike leans forward and tells him in a very irritated voice, "As you know, Mr. Lin likes to talk at length about his many business ventures. First, he showed me a film about Lin Enterprises. Then, we had lunch and continued to talk about some of his projects in Dalian and Guangzhou. Actually, it was quite an interesting afternoon. Since my company is in the trading business, shipping is quite important to us. I was hoping to find an opportunity to sell him something for his business."

"Just what is your company's business, Mr. Hernandez?"

"You know very well, don't you?"

"Please stop evading me, and tell me in your own words some of your projects."

Now he's got to be careful. They've probably done extensive research into Mercantil S. A. "We trade commodities such as iron ore, chrome ore, refractory clay, steel shapes, and wire products principally between Asia and the Americas. We've imported pipe from the Benelux mills for the oil and gas business in Venezuela."

"Why do you want a fast boat? Are you also smugglers?"

"Now, wait a minute. You're accusing us of illegal activity. If you have evidence, present it, or stop this line of badgering. Sir, I consider this interview concluded. If you have evidence, arrest me, or I'm leaving," he says quite forcibly and starts to stand up.

Zhu quickly and firmly motions Mike to sit down, and he stops but does not sit. "Mr. Hernandez, we are charged with protecting the citizens of China from any harmful activity. I am fulfilling my responsibility as director of state security for this region. Please know that we mean no harm to people who obey our laws. You may go now. Hopefully you will not give me any cause to call you in again. If you should, our next meeting will not be so cordial."

His demeanor is quite stern as he motions Mike to the door. "Mr. Wong will take you back to your apartment."

Mike doesn't know what caused them to put him under surveillance, but it's clear they've got a twenty-four-hour tail on him. They most likely have his phone and room bugged. It's a good thing he's hidden his notes from Lin's meeting. They've probably searched his room while he's been with Zhu. It's interesting that Zhu didn't ask about Lin's project at Jiangnan, where the new ships are being built. Maybe he's holding back on that until Mike sees Lin again. Based on this morning's tête-à-tête, Mike will have to reconsider accepting Lin's invitation to see the new ship. Since they're following him closely, that would be too dangerous. It would certainly earn him another visit with Zhu. The only safe and reasonable channel Mike has open is Mrs. Lao. Since they're making preparations for the launching of the boat, it would be reasonable for him to go to their office. But right now he needs to be cool for a few days. While he waits for the boat to be finished, Madam Liang will have time to find out what she can through her sources. If she doesn't come up with something, all he'll have to show for his time here is a large expense account and the information from Lin. Minton won't be happy about that.

Mike decides to avoid suspicion by going on a shopping trip to Nanjing Road this afternoon. East Nanjing Road above the Bund precinct features European-style restaurants. It's close to the Central Market, an old outdoor market. Still further west are most of Shanghai's oldest and largest department stores, as well as some historic restaurants and colorful cafes. A few of the high-fashion houses are here, places like Louis Vitton, Dior, and Chanel. Very few Chinese can afford such luxury, but apparently industrialists and high-level politicians can. It's a curious mix for a socialist state to have these haute couture houses here with actually tens of millions starving just a few miles away in the countryside. Nevertheless, it's a very pleasant stroll. His hope is that his MSS friends are enjoying it as well. Zhu's boys can spend the day watching him go in and out of shops alone and riding buses without making any contact with anyone. It would be fun if it weren't so serious. Zhu might decide to grab him just to be mean and see if he can force something out of Mike through more and tougher questioning. He's correct that he can hold Mike, and no one would know he was missing. Mike doesn't even know if Panama has a consulate in Beijing, although it wouldn't do him any good if it did.

A week after his chat with Zhu, Mike receives a call from Mrs. Lao. She tells him that Yang wants to talk with him about progress on the boat. A car will collect him the next morning to deliver him to CSSC. This is good. It saves his initiating a call to her. When he arrives, she greets him and takes him to the dining room for tea. Selecting a table in a corner, she explains in a quiet voice, "There is no meeting. I just heard about your meeting with Mr. Zhu at MSS. What was it about?"

"He grilled me quite thoroughly regarding my meetings with you, Madam Liang, and Mr. Lin. We got into a heated confrontation, where he threatened to detain me incommunicado."

"Oh, dear; that would be very bad. We must bring this business along. For your information, Mr. Yang is planning on the launch in the last week in March or first week in April. Of course you will want to be there for the traditional ceremony. We always have a Buddhist priest bless the ship as it is being launched. On the other side, Madam Liang's sources have been successful in obtaining some documentation on the new ships. I've not seen it yet, but she says it is a schema of the design with some details. She believes it is what you need."

"That is great news. How will she deliver the documents to me?"

"She will give them to me, and the next time you come here to sign off on the vessel after initial sea trials, I will give them to you. It will be easy to conceal them since I understand they have been reduced to microfiche."

Two days before the launch, Mrs. Lao calls Mike back to CSSC. They have a short meeting with Zhang, and then he turns Mike over to Mrs. Lao to finalize details. Once in her office, she closes the door. Assuming that the office is bugged, she hands him a packet of documents and says, "Here are your final documents for you to review. I'm certain that you will enjoy the launch ceremony. After the sea trial, please come back for the document sign-ing giving the boat over to your company." When he looks quizzically at her, she simply smiles. He gets it. The documents on the new ships will be avail-able then.

After a short, low-power sea trial, the boat will get its final outfitting. While they are completing the outfitting, Mike should be able to leave Shanghai. The fitting-out of a vessel can last weeks or even months for a large ship. The process can include completion of the superstructure and installation of the engines, interior equipment, and systems, including finishing interior spaces. In this case, since the vessel is small, most of the superstructure and engine installation have been completed. Equipment and systems are nearly finished. The only things to be completed are the furnishings. The boat will be ready for a short trial under low power in a few days. After that, Mike can leave, and Rosa can come and take possession of the boat. She's very astute, and he's cer-tain she can carry it off without any problem. Mission accomplished, almost.

Mike still has to leave without creating any suspicion or being detained. Since he knows MSS are watching every move, including his departure, he'll just be cool until a week or so after the sea trial.

The first week in April, the boat is launched, partially outfitted, and ready for a short sea trial a few miles out of the mouth of the Huangpu into the East China Sea. The crew consists of a helmsman, two engineers to check out the engines and systems, and a couple deckhands. Mrs. Lao has assigned the crew. At 0900 Mike gives the command to the helmsman to start the engines and cast off. They float unsteadily into the river's current until the propellers engage. Now they have command of the vessel. The tide is running out, and there is an offshore breeze, so they move steadily downriver. Mike tests the controls and gives the helmsman orders to make small heading changes back and forth as they progress down this big river. The Huangpu is over a thousand feet wide on average and over twenty-five feet deep. Once they leave the river and enter the East China Sea, the current becomes more agitated due to the inflow of the mighty Yangtze River descending from the north. Nevertheless, the boat responds easily to his commands. He orders an increase to half power, and the boat lurches forward. They feel the power of the twin engines. Mike's confident that this baby can fly. He insisted that the machineguns be installed and ammunition on board to test the guns. After a few miles south, there are no vessels in sight. He pushes the buttons to raise the guns. Moving first to the starboard side, he checks the gun and then get into position to fire it. After a few quick bursts, he moves to the port weapon and repeats the firing. All goes well. He lowers the weapons back under deck and gives the command to reverse course back to the Huangpu. Running against the heavy current and a port beam wind causes some shuddering but little listing and no yawing. Once back in the dock, Mike turns the boat over to the yard superintendent with a short punch list of small items. He's satisfied that they have bought the navy a seaworthy vessel. In a few days, he'll take her back out for a complete sea trial under full power. The next stop will be CSSC to sign papers with Mrs. Lao accepting the vessel and hopefully picking up the documents that Madam Liang has obtained. She's given him a bank account in Hong Kong where the navy can send payment for her and Madam Liang's services.

A week later a heavy April rainstorm is lashing Shanghai. The trees are bending under the wind. Their fresh spring blossoms are being ripped off their branches and blown across the streets. Papers and trash bounce along, and pedestrians cower from the wind gusts as they hurry toward their destinations. This great metropolis is dark and gray despite the bright-red and yellow decorations of storefronts. It's not a good day for a full-power sea trial. Mike decides that after he sees Mrs. Lao, he'll go to the boat and tell the crew to take the day off. They'll go out as soon as this front passes.

Shaking the rain off his umbrella, coat, and briefcase he waits in the CSSC lobby for Mrs. Lao. Presently, she hurries in, excusing herself for being late. She motions him to follow her to her office. Once there, they make small talk before she asks if he's satisfied with the vessel.

"I had planned to take it out for its final trial this morning, but the storm is making the sea too rough. It would be a good test of seaworthiness, but I'm certain that based on the first trial, there will be no problem."

"Very well; here are your documents signing the vessel over to Mercantil S. A." As she hands them to him, she holds on for a moment. Mike pulls on the envelope. She says, "I better put it in a plastic envelope to keep it dry." Then she releases it with an enigmatic smile. He nods and thanks her, more for the secret warship plans microfiche inside than for the little boat documents.

"After the trial, we'll have to celebrate. May I take you to dinner then?"

"That would be most enjoyable. I look forward to hearing that all went well."

It looks like the mission is nearly completed and Mike will be able to leave soon. His first thought is, "Where is Grace? Is she okay? What about her mother?" How great it will be to see her again. Hopefully, this separation has not been too much for her.

Chapter 15

Arrested

April 1971
Shanghai

When Mike reaches the front door, he sees there are taxis standing in the rain. He flips up and buttons his coat collar while opening his umbrella. The storm has not given up yet. Head down, he steps off into the street, and suddenly two men grab his arms. He looks up and sees Wong and Guo, the MSS agents. "Mr. Zhu wishes to speak with you," Guo mutters as he tugs Mike behind him into the backseat of the MSS car. Wong jumps into the front and tells the young driver to go to MSS headquarters.

"What is this?"

"Mr. Zhu wishes to speak with you," he repeats. Wong turns around and volunteers with a cynical smile that Zhu has evidence that Mike is not who he says he is.

Mike thinks quickly to himself, I don't have any idea what that is, but it can't be good. If they take me in now and look into my briefcase, I'm a dead man. They'll run the microfiche and discover that I'm a spy. They know where the fiche came from, and Mrs. Lao will also be caught up. This is what my friends in the intell business call deep shit.

With the briefcase between him and Guo, Mike reaches down the outside of his right leg. "You jerk, you hurt my leg," he yells as he reaches for the little Walther PPK pistol in his calf holster. He's been carrying it ever since his session with Zhu. In one motion he pulls it out and fires it point blank into Guo's right eye. As Guo's head slams back against the doorframe, Mike turns and unloads the second shot into Wong's left ear. The man bounces against the door and rebounds into the driver. The pounding thunder, driving rain on the roof and a bloody dead man on his shoulder totally terrorizes the driver, who screams, swerves the car, and stops. Mike jams the gun against his neck and tells him to drive quickly to the Huangpu shipyard. With terror in his eyes, the young man stomps on the gas, and they careen through the slippery, wet streets.

The guard at the shipyard recognizes the MSS license plate and waves them through. The car windows are steamed, and he can't see the chaos inside. Mike directs the driver to the boat. As they pull up, Mike tells him to run to the stern line and cast it off. He nods, thinking Mike's going to shoot him. Mike takes care of the bow line. There are only three crewmen in the cabin on board smoking cigarettes. They look at Mike casting off and wonder what's happening. The other crewmen must have gone ashore, not thinking they would be needed because of the storm.

Mike's mind is racing. I know these men are loyal to Mrs. Lao, so I tell them quickly to start the engines, and I'll explain when we're underway. I figure I've got at least thirty minutes before Zhu finds out what happened. He'll probably send out gunboats to intercept us. Fortunately, this boat is faster than anything the Chinese have, I believe. With the storm still raging, he can't get aircraft into the air. On top of all that, the storm is going to make it difficult to find us. We have a low profile, so radar probably can't pick us up amid the high, surging seas. He also doesn't know where to look for us. Come to think of it, neither do I.

Without any charts on board, Mike has to dead reckon them toward Okinawa. America maintains air and naval units there. It's about five hundred miles east-southeast from Shanghai. The good news is they should have full tanks since they had planned a full-power sea trial for today. The downside is that this vessel is designed for a four-hundred-mile range. With the high seas, even that will be cut back. Bottom line, even if they get away from China, they'll still be more than one hundred miles short of Okinawa, provided the storm doesn't capsize them on the way. Okinawa is the closest friendly port, even though it's not a reachable goal.

All that goes through his mind before he has time to talk to the crew. Fortunately, they obey without question, and he tells the helmsman to take them out of the river and into the middle of the East China Sea. From there, his heading is to be south-southeast 130 degrees until further notice. Mike calls the deckhand into the wheelhouse and explains to both of them that they are headed for Okinawa. If they want to return to China, he'll send them back, and they can claim they had no choice but to go with him. Next, he goes below to the engineer and repeats the story. This is the most critical person because he can foul the engine, and they will just drift until picked up by the Chinese coast guard. Again, Mike's lucky. He's happy to get out of China.

The storm is still surging. Back in the wheelhouse Mike tells the helmsman to turn on the radio and listen for reports of the storm's movement. But under no condition is he to transmit anything. He knows the Chinese will be listening for radio signals to try to locate the boat. The storm is keeping their speed down to about fifteen knots as they fight through five-foot waves. Mike and the engineer examine all below-deck surfaces for signs of leaks. So far the little boat is watertight. All they can do now is continue on their heading and wait for the storm to subside.

There's no food or drink aboard except for some water in the small galley reservoir. Mike looks at his watch. It's 1700. The storm seems to be lessening slightly. It might be moving northeast and leaving them behind. They probably left Shanghai about 1000, so seven hours at ten to fifteen knots puts them only about eighty or ninety miles off the China coast, plus or minus any current drift. They still have maybe three hours of light for the Chinese to find them. As the wind abates and the sea calms, they pick up speed to about twenty knots. They'll still be in Chinese territorial waters until dark. Actually, if the Chinese find them, Mike doubts they'll have any qualms about blowing them out of the water no matter where they are. "If I was in their shoes," he thinks, "I would do the same thing. You can always apologize afterward."

As they leave the worst of the storm behind, they cruise at twenty-five knots for the next hour. That's as fast as they can go in this still-turbulent sea. Suddenly, he hears a roar overhead. Looking up and astern, he sees a helicopter coming up behind them. The wind is buffeting it a bit, but he's holding his course steadily toward them. Mike points him out to the helmsman, who swears and pushes the throttle forward without waiting for an order. They're bouncing along at nearly thirty knots. Within a long, agonizing minute, the chopper is abeam. There is a crewman waving at them. He's indicating that they should turn around and head back toward China. They wave back at him but continue toward Okinawa, still over four hundred miles away and outside the patrol path of US aircraft.

When he sees they aren't complying, he pulls out a machine gun and shows that he will shoot them if they don't. The helmsman turns toward the plane and drives underneath him. In a few seconds, the pilot sees his game and banks away, exposing them again to the gunman. Seeing that they're not going to play, he fires across the bow. They're totally open to him. The wheelhouse is bulletproof, but the hull is only reinforced aluminum. With the air turbulence, the gunner's aim is erratic. Still, the little boat can't stand up to any machinegun bullets. Mike tells the helmsman to go underneath again while he raises the two machineguns from below deck. He spins the port gun toward the chopper and loads it for firing. Quickly the chopper banks away. He drops off a couple hundred yards while he figures out what to do. Mike doesn't see guns sticking out of the nose of the fuselage. This is not a gunship, thank god.

Mike's guess is he has reported finding them and their refusal to return. Somewhere back there, people in fancy uniforms covered with medals and gold are debating whether or not to kill us. He doubts that in a few minutes there will be anyone voting against it. Sure enough, slowly the pilot reduces the distance to the boat, and when he reaches about three hundred yards, the gunner fires a burst at them. The bullets hit the water well behind them. He was just testing the wind and distance. Now the pilot comes in faster and lower, only fifty feet off the waves. Another burst goes over their heads. He's got them bracketed. No time to wait. Mike tracks the bird and let's loose a test burst. With the bouncing of the boat, it's very difficult to get a bead on him. The helmsman starts weaving back and forth. That makes it harder for the helicopter to hit the boat and vice versa. Finally, the pilot guns his ship as if running up to broadside them. The wind is making it hard on the gunner, who is bouncing as he tries to bring his machinegun to bear on the boat. He squeezes off a couple rounds, and Mike feels a couple hit the boat.

He holds on to the gun with all his strength. Then, he squeezes the trigger and hold its. A long burst flashes and explodes out of the muzzle. The bullets stitch the chopper. It shudders and momentarily plunges almost into the waves. Either the pilot or copilot must have been hit. Someone grabs the controls just in time to keep from hitting the water. As it slows and rises, Mike has the helmsman pull away about two hundred yards. Mike fires again because the chopper is still within range. Now the pilot has to think what to do. Slowly, he pulls up and maintains a station about a quarter-mile astern.

The weather is improving, and as the sun slowly sinks toward the China mainland, the chopper turns and heads west. He's probably running low on fuel. He's called in and told command where they are. He's given attack aircraft coordinates and a heading to them. Although they're clearly still in Chinese waters, it's time to forget protocol and save their ass.

Mike gets on the radio and sends out an SOS on the guard frequency. That is an open frequency that everyone should be monitoring for just such a case. His hope is that a US P3V flying from Taiwan to Okinawa or Okinawa to Japan will hear them and turn their way. They are required to have a spare radio on board turned to the guard frequency. They might even scramble some F-16s out of Kadena Air Base or F-100s out of NAS Naha on Okinawa to give some protection if the Chinese air force finds the boat. They might even get lucky and have a fishing boat or other vessel in the area come to their aid. It's a deadly race to see who finds them first.

In a few minutes, Mike sees a fishing trawler off their starboard beam. It's flying a Chinese flag, so he orders the helmsman to keep the speed up and leave it far behind. Then comes the bad news in the form of two MIG fighter jets with Chinese markings. They roar over at about five hundred feet and begin a long turn back. This time they slow slightly and drop to one hundred feet right across the bow. Their message is clear: turn back. Instead, the helmsman guns the engine and begins evasive turns. Within two minutes they are back, and this time they fire across the bow. This second message is unequivocal. The next pass will be our last few minutes afloat and possibly alive.

Mike's fifty-caliber machine guns might be lucky and hit them the next time around, but it will be their last act because the MIGs can easily blow them out of the water with their twin 23 mm NR cannons. Mike orders the deckhand to break out the inflatable life raft. As he sees them making a turn to come back, he asks the deckhand for his knife. Mike slashes the plastic seat cover behind the helmsman and makes a quick wrap around the microfiche packet. The fiche and his notes from Lin's visit are in the plastic bag, but he wants to provide as much cushioning as he can. He's still wearing the suit he wore in the meeting with Mrs. Lao. Now it's soaked with seawater. He wonders if Minton will buy him a new suit when he gets back to Pearl, if he does. Mike pulls his jacket open, tears the shirt buttons from their holes, and jams the large package under his left armpit. Then, he snaps the life jacket closed and prepares everyone to abandon ship.

The fighters are coming at them no more than one hundred feet off the surface. Maybe it will be three seconds before they catch the first and last salvo. But then, in the last half mile, they suddenly pull up without firing. What the hell is going on? The deckhand pokes Mike's shoulder and points off the port bow. A mile away is another vessel. It isn't very big, and it isn't a warship. It's a freighter. The ship is low in the water, obviously heavily laden with cargo. Since they're only a hundred or so miles off China, they're probably headed for Taiwan or a coastal city in southern China. Astern they're flying the red ball of the Japanese flag. The deckhand jumps up on the bow and starts yelling and waving.

The jets have seen the ship and are reconsidering their attack. It doesn't take long. Within three minutes they are coming back, and their intent is clear. This isn't going to be a farewell salute and return to base. They're going to take the boat and crew out no matter who the witness is. It's like Mike thought before. They can always apologize afterward, but they won't.

The first shots hit the water about fifty yards short. Then, the next burst rips into the bow and tears the deckhand apart, throwing his body angrily into the sea. As the wingman lines up his shot, the engineer, helmsman, and Mike dive off the stern. He holds onto the lanyard connected to the raft. Number two fires, and the aluminum structure is shattered in a million pieces as the cannon shells disintegrate the hull and cabin.

Mike bobs back up to the surface and looks for his shipmates. First one and then the other surfaces. Mike's still holding the lanyard but isn't going to deploy the raft until the MIGs decide they've done their job and head home. It's only another minute before they come roaring back at one hundred feet to see their handiwork. Passing over the shattered remains of the sinking boat, they pull up and rapidly gain altitude, homeward bound.

Now it's safe to deploy the raft. Mike holds onto the gunwale while they fall in. It's an eight-man raft so there is plenty of room. He hopes its outfitting has been completed with flares, oars, and signal lights. In a few minutes, they collect themselves and check each other. No wounds but probably a lot of bruises that will begin to ache once the adrenaline wears off. They look eastward for the freighter. All they can see is the trail of his smoke slowly pulling away. "I guess he doesn't want any part of whatever he just witnessed," Mike thinks.

Taking stock, they find themselves still a couple hundred miles west of Okinawa at some unknown latitude. It will be dark soon. They have no food or water and only a tarp to cover them. If they huddle close together, they'll share some body warmth, but it won't be much. The hope is the SOS was picked up by someone who cares enough to investigate. The raft has a transmitter that continually sends a distress signal also. Mike asks the men which direction the current flows in this area. They tell him the currents vary by latitude. Generally, the flow is northward out of the South China Sea. But as they go farther north, the Japanese Sea currents come into play and tend to push eastward. He's certain that they're well south of that, so they will probably just drift north parallel to Okinawa. This will put them in shipping lanes, so they might be spotted before long by freighters or fishing boats. The navy has a picket line of ships and planes running north and south through this area also. The bad news is its getting dark, and the wind is cold. Most likely they're going to spend the night here. They spoon their bodies and wrap the tarp around them like a giant tortilla. There's little chance of a rescue in the dark, so they don't need anyone on watch. Some healing sleep is called for.

By morning, they're all wet and shivering. The engineer is coughing and spitting blood. He probably swallowed a lot of seawater. Fortunately, the sea is calm now, with only a slight breeze off the mainland. Swells are rolling lazily eastward. That will help move them toward the Ryukyu Islands, where Okinawa is the center. The worst part, besides the cold, is thirst. They have no fresh water on board. As the sun comes up, they begin to feel a bit of warmth. It's only April, so it won't get hot, if at all, until around midday.

Mike positions them around the raft so that they each have a different vista. This way they shouldn't miss any passing vessels. The morning hours drift very slowly. Taking inventory of the raft's equipment, Mike doesn't find the usual survival items like fishing equipment and any food rations. All they have are a signaling mirror and a flare gun.

Around noon they hear the sound of aircraft engines. They're props, not jets. That probably means a patrol plane. Could be a navy P3V. In a few minutes, they can see it at about a thousand feet heading south. The men jump up and wave frantically, nearly falling overboard. Mike grabs the flare gun and waits to see if the plane is coming their way. He's several miles east at about thirty degrees off their starboard bow. He fires the gun, and thank god, it works. The flare arcs into the sky in the plane's direction. They wait. No reaction. The plane is continuing to pass them headed south. Quickly he loads and fires another flare. Again, no reaction. They slump back into the raft as the plane passes. Then, there is a change in the pitch of the engines. He's circling around. Maybe he saw the flare after all. Yes. Yes. Here he comes. Passing over at five hundred feet, he waggles his wings. Slowly, he turns around and drops down to two hundred feet. They can see the copilot and crewmen waving at them. Then something drops from the plane and nearly hits the raft. The engineer leans into the oars, and, in a few minutes, they snag the packet. It's a message telling them they have diverted a destroyer escort in their direction at flank speed. The ship should be here in a couple hours. There is a note that there are Chinese vessels in the area, and they will stay on station as protection until the DE arrives.

After the ship picks the three men up in late afternoon, they're met by a coast guard cutter out of Okinawa that will bring them to port. The skipper wants to know who these three are and what they're doing in the middle of the East China Sea.

They have no ID. Mike has a full beard and unruly long hair. He keeps his cover by telling him in Spanish that he is Miguel Hernandez, special agent for naval intelligence out of Pearl Harbor. Fortunately, there is a crewman who understands Spanish. Mike tells him to verify this by having Okinawa Communications contact Commander Minton at CINCPAC. He does. While they wait, they trade their soggy attire for a shower, navy fatigues, and food. It's been about eighteen hours since they've eaten.

Mike's primary concern is the microfiche. Once settled, he has time to examine the wet packet. He wipes it off and then removes the outer cover. He can see that the plastic bag is intact. But it looks a little steamy. His body heat probably warmed the incipient moisture and created the steam. Sliding the fiche out with great sensitivity, he blots them with some tissue. He can't tell if they're damaged or not. He'll have to wait to find out once they reach port. His notes are a little damp but generally readable.

By the time they're pulling into port the next morning, someone has talked to Minton and cleared Mike's story. He leaves the engineer and helmsman with the Shore Patrol. He tells them how they made the escape possible and should be well treated. Without these men, Mike would be in a Shanghai jail today.

It's a short ride from the pier to NAS Naha, where he's shown into the CO's office. His fatigues show no insignia, of course, since they believe he's a contract civilian agent. The CO wants to know the story, but Mike respectfully tells him that he's under the command of navy intell in Hawaii and cannot disclose anything of his activity. The CO must talk to Minton if he needs to know how to handle this. The captain probes, but Mike remains silent. The man has already talked to Minton. He's just curious to find out some of the interesting stuff from the mission. Mike is dismissed with a wry smile from the captain. He tells his aide to make arrangements for Mike on the next plane to Pearl. He's given clean clothes and checked into a BOQ for some much-needed rest and food.

Lying back on his bed with a full stomach and a glass of scotch to warm him, he's headed home after a year on this mission. His thoughts immediately go to Grace. They've not had contact for a year. A lot can happen in that much time. He wonders if she's well, where she is, how her mother is, and how she's dealing with Jerry. He's missed her so much. She's such a clever woman that she would make a great teammate in the covert game.

Chapter 16

Home in Pearl

May 1971
Pearl Harbor

Mike lands on Oahu in early morning as the sun is just starting its climb over Diamond Head. As always the air is fragrant, so delicious you can almost eat it. Immediately, he's picked up by two marines and escorted to Hotel Solitary, back where he started thirteen months ago. He finds clean pajamas on the bed, underwear in the bureau, and a shirt and slacks in the closet. Along with that is a new khaki uniform. You have to hand it to Minton. He's one fine man. There's also an envelope on the table. When he opens it, the message is that he's to report to Minton's office at 1300. In the meantime he can't call out on this phone, so there's no way he can contact Grace's mother.

Suddenly in the midst of his thoughts, there is a knock at the door. This is really a surprise. When he opens it, he finds a small Asian man in a white smock and a bag in this hand. "Good morning, sir. I am Somaya, your barber. I've been instructed to cut your hair and give you a shave. It looks like you need one."

Mike gets it. This ends his disguise. Miguel is leaving, and Michael is coming back. What a load off his back. There's a lump in his throat. After a year playing a role that could get him killed or worse, he's finally off the hook. "Come in, Mr. Somaya. You're going to earn your pay today."

At 1250 he arrives in Minton's reception area. Then, minutes later, Minton opens the door to his office. "Welcome back, Mike," Minton says a great deal of warmth. "You've proven yourself again. I'm certain there is another citation on its way. You look like you've had a rough time. Are you okay?"

"Yes, sir. It was a bit touchy leaving Shanghai. They really didn't want me to go. I had to shoot my way out. MSS doesn't know why I was there, but they're probably giving my contacts at CSSC a rough time about it."

"I understand you have a package for me. Tell me about your escape."

"Yes, sir. This envelope has my notes regarding the electronics of the ships as well as microfiche diagrams of the hull, deck, and weaponry. Somehow the paper and fiche survived a bath in the East China Sea. There was some small damage to the paper, but more than eighty percent came through in readable condition. I can elaborate on it from memory. I was fortunate to partner with a Madam Liang and a Mrs. Lao. They were invaluable. Madam Liang's people got the microfiche for me. They need to be rewarded handsomely. We may need them again someday. Here is a bank account number at HSBC where you can send the money. I suggest about a hundred thousand dollars will be fair."

"Well done. I'll take care of the money. We'll want to spend some time going over the documents with you and any other intell you picked up about shipbuilding in Shanghai or China. There'll be some top-secret briefings with the admiral's staff and others with a need-to-know. After that, why don't you take a couple weeks off and decompress? You've earned a lot of leave time and back pay. I'll have your gear sent over from storage. Check into the BOQ now. Michael Holmes is back."

That was exactly what he wanted to hear. Those months in Shanghai were intense because he could never relax. Playing the part of another man doesn't allow you to turn off for an instant. It's just like being on stage, except if you blow your lines; you get more than a bad review in the *Times*. You get relieved of the role, the hard way.

While Mike was flying back from Okinawa, he let down a year's worth of tension and penned a letter to Grace. He figures he'll hand it to her when he sees her.

May 20, 1971

Dear C. J.,

I'm on my way back to Pearl. It will be a great relief getting back to the States. Of course the highlight will be seeing you. I just hope you are well and will be as happy to see me.

It will also be a relief to be out of the role I had to play for the past year. Even though it's over, I can't talk about it. The pressure for over a year was steady and the danger ever present. Still it wasn't anything compared to being on the ground in close combat. Nevertheless, suffice to say it was successful.

Now, I can relax for a while, hopefully with you, before the navy comes up with another crazy mission. Sometimes I wonder where they get these ideas.

I fantasize about a group of men sitting in a smoke-filled room asking, "What kind of an insane assignment can we think up for Holmes this time?"

Well, until they do, I hope that you and I can have some time together. I'll be happy to see your mom again. I hope she's well. Of course I don't know your situation with Jerry. I'll just have to wait to find out.

Anxiously,
Sherlock

After Minton dismisses him, Mike checks into the BOQ, takes a shower, and rests for a bit to get his land legs back and brain functioning again. He's still feeling some of the effects of his bath in the East China Sea.

When he feels that he's somewhat functional, he takes a deep breath and picks up the phone to dial out to Mrs. Liu's number. He's had it memorized for a year as he ran repeated scenarios of what it would be like when he hears Grace's voice. In a few seconds, a recorded voice comes on the line and says, "This number has been disconnected." Maybe his memory isn't as good as he thought it was. He rummages through the desk and finds the local phone book. Nervously fumbling through the pages, he locates the number. It's the one he believes he dialed.

Maybe he made a mistake. Now his hand is shaking. He picks up the receiver and dials again very slowly and carefully. Again, the recording tells him the number has been disconnected. Now what? Back to the phone book. He thinks he'll look for Jerry Donaldson. "I don't know what I'll do if he answers. Wait a minute, you dunce; he's in Moffett. Get a grip, Holmes." He replaces the receiver and lies back on the bed. Now what? "I've got to get a car somewhere and drive up to Mrs. Liu's house."

Mike desperately needs some sleep. He didn't get a wink on the plane coming back, too exhausted from the sea trial and too nervous to sleep. But now that the mission is complete, he closes his eyes for just a minute. There's a knock on the door. A man is standing there with his gear. Mike thanks him and lays it out on the bed. It's been cooped up for a year in a humid climate, and it smells like it. He shakes the uniforms and mufti out and hangs them in the closet. He puts the odds and ends away in the desk and bureau. Probably need to send it all to the laundry tomorrow. There is a year's worth of back pay in the bank, so he can afford to rent a car and spend some to find out what's happened while he's been away.

By 1600 he's in the rental car headed for Nuuanu Valley. He makes a wrong turn on the winding streets since his mind and memory aren't at full speed yet. Finally he pulls up in front of Mrs. Liu's house. When he mounts the steps onto the porch, the house seems very quiet. He rings the doorbell. No answer. He tries to see into the draped window and can make out furniture. Someone lives here. A walk around the house confirms it's occupied. As he reaches the backyard, a neighbor lady sees him looking around. She asks, "Can I help you?"

"I'm a friend of Mrs. Liu and her daughter. I'm a naval officer. I've just returned from a deployment. Do you know where Mrs. Liu is?"

"I guess you didn't know. Mrs. Liu passed away almost a year ago. The house was sold, and there is an older couple living here now. They're very nice people. I don't know anything about Mrs. Liu's daughter; her name is Grace, isn't it?"

"Yes. I didn't know about Mrs. Liu. I remember that she wasn't doing so well, but I didn't know that she died. I'm so sorry. She was a very sweet lady. I liked her very much. And you say you don't know Grace's whereabouts?"

The lady nods. "She didn't tell us where she was going when she locked up the house after selling it. She was a lovely young woman."

"Yes. That's true. Thank you." With that, Mike walks slowly back to the front of the house and takes a last look, remembering the night with Grace and her mother. Getting back into the car, he has a thought. I'll go to the Chinese Cultural Center. Grace worked there part time when she lived here. That was before Jerry was transferred to Moffett. Maybe when she was back caring for her mother, she might have dropped in at the center to tell them what was happening. She could have gone there after her mother passed just to say good-bye.

He starts the car and eases it back downhill to town. At the center a very sweet little Chinese lady who looks to be a hundred years old is at the reception desk.

She says, "Good morning."

He replies, "*Zǎoshang hǎo.*"

She smiles so prettily. "Your Chinese pronunciation is very good. What can I do for you?"

"I'm a friend of Grace—I mean Liu Chan-juan. I understand her mother passed away, and I'm trying to locate Chan-juan. Do you know where she has gone?"

"I don't know. I'm just a part-time volunteer. You should talk to our director, Miss Ming. I'll call her."

In a few minutes, a middle-aged Chinese woman comes out and shakes Mike's hand. "I'm Miss Ming. You want to know about Grace, is that correct?"

"Yes, Grace and I met here a couple years ago and became good friends. I've been in WestPac for several months and lost contact with her. Do you know where she went after her mother passed?"

"I wasn't here when she came to say good-bye, but I was told that she went to the mainland. I think her husband is stationed somewhere over there. I don't have her address. I'm sorry."

"I understand. Thank you very much." Turning to the old lady at the desk, he says, "*Xiè xiè*." Her sweet face lights up like a Christmas tree, and she gives him a slight bow.

Mike drives back to the BOQ. He's perplexed and restless. He walks around the grounds of the BOQ to try to draw off some of the tension. He doesn't know how to contact Grace at Moffett without creating a problem for her. She must be with Jerry there or some other place. Slow down, Holmes. Get your body and mind back together. It's been a rough year. You need to think, old boy. Even if this is the end of a beautiful idea, hold on. You're a young man. Don't go bonkers just yet. You have a long road ahead. Chin up, old chap. Carry on.

Chapter 17

Hong Kong Rebound

June 1971
Hong Kong

After a tedious month of briefings and meetings, Mike's just getting settled into his new job in the strategic section of CINCPAC's intelligence function. Then, he is summoned by Captain Bradley. "Holmes, you're our China hand. You've become a very valuable man. You have the touch when it comes to working undercover in the Chinese world. We've got a new mission that will build on that. This shouldn't be as dangerous, but it's even more important than the Shanghai case. You'll be the lead man in Hong Kong.

The goal is straightforward. It's strategic rather than weapon focused. Find out all you can about China's military plans, strategy, and weapons development. Obviously, since you can't travel in the PRC, you're going to have to be very clever in finding agents. Just like in Shanghai, you're going in deep cover. But this time there will be no physical disguise. Your cover will be that you're a writer doing research for a book on political economics in Asia. I say deep cover since no one, including our people in Hong Kong, will know who you really are. My new XO, Commander Jack Tweed, just came on board. He'll brief you and be your sole contact while you're in Hong Kong. He'll provide whatever you need to carry out your mission. Is that clear?"

I think, Yessiree Bob, Uncle Bradley. Will that be sufficient for now? I shan't be away more than a fortnight. Are these people crazy? They want me to be a spy in absentia with a wide open, nonspecific mission? How will I or how will they know if I've been successful? The United States does not have formal recognition in place with China, so clearly I can't travel or operate on the mainland. Hong Kong is as close as I can come. How the hell do you spy on a country when you aren't in it, flying over it, or otherwise connected to it? When I was successful in Shanghai, it was because I had a specific target—the new ships—and was in the city for several months. I was in such deep cover that it was like working out of a manhole. But at least I was in the city and could see, meet, and talk with people. I'm told that I can communicate with Commander Tweed via a dedicated secure telephone line that the Brits have leased to us. My Hong Kong apartment building is owned by Uncle Sam, and the apartment is used only by US personnel.

The next morning Mike heads for Commander Tweed's office. To say his greeting is cool is like saying absolute zero is cold. "Good morning, Holmes. Bradley seems to have an exalted opinion of your work. I'm not certain that I concur. Your escapade in Shanghai took a very long time and was extremely expensive, and the value of the data you obtained is still unclear."

"Have you seen the data, sir?"

"Only a small part and it does not appear to be all that useful."

"Do you have a background in physics or electronics, sir?'

"No. Accounting and law. Nevertheless, they're throwing you back into China and expecting your performance will improve. I want you to understand that you will operate on a stringent budget this time. You will have a small stipend to spend, and in no way are you to go over that amount. As regards reporting, you are to cable me a detailed coded report of your activity and spending once a month. Call only if there is an emergency. Be on time, or I will cut off your account at the HKSB. This is not a free ride like Shanghai was. Here are your orders. Study them carefully, and do not go off on some wild scheme, or I'll snap you back here so fast you'll be looking for a career outside of the US Navy. Do you understand me?"

"Aye, aye, sir."

What's his problem? Where did he come from? Mike goes to the intell library and look up Tweed's career. No wonder. This is his first field assignment. He's spent the previous twenty some years in DC navigating a desk. I'll be jiggered, guv. His background is in the two worst disciplines for clandestine work. Someone must have sent him to CINCPAC to see how cheaply it can be run. This job isn't difficult enough. Now he has to cope with Happy Jack too.

On top of dealing with him, there is one other problem. In Shanghai they speak Mandarin Chinese. In Hong Kong they speak Cantonese, which is quite different. It's not like British English versus American English. In Hong Kong, Mandarin won't get him very far. He learned that on his last excursion.

The good news about this mission, if there is any, Mike thinks, is that I don't have to report to anyone on site. I'm free to do my job and report only to CINCPAC Intell through Tweed. The British crown colony of Hong Kong is an open city. People from all countries with all purposes live or pass through here. They all want something, something they probably have no right to have, and that's why Hong Kong exists. It is a trader's and spy's paradise. Like Shanghai, only a smaller, tighter bundle.

"I'm thinking, in case anyone shows an interest in me and my activities, my cover story is that I'm a writer, and my name is Matt Henderson. Given my cover, it's natural for me to go about poking in holes and asking questions. So long as I don't break any laws, the authorities will probably ignore me. My behavior won't be that different from the many adventurers pursuing their nefarious goals. On the other hand, I'm not so naïve as to believe that there isn't an army of Chinese communist operatives hiding behind every pagoda. All in all, this is clearly the embodiment of the Chinese admonition, *May you live in interesting times.*

Over the past month Mike's tried to trace Grace without success. Even a check on Jerry comes up negative. Before he can do any more research on Grace's whereabouts, Mike's on a flight to Hong Kong. His spirit is low. His love has disappeared. Still he's got to perform.

If his entry into Hong Kong is a precursor of his time there, it's going to be more than mildly exciting. He's already had the joy of the Kai Tak heart attack. This time the thrill is boosted because they land in a driving, windy rainstorm. Barf bags are in operation throughout the aircraft. An hour after the roller-coaster ride into Kai Tak, he's on Hong Kong Island in the apartment that is his new home. His district is a couple blocks south of Hollywood Road, aptly named SoHo. The building has four levels with a secure garage on the ground floor. He's on the fourth floor with a balcony. The view is restricted by the forest of skyscrapers starting just a block away. The unit is nicely furnished, and the plumbing is up to date. All in all, it's quite comfortable.

Mike's first step once he's settled is just to cast as wide a net as possible in getting acquainted across several factions from business to sports and military. He begins by hanging out in the finest hotels and pubs, sopping up too many gin and tonics and wrangling invitations to the prestigious clubs. Although everyone likes to talk to writers, it's very slow, repetitive, and often frustrating work requiring the greatest degree of sensitivity.

Underneath it, Mike needs to recruit agents who have tentacles into the military establishment on the mainland. Cricket, football—we call it soccer—basketball, badminton, table tennis, cycling, and equestrian events draw big crowds. At the amateur or club-level Hong Kong Park, among other venues, is the site of weekly games. He starts to hang out and talk to people at these events. Eventually, they invite him to join in. He's not adept at cricket or soccer, but he can play a bit of basketball, at least at this level. One sport leads to another, and within about three months, he's got a busy weekend schedule of team activities. By late summer, the social whirl intensifies with holiday parties. He meets more people and gradually builds up an acquaintanceship of business and some military people. This is fun in some regards, although it is lonely and slow to show progress. His rationale is that you have to till the soil before you can plant seeds and eventually harvest something.

One day, when the humidity isn't strangling, Mike decides to spend an afternoon strolling through the better stores in the Landmark Mall. Landmark, also called Central by some, is the retail center of the island. Every high-end store is there. It's a great place to troll for prospects. The thing about spies is they come in all sizes, shapes, and looks. Almost all like and need money. He's about to call it a day as he ambles slowly through one of the upscale shops. At one counter is a twenty-something-year-old Chinese woman looking enviously at the luxury on display. As he saunters past her, she looks up and smiles. In heavily accented English, she remarks enviously, "So pretty, so expensive."

He takes a guess and answers her in Mandarin. She's startled. She steps back and looks him up and down. "You speak Mandarin?" she asks in Mandarin.

"*Shì de, wǒ yuànyì*" (Yes, I do).

She beams and takes off speaking a mile a minute. Within a few sentences she's given him half her life. She says her name is Jinjing. She lives in Beijing and works at the Guófángbù, the Ministry of National Defense. Bingo! Once a pure heart pays off.

MND is a liaison center that represents the PLA with foreign militaries in cooperative projects. It's the nerve center for organization, equipment, and scientific military research. At this time the MND has no minister in charge due to the upset of the Cultural Revolution and the death of the previous minister, Lin Biao, in a suspicious plane crash last September.

Jinjing babbles on about how she comes to Hong Kong frequently to meet with British and Asian military. She talks about how nice it is to see the opulence of the colony but contrarily how unsettling it is not to be able to participate in it. "So expensive, so expensive," she repeats.

He agrees with her how nice it must be to be wealthy and how unfair it is that the two of them are not. The conversation is light and humorous. She's a fun person, a bit young for him, but nevertheless, enjoyable. After a few more comments, he invites her to continue their chat over a cup of tea at one of the shops in the mall. She accepts immediately. The more they talk, the more he sees that this girl is quite bright. She volunteers that she's a department head in the equipment division. Yet, for all her intelligence, she's very fresh and seemingly naïve. When she asks what he does, Mike says, "I'm a writer here doing research on a book. Like many people, she responds with, "I could write a book. The things I know would surprise people."

He teases her by asking in a disbelieving voice, "Like what?"

She pauses for a second, surprised that he challenged her. He's pushing her in the hope that she'll talk about her work and what she sees through the MND. "Well, I know what you call the 'inside story' about weapons-development strategy, mistakes being made, money being wasted, what types of projects are working, which ones aren't, which people are effective, and which programs are wasting everyone's time; things like that."

"There would probably be readers very interested in that. Why don't you do it?"

"I never really thought about it. You say you're a writer. Where does one start?"

"You start with a general topic that you know well and that interests you. Then, think about what the specific issues are and who would you be writing for—who are your readers? You might rough out an outline or just start writing and see where it goes. Once you're started, we can think about how you're going to be published."

"I think I would write about the people and projects in MND. I know them very well. Which are the good results, which are the bad. People always like gossip. But I don't know any publishers. Besides, if I did publish what I know, I would be in big trouble."

"You have a good concept. It's true that people like to read that type of material."

"But how would I get it published so that I don't get into trouble?"

"You'd have to write under a pen name to keep yourself safe."

"But what about a publisher?"

"I could help you with that. I know someone who would love your story and would keep your identity a secret. If your material is really secret, something that no one outside of China's leadership knows, they would pay you quite well. They would deposit your royalties in a secret account here in Hong Kong. Then, when you come down here, you would have money to buy the pretty things you see. You'd make more money than you can imagine."

Her eyes light up for a moment as she envisions the money. "I have to think about it. If I do it, could you help me write it? I can write reports, but I don't know that I could write a book."

"Sure. If you decide to do it, I'll help you. For now, would you like to have dinner? We could eat at the hotel next door."

She almost jumps in his lap.

Dinner is a delight. Jinjing is a very intelligent young woman with a sense of humor and no pretense about her. She prattles on at length about the MND and its people and machinations. She tells Mike there is a great deal of consternation over the mysterious death of Lin Biao. "For many years he was a close confidant of Mao. Then, he started to do and say things that Mao didn't like. Until then everyone thought he would be Mao's successor. Suddenly, last year he was killed in a plane crash. Many think that Mao ordered it. Ever since he left, we've been without a director, and the operation is getting very loose."

She seems at ease with Mike, so he encourages her to babble on. By the end of the evening, they're good friends, in her eyes. He now calls her J. J. She tells him that she'll be in town through the weekend and, with a flirty look, asks if they could get together and do something.

"Would you like to go to the south side of the island to Aberdeen, Repulse Bay, and Stanley Market on Saturday?"

"That would be wonderful. How do we get there?"

"There is good bus service leaving from Central Terminal. Let's meet there about nine o'clock."

On Saturday she's waiting in the terminal dressed in red top and black slacks. She's carrying a large straw purse. A comfortable bus ride takes them to the south side of Hong Kong Island. The first stop is Aberdeen, where they take a small boat ride in the harbor to see the fishing boats. Some people use them as residences, hardly ever setting foot on dry land since vendors go from boat to boat with their goods. The only bad part is that there are no toilets on the boats.

They spend the day with lunch and sightseeing and going through the many shops. She runs in and out of them like a child in a candy store. In time her straw purse is full of trinkets, many probably made on the mainland.

Before they realize it, the shops are closing. When it's clear that the shopping binge is coming to an end, J. J. turns to Mike with a big smile. "I'm having so much fun. Can we stay over tonight and go back to the city tomorrow? It's so nice to be in a small town away from all the noise and people in the big city. Can we stay over, please?"

He thinks for a moment about an evening in a hotel with this pretty girl. It's more than tempting. Immediately Grace springs to mind and his heart aches. "It would be very nice, a great end to a great day. However, there is one issue that I didn't want to mention for fear it would spoil your fun."

"What's that?" she asks, somewhat alarmed.

"We've been followed all day. Probably MSS men."

"What? Where?"

"Face me, and look past my left shoulder casually as you talk to me. Don't stare. Do you see two men in gray suits and black jackets?"

"Yes."

"They've been there all day. They got on the bus at Central, and they've shadowed us the whole way. Are they here to protect you or spy on you or me?"

"No, I don't know them."

"If we just go back to the city and separate there, I can't see how they can make anything out of today to harm you. We've just been tourists." Surreptitiously Mike's wondering if he's the target. But there is no reason as yet for him to be followed.

"The *hundan*" (bastards), she mutters. "You're right. They look like MSS. *Tā mā de tāmen* (Fuck them). Why would those *hundan* be following me?"

"You must be a person of importance. Are you? Do you hold a critical top-secret job at MND that you haven't mentioned?"

She glances in their direction. Then, she takes his arm and turns him toward the intercity bus terminal. "A lot of very sensitive, highly classified information comes across my desk. I never thought about it before. It's just my job. Like I told you, I know about many sensitive matters. Okay. We'll show those *hundan*. Let's go have a wonderful dinner in Aberdeen and then go back."

Three hours later, he puts J. J. in a taxi at Central Terminal and takes one himself to his apartment. He could have gone with her and dropped her off, but since he doesn't know what's behind the surveillance, this is a safer, more innocent move. They've agreed to have dinner on Monday since she's leaving Tuesday morning for Beijing. He suggests Lao Shang Hai in Wan Chai. When she says that she likes Shanghai cuisine, they make a date at 7:00 p.m.

The restaurant lives up to its reputation. It's beautifully decorated, and there's soft music in the background that no one can hear because of the table chatter. Shanghai cuisine stresses keeping the original flavors of the food. The goal is to be light in flavor and beautiful in presentation. Fish, crab, or chicken are marinated with spirits and can be cooked, steamed, or raw. Sugar is often added to soy sauce to create a pleasant sweetness.

Over dinner they discuss quietly the information for her book. It's become an exciting prospect to her, realizing that she has great intelligence to share. At the end of dinner, Mike says, "Let's get together when you come back next month." The MSS men are in the restaurant again, watching them. So they pick a date—Saturday, July 6, at 6:00 p.m. at a different restaurant. Mike tells her some ways to evade their surveillance next time.

※ ※

At 1800 on 6 July, Mike's sitting in a corner at the new rendezvous waiting a bit nervously for J. J. Will she show up? Maybe the MSS have scared her off. As he's scanning the scene, J. J. comes bouncing through the door with a huge smile on her face. She sees him and almost dives into his arms. "I'm so happy to see you, Matt. I've missed you," she gushes, giving him a big hug.

"I'm happy to see you too. Have a seat and tell me what you've been doing for the last month, but, by the way, don't talk too loud."

"Why?"

"Because your two friends just came in."

"My friends?"

"Yes, the *hundans*. They're tailing you again. Don't look."

"Those *pigus* (asses). I thought I lost them. Why don't they leave me alone?"

"Never mind them. Let's order a drink. Would you like tea or something stronger?"

"I like white wine; just a bit sweet. You order for me," she says, reaching for his hand.

"I've spent a great deal of time and thought deciding what type of information people would like to read. I brought a few documents as examples, and I want your opinion. I have some papers in my purse. I left a large report in my suitcase at the hotel. We can look at the papers here if the *hundan* ever leave us alone."

"No, I have a better idea. I want to buy you a present."

"A present, why?"

"Because I like you, and I want you to have something nice to take back with you as a remembrance of our time together in Hong Kong."

"That is so sweet."

"After dinner, we'll take a taxi to Landmark. You can choose something from one of the stores there."

"Oh, they're so expensive."

"Don't worry about it. My publisher gave me some research money as an advance on my book. Let's eat. Then we can go shopping, and later you can show me what you've brought."

By eight o'clock, they're walking through the Landmark Mall. "What would you really like to have that you can use all the time? I don't want you to have something and just put in a closet or drawer."

"I love Louis Vuitton. But his purses are so expensive."

"Let's go take a look. Maybe they have a sale going on."

She's right. Louie is no slouch. His stuff is top drawer. Mike's ready to go all the way and buy her a handbag. Screw Tweed; he can just eat it. After looking for half an hour, she decides that a handbag would be too visible in Beijing. She opts for a brown-and-tan, monogrammed, coated-canvas French clutch purse with a brass snap and zipper. After he pays for it with Tweed's money, she takes his arm, and they stroll through Landmark as though she is the queen.

"Now we need to get rid of your friends. See the large group of people watching the dancers in the atrium? Just move slowly through the crowd as though you were a snake." Gradually, they slither toward the far edge of the crowd. Being taller than the average local people, Mike has to move slowly and occasionally duck in behind a big man or a large woman with a big hat. The people are clapping for the performers and swaying to the music, creating movement and distraction. Within ten minutes they're on the other side, just a few steps from Dior's. He guides her to the far side of the store, and they quickly duck out the exit. It's not an accident that they're very near the taxi queue. He looks back as they enter the cab and doesn't see their shadows. When he gives the driver instructions to his apartment, J. J. looks at him, and slowly a smile envelops her face. She sits back and closes her eyes. Within twenty minutes, they're riding the elevator to his rooms.

"Very nice," she remarks, looking around the unit. "Do all your girlfriends like it?" she teases.

"I don't have any girlfriends."

"A handsome man like you, so talented and sensitive, I can't believe you don't have several waiting on you all the time."

"Believe what you like. I'm here to do a job, and there is no time for romance. Let's see what you've brought."

She gives him a little pouting look and reaches into her handbag. Out come a half-dozen pages that she hands him.

"Excuse me. I forgot my manners. Would you like something to drink—tea, wine?"

"No, thank you," she answers curtly.

They sit at the dining table with the papers spread out. There are a few illustrations, but mostly it's text. Mike reads through them slowly. She's brought a report on the development plans of a major weapon system. He thinks, "This is great. It's exactly what I would have asked for."

"Let's go out on the balcony. It's a beautiful night." He wants to get out of earshot on the small chance that the place is bugged. "This is a great start, J. J. What do you have in your suitcase at the hotel?"

She understands the caution. Moving close to him, she says quietly in a mock-husky voice, "It's a journal that the senior officers use to discuss their ideas about warfare and weaponry in the coming years. Part of my job is to maintain a library on military equipment. There are a number of other periodicals like that, but this is the most important one."

By now she is pressing herself against him. "I'm like a top-secret librarian. The difference is I know what happens to these weapons systems. I think this would make very interesting reading if we can decide what to write and how to keep me out of trouble with Beijing. What do you think?" she almost whispers in his ear while rubbing his back.

He eases off and thinks, "This is priceless. If she didn't deliver anything more than this, it would still be a windfall. Now I have to work out how I'm going to obtain the journal without jeopardizing either J. J. or me."

"J. J., this sounds like just what we need for a great exposé book. We'll find a way to publish it that doesn't hurt you. But for now the problem is, how are we going to transfer the document from your hotel room to me? We must assume everyone at the hotel is in the employ of the MSS. I know that isn't true, but we have to be totally cautious. Second, we have to believe the MSS that we shook are at the hotel waiting for you to return. They could even be in your room. If that is the case, they could have opened your suitcase and seen the journal."

"I can explain that. I have to carry many classified documents with me on these trips. I have the documents with me so that our delegates can have them for reference in their discussions."

"Okay. Good. Next, how you can move them from your room to me without raising suspicions? You were wise not to bring them to dinner, considering that the *hundan* were watching us. They're probably pretty upset since they have to report they lost us. I can disguise myself to move about alone in your hotel, but if we were to appear together, they would probably see through the disguise. Let's go back in, have a drink, and think about this."

Mike brings out a bottle of cognac and pours a small bit for her. As he hands it to her at the table, she puts it down and steps into him. She kisses him. He puts down his drink and returns the gesture lightly.

"I think we've had enough talk for a while," she whispers in his ear and continues to press into him. "You know, I like you very much," she whispers and kisses him again.

This is too much. He has to respond. It's his duty, for the flag and country, of course. An hour later, they're getting dressed. His mind snaps back to Grace. Even though he doesn't know if he'll ever see her again there is no pleasure in being with someone else.

Mike takes her hand and brings her out to the balcony. "That was very sweet and so are you. It's a beautiful night and I'm sorry to break the spell, but I have it."

"Have what?"

"The solution to the transfer. Your hotel is going to have a fire alarm in the middle of the night."

"What? Why?"

"We need a distraction. Nothing is more distracting than a fire drill in a large building at two in the morning."

"How is that going to happen? How will it help?"

"In a few minutes, you're going back to the hotel by taxi and go to your room as though nothing has happened. If the MSS are around, they might ask you where you've been. You just tell them whatever story you can think of… except the truth. You might say we decided to take the Star Ferry across the harbor and back, just for fun and to see the boats and skyline at night. Or you can embarrass them by asking where they've been all night. They probably won't admit to tailing us."

"I don't want to go back tonight. I'd like to stay here."

"We'll have to save that for another time."

"Oooh, I understand. But this will be fun, playing with those *pigus.*"

"Here's the plan. You go back, get ready for bed, and get the report and any other document into a package where you can grab them quickly when the fire alarm goes off. I will have entered the hotel in disguise and gone up in the elevator to one floor above you. I think you said you were on six, correct?"

"Yes, that's right, 618."

"I'll set off the alarm at 2:05 a.m. and go down to your floor in the fire-stair exit. I'll give you two minutes from the time the alarm goes off for you to put on a long coat or bathrobe and hide the package under your garment. When you see people starting to pour out of their rooms and heading for the stairwell you get into the flow. When you step into the stairwell, move up against me as though someone has pushed you. Then, slide the package from your coat to the right half of mine. Mine has a large pocket on the inside, and you can just slip it into it. Here's the coat. See the pocket?

"Yes, yes, I understand. This is fun."

"I'll have put the left side of my coat around you as a blind. People won't be paying attention to us. They'll be anxious, fearful, or angry. Once the transfer has been made, you go down the stairs ahead of me. I'll make believe I have a limp and let people pass me. By the time you reach the street, move to the right. I'll be far behind. When I reach the street, I'll go left toward the taxi queue. I'll head home, and eventually you'll be allowed back into your room. Tomorrow morning, my dear girl, you'll return to Beijing. I'll see you next time you're in Hong Kong. Bring some more material, and we'll start to outline your book. And, by the way, I really enjoyed tonight—all of it."

The next week is action time. Mike cleans out everything that might be incriminating in case the MSS break in when he's not here. Then, he places a secure call to Tweed and alerts him to what has happened. Mike tells him simply to stand by for future developments. Tweed reminds him again about his tardiness in filing reports. What a jerk.

A few days later, Mike's door buzzer goes off. When he answers the intercom, a voice asks if he can come up. Mike asks who he is and he gives two names—Chan and Tang.

"Who are you?"

He says he's a friend of J. J. "Oh, yeah, friend—my ass." He's MSS. This conversation is inevitable. If Mike doesn't let them in, they'll wait for him to come out. It's better to do this on his turf, so he invites them up. Mike doesn't know how far these birds might go, so he tucks his .45 into the side cushion of his chair.

In a couple minutes, the doorbell rings, and through the peephole Mike sees two Chinese men, in gray suits, of course. He lets them in and tells them to have a seat on the sofa so that he has both of them in front of him, and they can't see his gun. Also, his back is to the sliding-glass balcony door. They have the light in their eyes, and Mike is in shadow. I learned to always sit with my back to the light, when I can.

They ask, "What was the nature of your relationship with Miss Wu?"

"Who? Miss Wu?" Mike asks, just for the fun of playing "who" and "Wu." It's like the old Abbott and Costello "Who's on first?" bit.

"How do you know Miss Jinjing Wu?"

"I didn't even know her last name. We just had a couple dates, which you undoubtedly know about."

"How long have you known her? Do you know what her occupation is in China?"

"I met her about a month ago. She just said she worked for the government. I wasn't interested in her work. You're getting too personal. This conversation is pointless. You're invading my privacy. You must leave now."

They glower at him, and as they stand, they do a quick visual sweep around the room. Seeing nothing, they leave and note that they may want to talk to him again. He's surprised that they leave so easily. They probably just wanted to see the apartment in case they come back some day.

Mike thinks, "I don't know if I'll see them again, but I'm certain that I am now under twenty-four-hour surveillance. I wonder how J. J. is going with them."

Chapter 18

Death Squad Attack

July 1971
Hong Kong

Mike's door buzzer sounds. "Who is it?"

"It's me, J. J."

What the hell is this? "Where are you? Are you downstairs?"

"Yes, please come down and help me with my luggage. It's too heavy for me."

In a flash he's into the elevator and landing on the ground floor. J. J. jumps into his arms and gives him a big kiss. "Surprise!"

No shit, Sherlock. He grabs her bags and throws them into the elevator, pushing her quickly in behind them.

"Aren't you glad to see me?" she pouts.

"Of course, but I'm certain I'm under surveillance. Did you see a car with some men in it down the block? It's been there all week."

"I didn't see one, but I really wasn't looking. What's happening?"

"I had two visitors from MSS recently. You and I are under suspicion for something. It could be anything, but the point is we are being followed openly now."

"Yes, I know that. I also had a session with MSS. I told them we've just had a couple dates. What did you tell them?"

He motions her to stop talking and leads her onto the balcony in case the apartment has been bugged recently. "I said exactly the same thing. But in my case, I've met a lot of people in my short time here, and they find my behavior suspicious."

"Why would they do that?"

"Well, it's a long story. I'll tell you later. For now we need to decide how to protect you, not to mention me, in the process. Tell me, how did you get here?"

"After my visit from the MSS, I realized that I was under suspicion, and from now on my life would be a nightmare. So I decided to defect."

"Defect?"

"Yes, you know. Ask for asylum at the British headquarters or the US consulate. You'll help me, won't you?"

"Sure, but how did you get away?"

"I was due to fly out this morning from Beijing to Hong Kong with my group from MND. They were to pick me up at my apartment at ten o'clock for a noon flight. Yesterday I gave a friend a spare key to my place. He came over and took my luggage during the day, including some presents for you, to his house. The MSS wasn't watching my apartment because I was in my office. After work, as usual I went home, had dinner, gathered some personal papers I would need, and turned off the lights as though I was going to bed.

"Then, I sat by the window for a couple of hours. About midnight I guess, the MSS decided I was truly asleep, and they left. I waited another hour, and when a new team didn't come to watch me, I left very quietly and walked the mile to my friend's place. Just before eleven at night, he had called China Air and made a reservation for me on the first flight out at seven thirty. At five thirty he drove me and my bags to the airport. When the counter opened at six, I paid for my ticket and got on the seven thirty flight. Pretty clever, don't you think?"

"Absolutely. You would make a great spy."

"When my group called to pick me up at ten o'clock, I was already within an hour of landing at Kai Tak. The MSS probably broke into my apartment and saw that I was gone. They would have started checking for me, and by the time they found out what I'd done, I was landing in Kowloon, British Crown Colony. Home safe. Ta-da," she exclaimed, throwing her arms around him and hugging with all her strength.

He holds her tenderly and smiles. What a great little gal. Then, he gives her a little kiss and hugs her again. What a woman this one is. She's not as naïve as he thought. But eventually, when she learns his game, she's going to be more than a little upset.

"Let's go inside. I want to show you the presents I brought you," she says.

"Presents?"

"You'll see. You're going to like them, I'm sure. They're going to make good reading eventually."

Once in the living room, she asks Mike to turn on the radio for some background noise and puts one of the suitcases on the dining room table. It's very heavy. When it's open, he sees it's full of paper—documents and drawings, most marked in pinyin: *Jue Mi*. Holy smoke—forty pounds of top-secret data from MND.

He looks at her with a smile and sees she's grinning from ear to ear. As she starts to say something, he puts his finger to his lips. He closes the suitcase and, with her following, takes it into the bedroom closet. She looks quizzically and then nods. He puts his arm around her shoulder in a loving way and walks her back out to the balcony.

"How did you get this through customs?"

"I go through all the time, so I know a lot of the agents. I always bring them little gifts, or I pass messages to their relatives. They're very grateful to me, so they never go through my luggage."

"Well, we have to decide how we're going to get ourselves and that suitcase out of here and to the consulate. I know they're watching this place. If we walk out with this, they'll surely grab it and us both."

He thinks to himself, "I'm going to call the consulate, tell them who I am, and have them come with several of his men and pick us up. It will blow my cover, but with this material from J. J., Captain Bradley will be more than happy. Tweed will have to go along. No time for admin details now."

Suddenly, the door buzzer from the lobby sounds. He guesses that's the MSS men who came before. They must have seen her arrive. He goes to the intercom and answers, "Yes, who is it?"

"Mr. Henderson, we know that Miss Wu is with you. We must speak with her."

"Miss Wu doesn't want to speak with you."

"Sir, this is a matter of the greatest importance. Miss Wu is wanted for questioning regarding the theft of secret documents from the People's Republic of China. We must speak with her *now*."

"If you want to talk with her, you will have to go through the proper channels. This is not China. The British insist on taking such matters through due process."

"Sir, I repeat for the last time. I must speak with her at this moment. I do not have time for the decadent bureaucratic processes of Great Britain."

"Well, you have no choice. If you do not leave immediately, I will call the police and have you arrested."

"That is no longer possible. This is your last chance to peacefully comply with my request. Miss Wu is a citizen of the People's Republic of China and is subject to our laws no matter where she may be."

"What do you mean no longer possible?"

"Check your telephone."

J. J. has heard all this and immediately picks up the phone. She puts it to her ear and then gives me a frightened look. She shakes her head. The line has been cut.

"Now will you let us in?"

"Never; you cannot break into this apartment. The police will hear of it from the noise you make and arrest you."

"That will be too late. What happens to us is of secondary importance. Miss Wu will not escape us, sir, and now, neither will you. Are you going to let us in, or do we have to break in?"

"You can try, but you will not succeed. I am a US naval intelligence officer. You will not harm Miss Wu, who is in my custody and is seeking political asylum."

J. J. looks at me with wonder in her eyes. Till now Mike was a writer doing research.

Suddenly, the building shivers as the front door is broken down.

Mike runs to the bedroom and grabs his navy-issue .45 pistol and his small Walther PPK, the one that he used to shoot his way out of Shanghai. He tosses that to J. J. "Shoot anyone who tries to harm you. It's not accurate at a long distance, so wait until they are closer than fifteen feet if you can. These guys are a death squad. They're willing to die if necessary to kidnap or kill you."

He can hear people running up the exit stairs. "J. J., balcony—look down the fire-escape ladder."

Seconds later, she yells to him, "There are two men at the bottom starting to climb up."

In the kitchen, he grabs two bottles of wine, breaks off their necks, and empties them. He pours them half-full of a bottle of Bacardi rum, which is very flammable. He tells J. J. to stuff the small hand towels into the necks of the wine bottles, and he pours the rum on one and a bottle of ninety-proof vodka on the other. "Take these outside, and when the men get to the second level, light the cloths, and one at a time, throw them against the wall by the ladder."

Now, there is pounding on the door. "Open the door. There is no escape."

Mike shoves the sofa, a large chair, and the heavy mahogany coffee table in front of the door. It's only a temporary barrier.

Hearing no answer, the MSS throw their shoulders into the door. It buckles but doesn't collapse because of the barrier. After two more tries to move the weight, there is a pause. Something is scratching on the door, and then there is an explosion that shatters the door. Mike gets a face and neck full of splinters, but his eyes are not cut. The muzzle of a machine pistol is pushed through the opening, and it sprays bullets around the room.

Mike takes careful aim, and as soon as a face appears, he fires three shots. There is a scream. "One down! I wonder how many agents are out there."

J. J.'s on the balcony. He hears her yell and then the sound of breaking glass. Someone below the balcony screams. Two down.

Again the machine pistol is shoved through the door and sprays the room. Mike's down on one side out of the line of fire. He lets go four more rounds through the opening. No sound. Then, there's another yell from the balcony and the sound of breaking glass. She missed. Five seconds later, the Walther goes off twice, followed by a scream. Three down.

A stun grenade flies into the room. Mike dives behind the kitchen wall and prays that J. J. is safe on the balcony. The concussion rips through the room, throwing furnishings around, lighting fire to the carpet, and blowing out the sliding-glass door.

In the street, he hears police sirens. The cavalry is coming. Realizing that the fight is now nearly over, the MSS make one last attempt at entry. Mike shoots the first man through the door with the last shot from his .45. Before he can reload, a second man dives through the shattered door opening. Mike jumps him and hits him with a shattered leg of the coffee table. He goes down and doesn't move. Mike hits him again just to make sure and then runs to the balcony.

J. J. is slumped on the floor with the gun in her lap and what looks like glass or shrapnel wounds all over her body and face. She's semiconscious, stunned from the grenade blast. She looks up at him and smiles faintly. "Got the *hundans*," she says and then passes out.

❦

As he scrambles back into the room to be sure that the bad guys are all dead or seriously incapacitated, a policeman tentatively peers into the room. "All clear, officer," Mike yells. Then, he returns to the balcony. The rest of the afternoon is spent getting J. J. to the hospital and treated for her wounds. They're painful and serious and will put her through a long recovery but will leave no lasting problems. It takes a doctor an hour to pick the splinters out of Mike's face and neck. All the little red spots make him look like he has measles.

Mike had asked the police to notify the consulate. Presently, two marines, the political attaché, and some other unidentified personnel arrive. Mike introduces himself to the attaché as a deep-cover operative. He gives him the short version of the day and promises a full recounting once they've recovered. Mike asks him to get in touch with Commander Tweed at Pearl to let him know he's okay and that he has a data present for him. Lastly, they need twenty-four-hour protection and a safe house for J. J. until she recovers. Then her case can be processed by the Brits.

In forty-eight hours, J. J. is awake and coherent. Mike tells her his story. She's unhappy because she imagined that they might be together once she is given asylum in Hong Kong. Her facial wounds make cosmetic surgery necessary, which is not all bad. With her new face and new identity, she can live safely in the colony or anywhere in Southeast Asia. That, along with a very large payment for the classified data, will guarantee that she can live comfortably.

"J. J., my dear girl, once you've recovered and are relocated, please get in touch with me through CINCPAC. Here is the address. You have been wonderful. I hate to leave you, but the Brits will take care of you. We'll send you enough money so that you can live comfortably wherever you are."

Mike calls Commander Tweed and brings him up to date. He seems concerned about Mike's health and safety. Then, he questions what Mike's spent this month. Wouldn't you know it, once an accountant, always an accountant. Then, he says the mission is complete.

No shit, Sherlock. He orders Mike as soon as possible to return to Pearl.

Within two weeks, Mike's "measles" spots have healed, and no infection has resulted. He catches a plane to Hawaii to report on the mission and the data he's supplied. Soon, he's ready for a short leave and then his next assignment. He thinks, "I hope I don't see Hong Kong for a long time. It's been pretty rough on me."

Chapter 19

Dangerous Games on Kauai

August 1971
Pearl Harbor, Hawaii

In Hawaii at CINCPAC in Pearl Harbor, Mike's welcomed somewhat coolly by Tweed. "Well, Holmes, you survived again. You seem to have a passion for messy exits. Messy and, I might add, expensive. What did you promise that woman who gave you the documents?"

"I left her with the British authorities and promised that she would be paid well for the intell she provided. I leave that up to Captain Bradley and the admiral."

"Very well; we'll need you around here for a couple weeks, and then you should take some leave. I'll let you know when you can be released. By the way, your promotion came through last week. Congratulations, Lieutenant Commander Holmes. Dismissed."

"What a great guy. It's certainly nice to have someone appreciate how you've laid your life on the line, isn't it? What's next?" He revisits his attempts to find Grace. He tries to locate Jerry at Moffett, but he's not on the VP squadron roster. Now, Mike doesn't know where he and Grace are.

Better slow down, take some time off, and get his body and mind back together. It's been a very taxing couple of missions. He needs time to think. Maybe this is actually the end of a beautiful idea. "Hold on, old boy. You're a young man. Perhaps this is a tragedy, but you have a long road ahead. Chin up, old boy. Carry on."

Mike's heard there is a new resort development on the north shore of Kauai, up near Hanalei. It's called Princeville: sun, surf, golf, Macallans, and

Montecristo. Sounds like paradise. He books a flight and a hotel for two weeks and takes off for the Garden Isle. Kauai and Niihau were the only two islands not conquered by King Kamayamaya. From the airport he catches the shuttle and relaxes for the leisurely trip along the east coast of Kauai. Already the slow rhythm of the islands is taking hold. This little island, far up the northwestern side of the Hawaiian chain, is not crowded like Oahu. He doesn't know the population but would be surprised if there are fifty thousand people on the whole island. The majority are on the south side and east coast. In thirty minutes the shuttle passes Kilauea on the north shore and, in a few miles, rounds the corner along the base of the mountains to look out toward Hanalei Bay. Although he's still very depressed over Grace's disappearance, there is a slowly growing feeling that he's approaching paradise. Hanalei is situated just north of the tropical cliffs that tower over the bay. It seems to be the edge of Shangri-La.

Mike checks into the hotel and immediately heads for the balcony off his room. The view is northwest overlooking the bay and out to the infinity of the North Pacific. A piña colada and a Montecristo with his feet up help make this blissful. His anxiety slowly dissipates. After the crowds, concrete, and tension of Shanghai and Hong Kong, he begins to melt. A call to the golf shop tells him he can join a threesome at 0900 tomorrow. Dinner is a delectable coconut-encrusted mahi mahi and luscious medley of fresh mangos, papayas, and bananas. After a cognac and a serene night's sleep, he's prepared for the links. He hasn't touched a club in over a year, so this should be interesting.

At 0800 Mike's at the practice range trying to find a swing that went on vacation a year ago. The lack of play shows immediately. The only thing he can do is relax, not try to hit fancy shots, and survive the round. When he walks up to the first tee, he finds his threesome consists of two men and one gorgeous woman. The older man introduces himself.

"I'm Gordon O. Douglas; you can just call me by my initials." He pauses for a second to see if Mike gets the joke. "I hate the name Gordon, so just call me Doug. This beautiful woman is my wife, Eleanor. Most people call her

Ellie. The gentleman is Leonard Levine, my executive assistant and all-around gopher. And, sir, how might we address you?"

Mike shakes hands all around and says, "I'm Mike Holmes."

"Any relationship to Sherlock?"

"Not in the least." He holds off his typical Edwardian retort. He doesn't think it appropriate right out of the box.

As they wait for the group in the fairway to hit their shots, Doug asks, "What do you do when you're not relaxing in paradise, Mike?"

"I'm a naval officer. I'm based at Pearl with CINCPAC."

"What's your designator?" he asks, showing some knowledge of the navy.

"I'm a line officer in intelligence."

"Did you say you're intelligent or in intelligence?" he quips, smiling.

"A little of the first and some of the second, periodically."

"Ho, ho. Clever boy. I did twenty-one years in the Seabees. Came out a commander."

"When did you serve, Commander?"

"Joined shortly after Pearl Harbor and retired in sixty-two."

"Where did you see action?"

"I built and rebuilt airstrips and whatever else needed from Guadalcanal to Iwo Jima and later in Japan and Korea during the Korean conflict. That's where I learned the construction business. It looks like the fairway is clear. Do you want to lead off, Mike?"

"I've been off on a twelve-month mission so I'm very rusty. Why don't you show us the way, Doug?"

He steps to the tee, waggles a couple of times, and sends a slight slice down the right side of the fairway. Leonard, who asked that Mike call him Len, tees it up and booms a shot down the middle. He's a player. When it's Mike's turn, he manages to keep it in the fairway some distance behind Len's shot. They move to the women's tees, and Ellie shows good form. Her shot is in the fairway about 160 yards.

Len says, "Mike, why don't you ride with me, while Doug and Ellie take the other cart?" The course is pretty new and a bit rough. The sod hasn't had a season to grow in, and the greens are somewhat uneven. The saving grace is the setting. On one side they're in the shadow of the great lava cliffs typical of the Islands. In front is the infinite ocean, and on the other side are a couple holes that burrow their way through the jungle. Palm trees and flowering bushes of several types line the fairways. The round goes well. When they finish, Doug shot something in the high eighties, Len in the high seventies, and Mike in the mid-eighties with a couple OBs. Ellie has a good swing but no touch around the greens. If she learns to chip and putt, her scores could be in the high eighties.

After they turn in the carts, Doug leads them to the lanai bar. While they're enjoying drinks, Mike asks Doug to tell about his construction business.

"It's mostly commercial-real-estate development. "I have a small project on the west side of Oahu and a piece of what's happening here in Princeville," he offers. "We work all over North America and some here in the other islands. There's a lot of future in Hawaii now that the jets are making it a shorter trip from the States and from Japan. The Japs love golf and love to travel. I expect we'll see hordes of them in coming years."

"Where are you based?"

"That's a good question isn't it, hon," he says, turning to Ellie.

"We have our main residence in San Francisco, but it seems we're never home," she explains.

"Ain't that the truth," adds Len.

"It should make you happy, Leonard," says Doug. "When you're away from home, I pay all your expenses, and you just bank everything," he remarks somewhat condescendingly.

Len says nothing, but his look is not one of appreciation.

"Well, Leonard and I have work to do. Ellie, do you want to stay and have another drink with Mike? Someone from the club will drive you home."

She nods and blows him a kiss as he and Len get up to leave.

"How about tomorrow, Mike? Want to give it a go again at nine o'clock?"

"Sure. I'll see you then, and maybe I can find the middle of the course. It's probably pretty nice out there but not as interesting as the places I was today."

"You did fine, son. I'm sure that once you're warmed up, you'll beat the pants off Leonard."

Len smiles weakly in response.

Once they've left Ellie moves to a chair next to Mike. She's a very pretty woman. Probably was a model or showgirl fifteen years ago. She looks at him in a way that he would swear is a sexual invitation, although she says nothing. He takes her to be a tease.

"Tell me more about yourself, Michael. Intelligence must be a fascinating business—all this spying and such."

"Ellie, it's not that glamorous. A lot of the time it's like being a librarian, just collecting and cataloging data."

"Oh, you're being too modest. Have you ever been captured by the bad guys or tortured or shot at?"

"Yes to all of that, but I assure you it isn't exciting. It's damned scary when it's happening."

"I'd like to see your wounds sometime," she coos with a sexy smile.

"No, you wouldn't. They're not pretty. See the scars on my kneecaps? Tell me about yourself. I'm sure that's more interesting."

"I grew up in southern California. Got into modeling and later was in a chorus in Vegas. I never went far in the business. The only assets I have are my tits and ass."

She waits for his reaction. He smiles and tries to keep from laughing. He was right. She's definitely a tease. He wonders if she ever goes beyond that.

"I met Doug, as we call him, at a show in Vegas. He's very nice, very rich, probably worth a billion, and I think he actually loves me for more than my T and A."

"I'm certain that he does. Tell me about Len."

"Lenny is Doug's gopher. He does anything and everything that Doug tells him to. I think he's actually smart but doesn't have much ambition. If he did, he wouldn't take Doug's condescending remarks. He's well paid, and he has a crush on me, so he sticks it out and suffers, poor dear."

"I see that Doug is hard on him. Well, I'm still recovering a bit from my last mission, so I think I'll shower and take a break before dinner. I look forward to seeing you again tomorrow."

"Me too, Michael," she says, raising her arms slowly, thrusting her breasts out slightly, and joining her hands behind her head that tilts slightly to one side. What a temptress. This woman knows exactly how she affects men, and she plays it all the way. The message is clear and is accented with that look in her eye.

The next morning they're off again at nine. It's a pleasant round, and Mike plays a bit better. At the nineteenth hole, Doug says, "Mike, if you don't have something planned, why don't you come over and have dinner with us? Leonard can pick you up. Our place is up on a bluff above Hanalei. There's a gorgeous view. It's difficult to find if you don't know how to get there."

Mike accepts, and at seven o'clock, Len arrives in a Jeep station wagon. "Hop in, Mike. Doug likes to go off road, so he has this tin can."

"Thanks, Len. How's it going with you folks? Do you spend a lot of time here?"

"Not really. We don't spend much time anywhere. Doug has a number of projects that we cycle through constantly."

"Does Ellie go along?"

"A lot of the time she does. If she didn't, I don't know if I could stand being with Doug."

"I noticed he's pretty hard on you. Why do you work for him?"

"He pays very, very well. Although he beats on me, he needs me. I do all the shit work that he hates. And just between you and me, I like being around Ellie. She's a fantastic woman, not to mention gorgeous."

"She's that, all right. Frankly, I find her to be a bit of a tease. Am I right?"

"Mike, this is a private conversation, right?"

"Of course."

"Yes, she's a tease. She plays around a little. I think Doug knows, but so long as she's discreet, he overlooks it."

"Does she tease you?"

"Not really," he says rather shyly. I don't believe him.

They follow a winding two-lane road up into the hills above Hanalei. Doug was right. Mike would never find it. When they turn off the paved road, he's surprised to find the property fenced, a gate across the gravel road, and a guard at the gate.

"Doug's concerned about safety. He's involved in some sensitive deals, hence the security."

Inside the grounds are beautiful. As Len parks the jeep, Ellie comes out, takes his arm, and leads him through a tropically themed living room out to a lanai that has a sweeping view of Hanalei Bay. "Doug will be here in a minute. He's on the phone. How are you feeling, Michael?"

He gives her his stock answer. "Better for having seen you, Eleanor."

She laughs and squeezes his arm. Doug and Len arrive simultaneously from different directions. The group settles into soft lounges. A servant brings a large pitcher of some tropical dynamite. Doug looks upset, and Ellie asks him, "What's the matter, honey? Who was on the phone?"

"It was that son of a bitch Bill Bracher. It's been two years since we finished our project in Mexico, and he's still bitching about it. He's in Honolulu and wants to come here to talk about it. I told him to give it up. It's over."

"I don't like him. I think he's dangerous," she says.

"I agree," says Len. "He's a wild man. You never know what he's going to do."

"Well, he'd better not show up here, or I'll finish him for good."

The evening wears on through drinks, dinner, and interesting tales from Doug of his adventures. When they turn to Mike, he tells them about the sniper in San Diego and his time aboard the *Ranger*, leaving out the story of the raid on the reinforcements and the abduction in Hong Kong.

About ten o'clock, everyone is winding down, and Len says he'll take Mike back to the hotel. Doug jumps in and says, "Mike, why don't you move up here with us? We've got five unused bedrooms. There's no sense spending money at the hotel. My driver can take you anywhere you want to go. Besides, you spend most of your time with us anyway. It would be a pleasure to have your smiling face around here. You can come back up here after golf tomorrow."

Len doesn't react, but Ellie agrees wholeheartedly. "Sure, Michael. Please come stay with us. We have everything you need here: a beautiful swimming pool, good food and drink, and quiet time for you to relax and recoup. And besides, you'll be here to keep me company when these two are working. Puleez."

He looks at each of them and then replies, "I guess I'm outnumbered. You've got a nonpaying guest."

When they finish their round the next day, they skip the nineteenth hole. Mike throws his bags into the back of their car, and they head up the hill. When they arrive a light lunch has been prepared. It's mostly finger food and some fruit drinks. Afterward Mike unpacks, showers, and takes a short nap. He's still feeling the effects of the time in Hong Kong. Maybe he picked up a bug.

The grounds of the property are a miniature tropical paradise. The house has seven bedrooms, nine baths, an office, and a large pool, with spa of course. There are paths leading out to vista points on the bluff. A day staff of seven includes a cook and kitchen helper, housekeeper, a gate guard, and a gardener/groundskeeper, plus a night gate guard and maid/cook who is on from 10:00 p.m. until 6:00 a.m. just in case someone gets hungry or needs something in the middle of the night.

No golf the next day. Doug and Len are working. Ellie suggests that after breakfast, she and Mike go into Hanalei, and she will show him around. Doug agrees that's a good idea. A kiss on the cheek for him, and away they go. They take the Jeep, and Ellie insists on driving down to town because she knows the way. "You can drive back," she says.

Hanalei is actually a village of just a couple hundred people. It's a farm town supplying local taro growers. It doesn't take long to walk the main street and have coffee at the bakery. It's breezy and humid, about eighty degrees, so they decide to drive west toward Wainiha and the end of the road. West and south of there are the Na Pali Cliffs. These sharp-edged lava cliffs, some as high as four thousand feet, plunge to barely accessible beaches and into the Pacific. After a short walk along the shoreline at Wainiha, they head back with Mike behind the wheel. By three, they're at the house and decide to go for a swim. Doug and Len are still working in the office side of the complex.

About five o'clock, the boys join them and order up drinks. A refreshing dinner features the typical Hawaiian fish, mahi mahi, cooked a special way. The fillets are placed in a baking pan and lemon juice is poured over them. Then, they're sprinkled with thyme and basil and topped with pineapple. A little milk is poured into the pan, not directly on the fish. The fish are baked about 25 minutes in a preheated oven. The result is fish that flakes easily with a fork. The lemon, herbs and milk combine in divine sauce.

After dinner they retire to the patio with drinks. Doug offers Mike a cigar. "Len doesn't like cigars, but you might. These are Montecristos."

"My favorite."

"You can't get these in the US, but I get them direct from a contact in Havana," Doug says proudly.

Mike rolls the cigar in his fingers and smells its distinct aroma. "These are wonderful, but I'm afraid they're not Cubans, Doug."

"Yes they are," he declares indignantly. "What makes you say something like that?"

"These are Dominicans made from the Cuban seed, but they're probably grown in one of the plantations north of Santo Domingo."

"Where do you get that? I was guaranteed they're Cubans"

"Look at the two labels. There is a style label, such as 'White, Casino No. 1 or Platinum. Plus there is the brand label, Montecristo. If you look closely you see that the tips of the labels are lined up. That means they were put on by a machine. In Havana they're put on by hand and they never line up exactly."

"Son of a bitch," Doug blurts out. "How did you notice that? I've been smoking them for years and never saw it."

"I didn't tell you when we met, but I'm part Sioux Indian. My Sioux cousins taught me to be observant. Aboriginal people live close to the land and are taught to notice the slightest variations. Also at Defense Investigative

Services school observation was pounded into us. The world is full of clues if one is observant."

The rest of the evening winds down, albeit with a subdued Doug.

In the morning at the breakfast table Doug says, "I'm going to give you folks a treat. I've booked a helicopter tour of the west coast for tomorrow. We'll fly down along the Na Pali coast nearly to Mana. Then we turn east and fly up into Waimea Canyon. You'll really get a kick out of that. It's almost as big as the Grand Canyon and a lot more interesting. We'll turn back to the coast and land at a beach for a picnic. We'll watch the sun go down in the west and then fly back at dusk. It's a beautiful ride in early evening with the moon and stars starting to come out. Have a good night's sleep. We'll head to the heliport about ten o'clock."

In the morning Doug comes into breakfast with a sour look on his face. "I've got a problem with the project at Manakuli on Oahu," he announces. "Leonard and I have to fly over there and get things straightened out before I have a catastrophe on my hands. So we're skipping breakfast and taking off now. We should be back tonight."

"Oh, honey, that's terrible. I really wanted to see the canyon and have a picnic on the beach. Are you sure you can't fix it from here?

"No, babe. It's a big mess. But, Ellie, you and Mike can go. No sense all of us missing the trip."

There's more back and forth, but Doug is adamant. Mike can tell Doug's really angry by whatever is happening on Oahu. In the end, it's settled. Ellie and Mike will go. Mike's not too comfortable with this but can't tell Doug why. So Mike goes back to his room and puts on a long-sleeve cotton shirt, Bermuda shorts, and canvas sneakers. He takes a light jacket in case of rain. When he comes out, he finds Ellie looking too sexy in a tight yellow top, short shorts, and sandals. By now the boys are gone. Her outfit stops him. She notices, of course, and smiles that damned suggestive smile. It's almost a leer. At ten they jump into the Jeep and head to the Island Sites Heliport southeast of Hanalei.

Their pilot is a young fellow who says his name is Phil. He's all suntan and bleached-blond hair. He offers, "You folks are going to love this trip. I've made it dozens of times, and my passengers always come back happy. We've got a picnic hamper including champagne just to ensure you have a good time."

They go through simple preflight instructions such as, "Don't stick your head out the window." Then, they take off and head out over Hanalei Bay. In the distance Mike can see clouds that might be bringing rain. They turn left along the coast. As they round the northwest corner of Kauai, the sharp-edged, thousand-foot-tall Na Pali Cliffs climb into view. It's breathtaking. The power that formed and reformed them must have been colossal. In half an hour, they've passed the cliffs, and as they near Mana, Phil turns the chopper to the northeast, heading for Waimea Canyon. There is rough air coming over the top of the canyon, so Phil drops them down to get under it.

The canyon is ten miles long and a couple miles wide with a number of arms that reach up into its interior. It rivals the Grand Canyon in many ways with its vistas, and it adds tropical foliage to the picture. As they near the head of the canyon, the thousand-foot-high walls seem ready to wrap their arms around then. Suddenly, a strong downdraft comes off the top and slams into them. The chopper shudders and drops off to one side. Then, there is a jolt as the tail rotor scrapes one of the lava ridges. It starts to spin and drop as the damaged rotor fails to provide lateral stability. In the blink of an eye, they've lost a couple hundred feet and hit the canyon floor just yards from the foot of the head wall.

Then, Phil curses. Ellie screams and falls on top of Mike as they bounce twice before settling at an awkward angle on the slanted floor. There's water running down the walls and threatening to swamp them.

"Ellie, are you all right?"

She doesn't answer for a few seconds. Then, she groans and says, "My leg is broken."

He manages to move gently out from under her. He helps her sit back, and then he looks for Phil. The young pilot is pulling himself out of the front door. There is a small gash on the side of his head, and he's cursing over and over. Once he's extracted himself from the ship, he turns and sees Mike. "We better get out of here before this catches on fire or we drown," he yells over the splash of the waterfall.

Together they pick up Ellie and stumble up to a small shelf about ten feet above the chopper. There doesn't seem to be any fire, but the water from the walls of the canyon is beginning to rise around the ship, which is acting like a leaky dam.

"There are some supplies in the back. I'll get them," Phil yells.

Mike looks at Ellie. Her eyes are closed. He feels her pulse, and it is strong but unsteady. She's probably in shock. He rolls her over so that her head is below her heart. In a few seconds, she opens her eyes. "What happened?" she asks.

"A downdraft threw us against the canyon wall and knocked our rotor blade off. We crashed. But now we're okay. There's no danger. Phil is getting supplies out of the chopper."

Phil throws up a two-foot-square bundle and then scrambles up to the shelf with the picnic hamper. "The basket survived, but I think the champagne might have been cracked." The bundle is a waterproof tarp wrapped around an inflatable mattress.

They all stop and take a few breaths as they assess their situation. Mike looks at Ellie's legs, and neither appears broken, although there is a big bruise below her left knee. He checks myself and finds only that one of his knees is stiffening and swelling. It must have hit the fuselage when Ellie fell on top of him. Phil sees their injuries. "There's a first-aid kit in the tarp, and there's still some ice in the hamper." He climbs back down to the ship and comes back with some straps and cushions that they can use to wrap and ice their legs.

"Well. Welcome to scenic Waimea Canyon, folks, courtesy of Island Sites."

"Phil, we have to figure out how we're going to get out of here. It'll be dark here in a couple hours. I don't know how mobile Ellie and I are going to be."

"No problem, Commander. Phil to the rescue! I'll hike out of here. It's nearly eight miles from here to the first civilization point. I do minimarathons, so I'm in good shape. I've got a flashlight to light the way when it gets dark in this hole. In the morning there will be a rescue crew up here to pull you two out."

"Good enough. It looks like it might rain. I'll make a little shelter with the tarp and the mattress. The mattress is for the water, but it will be a good cushion. We've got the picnic hamper, so we won't starve. It might get a bit cold tonight, but we can wrap the tarp around us. You just be careful going out. If you fall in a hole, we'll be in big trouble because no one knows where we are."

With that, Phil takes off down the stream to find a trail out of the canyon. Mike turns to Ellie. "How are you feeling?"

"I'm better. The ice pack on my bruise is taking the sting out of it. Would you like to dance?"

"Very funny. I think we're in for a storm tonight. I suggest we set up the mattress and tarp against the cliff out of the wind as much as possible. Then, we can eat some dinner before it gets dark. Hopefully the champagne didn't break. We can toast to our survival."

Once they've inflated the mattress and had dinner, they're over the initial shock and a bit more comfortable. It starts to rain lightly.

"I'm cold," Ellie complains in a pouty voice.

"Come over here and lie against me. I'm a furnace. I'll keep you warm."

She slides over on the mattress and snuggles up against Mike with a sneaky little smile. After a few minutes, she says, "Something's poking me in the butt."

"Sorry. I'm afraid it's just my imagination."

"Do you know what it is?" she asks in a little-girl voice.

"Yes, I do."

"Well, do you know what to do with it?"

"Yes, I do."

"Well, what's stopping you?"

"Your husband."

"Oh, don't let that worry you. Doug knows I like to play. He's well past sixty now and has lost interest in sex. Besides, we're more friends than lovers."

The fire down below is heating up. Other than one unintended quickie with J. J., Mike hasn't been with a woman since before meeting Grace. He's just too busy trying to make the world safe for democracy and, to be honest, is somewhat disinterested, because of Grace. Suddenly, Ellie turns her body to face Mike and gives him a voracious kiss while reaching into his bermudas. She strokes and squeezes. As Sherlock would say, "The game is on."

A swell of pent-up energy is released. Shorts are off, and they're together before he can think any more about it. Over the next hour, they try every known position possible in their restricted space.

"How did you like that, sailor boy," she asks while Mike's catching his breath.

He just looks at her.

"Well, you just relax and let Ellie take care of you." She starts slow, gradually building as her excitement grows. When they explode together, he thinks his heart will shatter. She lies on top of him for a long minute and then says, "I think I need a break. But don't you go anywhere. I'm not through with you."

In seconds they're falling asleep with her lying alongside him. Her head is on his right arm. The next thing he knows there's a hint of light in the sky. He feels something rubbing against him. Opening his eyes, he's looking into her face. It's the face of a woman on fire. He can't believe it. She wants more. He responds until finally, he rolls off, gasping for breath, she whispers, "You're terrific."

He thinks, "She's certainly a lot of fun, but she's no Grace."

After a short nap, he opens his eyes slowly to see that the rain has stopped. The sun is cresting the tops of the canyon spikes. Ellie is still lying next to him, sleeping with a little smile on her lips. He stirs to look around. She opens her eyes and smiles at him.

"My god, you're so good. I've never had such a good time."

He doesn't know what to say, so he asks her, "Are you hungry? I think there is still something to eat in the hamper. Our rescuers are on their way by now."

"I hope they don't get here too soon," she says with that look again.

In a few minutes there is a new sound. "Do you hear that? It sounds like a helicopter. They're coming to airlift us out of here."

"Airlift. What do you mean 'airlift'?"

"They'll hover above us, drop a harness in a cable, and pull us up into the ship. We better get our junk together and put it back into the helicopter. They'll come back for that too."

Thirty minutes later they're in the rescue chopper and on their way out of the canyon. When they drop into the Island Sites base, Doug and Leonard are waiting. Having spent a night in the canyon in just shirts and shorts, they look pretty ragged. Doug comes out to hug Ellie while Leonard hangs back. Inside the terminal there are two paramedics waiting to examine them. Ellie shows her bruised leg and some unexplained scratches from rolling around getting out of the chopper, she claims. Mike tells them he's fine. He doesn't need them looking at the scratches on his back.

Doug says, "Let's get you two home and cleaned up. Phil said you were okay but banged up a little. We were up all night worrying about you."

Soon they're back at the house for breakfast, shower, and a nap. Mike wakes up and dresses. It's midafternoon. There doesn't seem to be anyone in the house except the staff.

"Everyone is still asleep," the housekeeper tells him. How do you feel, Commander?"

"Just a little sore from the crash—nothing serious. I could use a cup of coffee, though, and just a little snack."

"I'll bring it out to the lanai. Sit in the sun. It will help you heal."

By the time the food and coffee arrive, Len wanders in. "Well, Mike, how are you? Any side effects from the adventure?" he adds with the slightest grin.

"I'm just sore from the crash. Ellie landed on top of me, and I slammed into the fuselage."

"That actually could have been pleasant."

"What are you implying, Len?" Mike replies with a stern face.

"Nothing. Nothing at all," he answers in a way that suggests maybe there is something.

Mike sips his drink and finishes the snack without another word. Then, he lies back and dozes in the warm sun. He opens his eyes as he hears Doug come in. "How are you feeling, Mike?

"I'm fine, Doug. But I don't want to do it again," he answers, half lying.

Presently, Ellie strolls in looking very rested and happy, one-night adventure fulfilled. They all agree that tomorrow is a rest day.

"That bastard Bracher called again," Doug blurts out. "He said he was going to fly up here tomorrow to talk to me. I told him to save his time and money. There's nothing to talk about. I added that I don't want to see him under any circumstances."

Len adds, "He never could take a hint. He's like a wild bull running in all directions looking for somebody to gore. It won't surprise me to see him at the gate."

Doug mumbles, "I'll tell Kamalo if he shows up at the gate to shoot the son of a bitch. Let's go over to the hotel and have some dinner. I need some fresh air."

Dinner turns out to be a very quiet, somewhat strained evening. They don't linger. Within two hours they're back at the house. Mike walks out with Doug to the bluff overlooking Hanalei Bay. There are lights from the village as well as a few residences spotted around the area. But all in all it is a beautiful, velvet-blue scene. Doug offers an original Cuban version of the Montecristo. It's a bit stronger than the Dominican derivative that Mike's been smoking. Nonetheless, with a Bailey's to soothe the palette, all is well.

"Michael, tell me a little about your training. You mentioned that you went to NIS and to this new place—Defensive Investigative Services, was it?"

"Yes."

"What was that like?"

"It was criminology. The school had civilian law enforcement officers, attorneys, and accountants as well as naval officers. We focused on general criminal investigation as opposed to typical intell work. It's a great combination." Mike goes on with more details about the curriculum and the overall experience.

"Maybe you can advise me about this asshole Bracher. What can I do to get him off my back?"

"You could get a restraining order if you can show that he's harassing or stalking you."

"That would be helpful. How about I just put out a contract on the prick?"

"That would be a more direct approach, but I wouldn't advise it."

"I know; just blowing smoke. He just pisses me off so much."

After Mike finishes the Monte and Bailey, he thinks it's time for bed.

"Maria, the night maid, is here by now. Would you ask her to bring me my little pitcher of piña coladas and a couple glasses? It's so peaceful here. I think I'll wait awhile before I return to reality. Tell Leonard that when he finishes the bid on the Steven's project, to bring it out here. I want to take a look at it before I go to bed."

"Sure," Mike says as he strolls off down the lighted path to the house. Following orders, he tells Maria that Doug wants his usual. Then, he stops at the office. "Len, Doug wants to see the Stevens bid before he goes to bed. He's up on the bluff waiting for you." With that he heads for bed, hoping that Doug will keep his cool about Bracher.

G.O.D. Disappears

August 1971
Princeville, Kauai

It's another perfect morning in Paradise. On the lanai, Mike sees Len, Kamalo, and Ellie. They're agitated over something.

Ellie sees him and asks nervously, "Michael, do you know where Doug is?"

"No, the last time I saw him was out on the bluff a little after ten o'clock. He asked me to have Maria bring him a pitcher of piña coladas and to tell Len to bring out the Stevens project bid when he finished it. I went to bed right after that."

"Well, he's not anywhere around here. The cars are here. Kamalo didn't see him at the gate, and Maria hasn't seen him either this morning. Mike, I'm getting worried."

"Don't fret. He probably just went for a walk this morning. He was a bit concerned last night about that Bracher fellow and maybe just wanted to think it through. Len, did you see him last night on the bluff?"

"No, when I got there, it was nearly eleven o'clock, and he wasn't there. His pitcher was on the little table, but he wasn't there. Either you or Maria was the last person to see him."

'Ellie, do you have Maria's phone number? I'll call her and ask if she saw him on the bluff."

Mike rings Maria's phone number, and a woman answers. "Good morning. I'm calling for Mrs. Douglas. Is Maria in? I need to speak to her."

After a long wait, Maria comes on the phone. "Maria, good morning. How are you?"

Hesitantly she answers, "I'm fine," in a flat voice.

"Maria, did you take the pitcher and two glasses out to Mr. Douglas last night like I asked you?"

"Yes, sir. Right away."

"Was he there when you got to the bluff?"

"Yes."

"Did he say anything unusual to you?"

"No," she answers quickly. "He didn't say anything except thank you and good night. Why are you asking me?"

"Mr. Douglas isn't here this morning, and I think you were the last person to see him last night."

"Well, he was fine when I saw him," she says firmly. "Besides, I think Mr. Levine saw him after I did."

After Mike hangs up, he asks Kamalo if he has any ideas about Doug's whereabouts. "Kamalo, he didn't go out the gate after you got here, right? What time do you come on duty?"

"My shift changes a leedle, but usually it eight in morning until six at night. Sometime he tell me go home early. When I come in dis morning, I see car tracks up to da gate, but dey back away. I ask da night guy. He say car just come toward gate about eleven but back away. We have security system on da gate. When car come up, floodlights go on. Den, in three seconds, lights go off, and two flash cameras fire. One take license plate, duther take windshield so we can see driver. Den, floodlights go back on. Our cars, dey still here. When I walk around dem to check dem, like I do every day when I come on, I see dey not warm from driving."

"Wait, you say we have photos of the car that came to the gate?"

"Ya. Here dey is. Dey Polaroid, see? Car is white Chevy, and you can read da plate."

"Excellent. I'll have the cops run the plate to see who the car belongs to. Kamalo, check the fence around the property. Look for signs of someone trying to get through or under. I'll go out to the bluff. Do you want to come along, Len?"

"Sure."

In a few minutes, they're on the pad overlooking Hanalei. The morning sun is glistening off the ocean. The constant trade winds are weak, and there are almost no waves. Not a good surfing day. The beach brudders will be unhappy. At the site they find the pitcher on the table and one glass. The pitcher's nearly full. The dirt is disturbed. It looks like there were a couple people milling about. "Did you walk around here when you were here?"

"No, as soon as I saw he wasn't there, I figured he went to bed. It was at little after eleven when I got here. I just turned around and went back down the path and to bed. I was beat from working on the bid."

"Did you see the pitcher and the glasses?"

"Yes. "They were on the table."

"Why didn't you take them back to the kitchen when you saw he was gone?"

"That's not my job."

Mike gives him a disdainful look. "I see. Go back and tell Ellie there's nothing here. I'm going to look around." When Len is gone, Mike looks closely at the dirt on the pad. It's clear that something happened here after he left Doug. The dirt is disturbed. There are several footprints, mostly blurred, but at least two that are clear. He kneels down and looks carefully at them. They look like a woman's sandal. Too small for Doug or Len. Mike thinks Ellie's are larger also. He doesn't know the size of the housemaid's feet, but she was gone by 7:00 p.m. So was the kitchen helper. "Maria is the only woman who might have left these. She claims she brought the pitcher and two glasses and then went directly back to the kitchen." Mike thinks, "I'll have to talk to her again if Doug doesn't show up." Being careful to avoid the footprints, he steps to the right side of the pad and looks down. Nothing but jungle below. Same on the left side. Gingerly, he steps toward the front. He can't get close because of the prints. Leaning as far over as possible, he sees that the edge is gouged out. All he can tell is that apparently at some time, something slid down the front edge of the site into the heavy undergrowth below. Maybe it's not new. He'll ask the gardener when he sees him. Someone could have looked over the edge, and it gave way. That's a long shot. It's a good hundred feet down to the dense vegetation. He can't see much from here. He thinks to himself, "If Doug doesn't show up soon, I'll have to take a closer look."

Back at the lanai Mike doesn't mention what he's just seen. No sense upsetting Ellie at this point. Addressing Len and Ellie, he says, "Well, I guess we'll just have to wait awhile till Doug comes back and explains himself."

❦

The cook brings a light breakfast, but no one is very hungry. They just pick at the fruit and nibble on croissants. Coffee is giving them some energy, but otherwise it's just questions and conjectures going around among the three of them.

Len finally says somewhat sarcastically, "You're the intelligence officer. What's happened?"

"If I knew, I'd tell you. We have no evidence of any sort at this point." He omits what he saw on the bluff. The only tangible things are the two photographs from the gate. "Len, you know this fellow Bracher. Does this look like him?"

"There's a lot of glare on the windshield, but it could be him."

"I'm sure that Doug will show up soon with some story. He probably went for a little hike to think. If we don't hear in a couple of hours, I'll check with the police and the clinic to learn if they've seen him."

"Oh, my god, Michael, do you think he might have been hurt? Do you think that Bracher fellow showed up and attacked him?"

"No, Ellie. There's no evidence that a stranger was anywhere on the property last night. According to Kamalo, the night guard said a car come to the gate, but it backed away as soon as the photos were taken. Kamalo and the gardener are checking the fence. They should be done by now. I'll go see if they found anything."

Mike finds Kamalo and the gardener, an older Japanese man, coming around the edge of the house. "We don' fine no holes in fence. Just some deeggin' outside in one place. Could be wild pigs from da hills," he reports and goes back to the gate.

Mike signals the gardener to come with him up the path to the bluff. Once on the pad, being careful to stay away from the footprints, he shows the old man the edge that has a gouge in it. The gardener says it's new. It wasn't there when he cleaned up the pad two days ago. He says it must have been something heavy to make that big a scrape on the edge. Then, he looks at Mike with enquiring eyes. Mike just shrugs his shoulders and tells the man that they won't let the others know about this for now. He nods knowingly.

In a couple hours, when Mike calls the police and the clinic, they have no information. He asks them to run the license plate. They don't even ask why. He's not surprised by the so-called law enforcement contingent. They're just two overweight beach-boy types with badges and weapons. He hopes they don't ever have to use the guns. His call to the local clinic draws another blank. By early afternoon he feels he's waited long enough. Quietly he tells the gardener and Kamalo to get the longest rope they can find and follow him up the path to the bluff. Cautioning Kamalo to keep this a secret, Mike makes a belay with the rope. With Kamalo and the gardener holding the end, he puts on gloves from the gardener and slowly goes over the edge wide of the gouge. That may be evidence in the footprints, and he doesn't want anyone to disturb it.

After fifty feet, he's into heavy foliage through a space that shows some breakage. He continues a few more feet. Now he's near the end of the rope. He sees something white just below. Inching to the very end of the rope and stretching as far as possible, he reaches out and grabs a small, torn piece of white cloth. It looks like part of a shirt. Doug was wearing a white shirt last night. Far below Mike can see something else that is not part of the jungle. But he can't go any farther. He signals Kamalo and the gardener, and slowly they pull him up with the fragment tucked inside his shirt.

When he reaches the top, he shows them what he's found. "I need to call the police rescue team. We may have an answer to Mr. Douglas's disappearance." Unfortunately, the footprints have been obliterated by the two men.

The three of them walk quickly down the path to the house. Ellie and the staff are milling restlessly around the kitchen. When she sees Mike come in all dirty, she knows something has happened. He describes the descent and shows her the shirt fragment.

"Oh, my god, that's Doug's shirt. It's the one he had on last night."

"Are you sure?"

"I'm positive. I bought it for him. I remember the open weave. Where did you find it?"

"It was in the vegetation below the bluff. He might have fallen over the edge. I'm going to call the rescue squad and get them here immediately. It's possible he's down there and still alive."

Ellie starts to cry, and Len puts his arms around her.

They're lucky the rescue team happens to be in Kilauea today. It's about ten miles from Kilauea to this property. Mike explains the situation and tells them that there may have a man still alive below the bluff. There's no hu-hu in Hawaii, especially on the outer islands. Nevertheless, within twenty minutes of the call, they hear a siren, and Kamalo goes to the gate to let them in. Three men come off the truck carrying ropes and hooks.

"It's this way," Mike yells, waving his hand and trotting up the path. At the edge of the bluff, he shows them the gouge and points out where he found the shirt fragment. "I couldn't go any farther because my rope wasn't long enough."

Quickly they organize the belay, and one man goes over the edge with the other two holding him. Mike takes one end of a second cable that will be needed if they find him, something, or somebody. In about ten minutes, the man yells, "I found him."

"Is he still alive?"

"I can't tell for sure, but I don't think so. I've got him hooked up. Pull."

They tie down his rope, and the three pull on the cable. The weight is very heavy, especially when he gets caught on the undergrowth. Vines and branches snag the body. Finally, Mike sees that it is Doug. He's showing no signs of life. They drag him over the edge. One man examines him while the other fellow and Mike pull the belayed man up the cliff.

"He has no pulse. He's already past rigor mortis. When did this happen?"

"We don't know for certain, but probably between eleven and twelve last night. That's more than fifteen hours ago."

"No wonder. We'll bag him and take him back to Lihue. They'll want to do an autopsy."

Mike concurs. "They'll look for alcohol or drugs in his system as well as injuries that caused the fall or death. If you'll bag him here, I'll go ahead and take his wife into the house, where she won't see you take him away. Thanks for coming quickly and for retrieving him."

When Mike comes down the path, Ellie is standing there with Len's arm still around her. She knows it isn't going to be good news. As soon as Mike comes off the path, she looks hopefully at him. He shakes his head as he approaches her. She leaves Len and runs into Mike's arms, sobbing.

"Let's go inside and sit down. Len, get her a drink."

❧ ❦

The rescue team will notify the Kauai police in Lihue. There's no one on the north coast who is capable of handling this case. Mike's not even certain that anyone in Lihue is capable either. At this point it's not clear if it was an accident, suicide, or murder. He thinks, "I might even be a prime suspect since Maria and I are the only persons who admit to having seen Doug last night. Plus, I'm capable of pushing him off the cliff. Little ninety-eight-pound Maria could never do it if she tried. I expect that I'll be here for some time."

Mike puts in a call to Commander Tweed. When he comes on the line, Mike briefs him on the situation. "Sir, it's most likely the investigator will want me to stick around at least until he clears me and maybe later to help in the investigation. Of course, that is up to you."

"I'll talk to the captain, and I expect he won't have any problem with that. You've got some leave time you can put toward it if necessary. Just report the progress so I can keep him in the loop. This might take a little time. Good hunting. Oh, by the way, you didn't do it, did you?"

"Very funny; what a thoughtful man. I can use my leave time to help on the investigation."

The next morning, the phone rings, and Len answers it. "It's for you—some detective from Lihue."

"Good morning, sir. Lieutenant Commander Michael Holmes speaking."

"Commander, this is Inspector Hiroshi Matsuyama, Kauai homicide section. I understand from the rescue team that you were the one who led them to the site of the incident."

"Yes, sir, that's correct."

"Do you have any evidence regarding what and how it happened?"

"All I know at this point is that Mr. Douglas either fell, jumped, or was pushed over the edge of the bluff here. He was found over one hundred feet into the jungle below. It happened sometime after ten o'clock the night before last. We didn't know where he was in the morning and didn't discover the point where he fell until later in the afternoon. I belayed down the cliff when I saw that and found a piece of his shirt. I couldn't go farther because my rope wasn't long enough. That's when I called the rescue team."

"I see. Keep everyone on site who was around on the night of his disappearance. I'll be there with my associate Detective Haamoa later today. We'll have the report of the autopsy by tomorrow."

After he hangs up, Mike assembles the group and reiterates what the detective said. Ellie goes with the housekeeper to her room to rest, and Mike motions Len to come outside with him.

"Len, I need to know as much as possible about Doug before the police get here. I don't want them bothering Ellie and the rest of the household any more than is necessary. First, do you have any idea of how he might have gone over the edge? Would he have had any reason to commit suicide?"

"I can't see Doug doing that."

"Does he have any major problems with his business?"

Len hesitated for at least ten seconds before answering. Mike can see him struggling with the question. "No one knows this except me, Doug's bankers, and some joint-venture partners. Actually, he's facing major problems in several of his big projects. If he can't get emergency financing, he could have to declare bankruptcy. He's a very proud man, as you could tell. Going BK would be extremely hard on him psychologically. It wouldn't surprise me if he took the easy way out."

"Financial disaster has done that for many a man. Underneath the façade, proud people are often very vulnerable to the possibility of failure. Their pride can't conceive of it. More than one has taken his or her life when faced with catastrophic failure. Any other possible reasons for a suicide?"

"I know he went to a specialist a couple months ago. When he came back, he didn't have his usual bravado. Maybe he got come bad news."

"Have you noticed any change in his behavior, physically? Is he just as lively now as he was a couple months ago?"

"He might have slowed down just a very little bit. He's had some flulike symptoms lately—cough, a little fever, you know. When I told him maybe he should take a little time off, he told me to mind my own business."

"The pathologist's report will tell us if there was any evidence of illness. I'm going to ask Ellie gently if she noticed any change in his health."

Mike waits on the lanai for Ellie to come out. He wants to talk to her before the detectives arrive. It's the same idea as he had with Len. He wants to prepare her for some serious questioning. These boys may be rough with her.

Ellie comes out around noon. She doesn't look too bad for a new widow. Mike suggests they take a walk around the grounds so she can get some fresh air. She agrees and takes his arm. Len looks at them strangely as they walk off. In Len's mind, Mike might be prime suspect. He knows Ellie likes Mike and realizes that with Doug gone, she will be a very rich lady, even if his business is in trouble. It could be a big temptation—maybe even a plot between the two of them. It's a story that the police might like. They prefer simple cases not requiring a lot of heavy investigative labor. Parking patrol is much easier.

"Ellie, how are you holding up? This is a terrible shock for all of us."

"I'm okay; as good as can be expected. It's hard to imagine a big, strong guy like Doug being gone. What do you think happened? Who could have pushed him? I know he wouldn't jump. He didn't have any reason to be depressed."

"Have you noticed any change in his physical behavior or habits in the last couple months?'

"He looks tired, but his schedule is so horrendous, that's no surprise."

"Any symptoms?"

"He seemed to have a small cold that lingered. But that's not unusual. He had a lung problem from working construction during the war. He must have breathed some toxic stuff during those jobs in the Pacific Islands."

"How were his projects going? How was the business? Did he seem worried?"

"Not really. He fussed a lot and cursed people for their lack of performance or going back on their word. But I took that with a grain of salt. It's nothing new."

"Ellie, there's another thing you should be prepared for, in case the detectives bring it up."

"What's that, Michael?"

"I believe Len is jealous of me. We both know he has a crush on you. I see the way he looks and acts around you. It's pretty obvious. I won't be surprised if someone on the staff brings it up. That might make him and you suspect. I have to ask you the next obvious question. It's none of my business, but you need to be prepared for it. The police might press it. Was Len ever your lover?"

"What? Don't be silly. He's not my type."

"Sorry to push this, but they probably will. You're going to be a very rich lady. It's natural for suspicious people to wonder if you two plotted to get rid of Doug."

"That's absurd. That is too, too crazy. We were never close."

"Not even casually?"

"Oh, my god. One night a few years ago, we were on a business trip with Doug. He had to go on a short side trip overnight. Len and I got drunk, and I was feeling neglected by Doug, and it happened. But this was the one and only time. Besides, he wasn't very good. Not like you."

"Wait a second Ellie. Get rid of that last sentence. The canyon absolutely never happened! Do you understand? If the police find out about it, both you and I will be in big trouble. They love something like this. So do juries. Do you understand how dangerous that incident would be? Erase it from your memory now!"

"Oh, yes. Sure, my god, I can see the reasoning and the suspicion. I'll remove it immediately. It's gone."

"They might push it really hard, and you can't give any clue—a look, a smile, nothing. I can't make this point too strongly. If they bring up the canyon, just tell them we tried to sleep and waited for the helicopter to bring us out. Nothing but nothing else happened. Period! This would disastrous for both or us. Also, I think you should wear something that doesn't reveal the bruise on your leg. That could start the questioning. There's no reason for them to bring that up unless Len suggests it. In that regard he might try to shift the blame off himself and pin Doug's fall on me or on both of us. I was the last one, besides little Maria, who admits to seeing him alive. Len says that Doug wasn't on the pad when he went out there about eleven. I don't know if he's telling the truth. He doesn't have an alibi for himself, so my bet is he will try to implicate one or both of us. Just know that we are on the spot if he tries. I've already called Maria and told her to come over. If she gets here soon, I'll have a chance to go over her story again before they arrive. But you get amnesia right now!"

If she falters, and they open that door, Mike thinks his goose could be cooked. Shit. He wouldn't be the first man who went to prison over a one-night fling.

Just as Ellie and he return from their walk, Maria arrives. Mike motions her to come with him. They walk out to the bluff where they can be alone so that he can go over her story again.

"Maria, the police will be here soon, and I want to go over your story again so that you will be prepared for the possibility of some hard questioning. You told me the other morning that you took the pitcher of piña coladas with two glasses out to him here. Go on from there."

"When I came out, he was sitting on the chair on the left. I brought the pitcher to him, and he said, 'Thank you. Have a seat, and have a drink with me. It's a beautiful night, and it's lonely out here.' I told him I don't drink, and I turned around and went inside."

"When I talked to you on the phone, you didn't say anything about him asking you to join him. Now you're changing your story. Which is it?"

Maria blushes, stammers, and starts wringing her hands. Mike is sure there is more that she doesn't want to talk about. "I forgot. When you called, I was very nervous, and I forgot that he asked me to have a drink with him."

"Why were you nervous? At that time we didn't know there was a problem. All we knew was that Mr. Douglas wasn't around the house. What would make you nervous unless you knew something you didn't want to tell me?"

"I don't know. I just got out of bed. I work until six o'clock, and I was asleep when you called."

"Maria. I know you didn't push Mr. Douglas off the bluff. You're not strong enough. You're not a suspect. But I feel that you know something you're not telling me. You said you brought two glasses. Mr. Levine says he saw only one glass when he got there. What could have happened to the second glass? The police can be very brutal in their questioning. If your story isn't clear and consistent, they will feel that, and then you could be in trouble. So tell me now so I can help you. Is there anything you haven't told me?"

"No. That's all. Nothing happened."

"That's what I mean. If you say nothing happened, they're going to think that something did happen, and they will be very hard on you. They might even take you to the station in Lihue for more questioning. That wouldn't be pleasant. So tell me the truth. What happened here the night before last?"

"Nothing. I tell you nothing happened. I didn't do anything."

Just then Len calls up the path. "The cops are here."

Marie is hiding something, but Mike doesn't have time to get it out of her now.

Chapter 21

Whodunit?

August 1971
Princeville

"Commander, I'm Inspector Matsuyama. This is Detective Haamoa." Matsuyama looks like he's in his fifties, maybe sixty. He's slight, balding, and rather taciturn to the point of being abrupt. Haamoa is a huge man, probably Samoan. He smiles, extends his hand for a crushing shake.

"I'm Michael Holmes. I'm in naval intelligence, and I have experience also in the defense investigative services."

Ignoring Mike's credentials, he replies, "Commander, I'd like you to repeat what you said on the phone, describing the situation. Then I want to see the site you mentioned where Mr. Douglas allegedly fell or was pushed."

"Or jumped, Inspector."

"Do you think it was a suicide?"

"At this point, we don't know." Mike repeats the original story and then adds the photos that he hands to the detective. "I've asked the local police to run the plates yesterday, but I haven't heard back from them."

Abruptly Matsuyama hands the photo showing the license number to Haamoa and tells him to call. Then, he says, "Let's go to the site."

Once there Mike shows him the gouge in the edge, and he leans over to see what is below. Without a word, he looks around at the dirt and sees there are no prints. Mike doesn't implicate Maria by telling him what he saw. "Let him find his own evidence before he jumps on her or any of us," Mike thinks.

He motions, and they go down the path. On the way, Matsuyama says, "Please assemble everyone in the living room."

Ellie, Len, Kamalo, Maria, and the day staff, including the gardener, are seated and looking anxious. "This is the whole household except for the night guard, who wasn't on duty when the incident happened, we think. He told Kamalo that no one entered the compound, and he gave us the photos of the car that approached the gate. If you need him, we can bring him here."

"Ladies and gentlemen, I am sorry to bother you at this time, but you understand that I must learn what happened here and who might be responsible for Mr. Douglas's accident. At this point I have made no decisions. I will need to speak privately with each of you. If you would all go on to the lanai with Detective Haamoa, I will proceed as quickly as possible."

Everyone stands up as he says, "Who was the last person to see Mr. Douglas?"

"That would be Maria," Mike says, pointing to her.

"Miss, please stay here. I'd like to speak to you first and construct a history of the events of the night Mr. Douglas disappeared."

"Inspector, I would like to be here while you talk to Maria."

He looks at Mike for a moment with a question on his lips but says nothing and nods. Haamoa sets a recorder in front of her. "Please don't be alarmed, miss. We want to make sure that we don't make any mistakes with your testimony."

The word "testimony" startles her, but Haamoa assures her she is not accused of anything and should not be afraid to tell the whole story. Over the next twenty minutes, Matsuyama questions Maria and goes back and forth a couple of times double-checking her statements. She doesn't mention the issue of the number of glasses. She stuns Mike when she adds something new to her story. She says, "Sometimes in the middle of the night, Mr. Douglas can't sleep. He comes to the kitchen, and I make him something to eat or drink. Then, he wants me to sit on his lap and talk to him while he eats."

"While you sit there, what happens?"

She stops for a long minute. He repeats the question. Still Maria hesitates.

"What aren't you telling us? Did he bother you?"

She nods her head, buries her face in her hands, and starts to cry. After a half minute, she looks at him with tears in her eyes and says, "Always he gave me some money, but I didn't kill him."

Matsuyama looks inquiringly at Mike as if to say, "Did you know this?"

He shakes his head and shrugs his shoulders.

The inspector says to her, "I'm sorry to put you through this, Maria. Don't worry. I know you didn't kill him. But why didn't you quit if he was bothering you?"

"I need the money. There are no good jobs here. I live with my sister and brother-in-law because I have no money."

"I understand. That's all for now. You can go for today. If I need to talk to you again, we'll call you. Don't worry. You've been very helpful."

When she's gone, he turns to Mike and asks, "Did you know about this?"

"Absolutely not. I questioned her in depth twice, and she never hinted about any past behavior by Mr. Douglas. I think there is more that she hasn't told us, don't you?"

"I agree. There could be. This does add to the picture, but this is not the time to press. I'll talk to her again, probably tomorrow after I'm finished with the others. Who is next?"

Mike says Len should be next and tells him that chronologically he was the next person in the scenario. When Len comes in, he is surprised to see Mike sitting there. Purposely Mike's not excused himself. He'll let Len object, and that will tell him that he's going to bring Mike into the picture. Maybe he can't blame him—he's just trying to protect himself, and Mike's a good red herring to throw in.

Matsuyama starts, "Mr. Levine, please tell us what happened that night."

Len looks at Mike and hesitates.

Mike waits several seconds and then asks pointedly, "Len, would you rather I leave?"

He nods with a look of chagrin. Mike walks out to the lanai.

On the lanai Ellie and the staff are waiting. Haamoa is making small talk with them to break the silence and the tension. In half an hour, Len comes out with a smug little smile on his face. He says, "Ellie, he wants to see you next."

She looks nervously at Mike, who smiles and gives her a thumbs-ups sign. He's not worried about her. She's no one's fool. Given the earlier admonishment, he knows she will handle Matsuyama.

Forty minutes later she's back on the lanai, and the cook and kitchen helper are with Matsuyama. They can only add background information since they were gone when Doug disappeared. Ellie looks at Len and Mike and says, "He asked me about my relationship with Doug and also my relationship with you two. I told him that Len has been working with Doug for almost six years and the relationship was good. Len, I didn't tell him how Doug treated you at times. That would just raise his suspicion of you."

Len nods and mouths, "Thank you."

"As for you, Michael, I just said that we met you just ten days ago, so there is no past history with you as it relates to any of us."

Within less than an hour, Matsuyama has finished his interrogations. He comes out on the lanai and says very succinctly without any expression, "That will be all for today. We should have an autopsy report within a day or two. We'll also have the ownership of the car that came to the gate that night. When I have that data, I will come back and continue my investigation. Please do not leave the area."

It's the following Monday when Haamoa calls and tells Mike that they have the autopsy report and will be coming back on Tuesday or Wednesday. He volunteers that they have a new case of a tourist who was found dead on the weekend in her hotel room. "We're really busy. When it rains, it pours," he says, laughing. Sick cop joke.

Wednesday morning they arrive unannounced at the gate. Mike thinks, "This is stupid. We could be in the village or elsewhere. They didn't tell us we were under house arrest." In fact, that is just what has happened. Ellie and Len have driven into Hanalei just to get away from the atmosphere of the house.

"Good morning, Inspector," Mike greets him and nods to Haamoa as well, who is still smiling. Mike has a sense that Haamoa doesn't feel the gravity of the situation. "I'm afraid that Mrs. Douglas and Len are in town at the moment. They should be back within an hour at most."

"It's no matter. I want to go over the pathologist's report with you before I talk to them. By the way, the license plate identified the vehicle as belonging to a car rental company at the Lihue Airport. The renter was a Mr. William Bracher. Haamoa is trying to find him. The car was returned the morning that Mr. Douglas disappeared. According to the night guard, the driver didn't get out of the car, so I don't expect to learn anything about him. Your DIS experience may prove helpful with the autopsy report. I talked to the pathologist, and in summary, she pointed out several injuries that may have been the cause of death or contributed to it. There are cervical fractures and a ruptured spleen that probably resulted from the impact of the fall. There is no sign of a fight. Here is the pathologist's report and conclusions."

> The abdominal cavity was opened, and 2000 ml of unclotted blood was removed. The spleen had deep fractures and had been avulsed from its pedicle with transection of the splenic artery and vein. Examination of the brain revealed a lacerated brainstem with 180 ml of unclotted blood in the cranial cavity. There were no circumferential bruises of the neck and no apparent defensive wounds of the hands. The lungs showed signs of pleural mesothelioma, but this is unrelated to the case. Death was the result of multiple trauma.

"So apparently Mr. Douglas was not fighting with someone before he went over the bluff."

"Well, now we know what happened, but we still don't know how it happened and what or who caused it."

"Mr. Levine made a strong point when I talked to him that perhaps you and/or Mrs. Douglas were involved. He doesn't seem to like you."

"Yes, that is quite clear. He has a crush on Mrs. Douglas that is not reciprocated, and he sees me as getting in the middle, I think. I've only been around these people for about ten days. There hasn't been time to develop much of a relationship with any of them. Doug invited me to stay here, so he obviously didn't see me as any type of threat. Besides that, I have an exemplary personal and service record. Finally, I don't believe that Mrs. Douglas has any romantic feelings about me.

"However, did you see the note about the lungs? Len had said that Doug had been to a doctor a couple months ago and that recently he had shown signs of fatigue. Along with that, he said Doug's business is in trouble to the point of possibly filing bankruptcy. Did he tell you that?"

"No, he did not."

"If you add that to the mix, Inspector, we can't rule out suicide, wouldn't you agree?"

"Yes, I don't believe Mr. Levine was truthful with me, and now this confirms it."

"Inspector, my view is that he is just trying to remove any suspicion about him being the perpetrator. It's well known among the staff that Douglas treated Len poorly. He always referred to him as Leonard rather than Len. When Doug felt like it, he called him Mr. Levine sarcastically or LIL, Len's initials. That really upset Len because Doug said it like Len was a sissy."

"It could be that in a fit of anger Len pushed him, but there is no evidence of a fight," Matsuyama says. "Yet, given the right circumstances, a single push on Doug's back or chest could have sent him over the cliff. Len's big enough to do that. If it isn't Len or you or even Mrs. Douglas, that leaves Kamalo, who wasn't here that night, or the night guard, who has no apparent motive for either of them. Last is Maria; she's too small to push Douglas. He weighed well over two hundred pounds. I'm going to talk to Levine again, and I'd also like to talk to Maria. She's not under suspicion, but she might have seen or heard something and is afraid to tell me. Please call Maria and ask her to come up. I'll talk to Len while I wait for her. Maybe I can find a motive. I'll also talk to Mrs. Douglas again."

Mike puts a call in to Maria and asks her to come back. She's very frightened, but he assures her that they know she did not cause Doug to fall. Shortly after he called, Len and Ellie returned from Hanalei. Matsuyama took Len out to the bluff. The old boy is more clever than he has shown. If Len was involved, he might be nervous returning to the scene of the fall. Matsuyama had Haamoa come also, probably in case Len reacted violently.

When they're gone, Ellie and Mike sit in the living room. "Michael, what's happening? Who does the inspector think pushed Doug off the bluff?"

"He really has no clues, but he thinks that Len worked too hard to implicate me, and possibly even you, in a conspiracy to get rid of Doug. He's beginning to believe that Len had something to do with it. Do you think Len might be involved?"

"That bastard. I didn't tell the inspector how poorly Doug treated Len at times. I could have suggested that Len could have a motive based on Doug's treatment. I could have told the inspector that Doug often yelled at Len and accused him of making mistakes that cost us a lot of money. But I didn't. If I'm questioned again, I won't hold back. Also, there's a provision that if something happens to Doug Len will receive a lump sum payment of I think about two millions dollars to help wind down the business and sell off the assets. How's that for a motive?"

It is a long hour before Matsuyama finishes with Len. When he comes down the path, Len is flushed and sweating. Matsuyama must have gone after him pretty hard. Just then Maria arrives. Mike takes her aside and tells her again not to worry. She's not a suspect. The inspector spends about twenty minutes with her, and when she comes out, she doesn't look bad. Apparently, he hasn't beaten on her.

In a few minutes, Matsuyama and Haamoa come into the living room where the four of them are sitting and announces, "That's all for today. I'm going to have Haamoa check some points, and I'll get back to you in a day or two." Everyone except Len looks relieved.

Maria says to Mike, "My brother-in-law drove me up here, but he had to go to work. Can someone drive me home?"

"I'll take you, Maria. I'll have Kamalo bring the car around."

Once they start down the road to town, Maria is very quiet. "Are you okay, Maria?"

"Yes."

"Was the inspector hard on you?"

"No, but he keeps asking about when I took the drinks to Mr. Douglas and what happened then. I've told him the same story several times, and he just keeps asking about it. Why is that?"

Mike finds a vista turnout off the road and stops at a spot that overlooks Hanalei Bay. The sun is shining brightly in a cloudless sky. It's bouncing off the blue ocean and flashing over the waves. The day is already quite warm, and the car windows are down to catch some breeze. Maria seems to be sweating a little.

"Maria, The inspector keeps asking because he believes there is something about that night you haven't told him. He knows you didn't shove Mr. Douglas off the bluff, but he feels certain that more happened, and you're not telling all. Was there more?"

"I'm scared, Commander. I didn't do anything to hurt anyone. Why does he keep after me?"

"There is just a feeling that something happened after Doug asked you to sit down and have a drink with him. Did something happen, Maria?"

Maria is silent. It's clear that she's covering up.

"Maria, you're not in trouble. Believe me. But if you don't talk, Matsuyama is going to keep after you until you do. He could make things very uncomfortable for you. Like I said earlier, he could take you to police headquarters in Lihue and question you there. That would not be pleasant. Please, Maria, tell me what else happened so I can protect you."

She looks down at her hands and then out the window. When she turns back to Mike, there are tears in her eyes. "I didn't touch him. After I told him I don't drink, he poured some piña into a glass. He got up with a nasty smile on his face and came around to my chair. I was very scared. I didn't know what he was going to do to me. I jumped up, and he stepped back. One of his feet caught the edge of the pad, and he staggered back and then fell off, still holding the glass. That's why Mr. Levine saw only one glass when he came up. I didn't touch him—I swear it. I didn't touch him," she blurts out and buries her face in her lap.

Mike puts his arm around her shoulders and pulls her up.

"We know you didn't push him, but we didn't know how he went over the edge. We even thought Mr. Levine might have come up there after you left, got into a fight with Mr. Douglas, and pushed him off. You can relax. I'll help you write a statement for Matsuyama repeating what you just told me. I know he will accept it, because it will close the case for him, and it will look like he solved it."

The next morning, Mike calls Matsuyama and tells him what happened. The following morning, the inspector makes a final trip up from Lihue to talk to Maria. They go into the living room again, and Mike gives him her statement. She repeats it almost verbatim. He asks a couple clarifying questions, thanks her for her testimony, and dismisses her.

"I knew she was hiding something. This solves it. I will file my report, and the case will be closed: accidental death from a fall off the bluff. We have a witness, so that does it. Thanks for your assistance, Commander."

The case is closed, and Mike has to go back to Pearl. Before he goes, he counsels Ellie on settling Doug's estate. "Ellie, you should work with Doug's lawyers and bankers and Len to sell everything to other developers. You need to keep Len on for a year to help with the disposition of assets. He would have all the details on Doug's projects and their status. Then give him his separation bonus. As for Maria, she endured Doug's advances and deserves some compensation. You could set up a trust to disperse Maria's salary for a couple more years while she goes about trying to find a new job in the local market. It will be a very small amount out of your total assets. But it will be very important for her. Finally, no matter how much you inherit from the sale of assets, it should be well over a couple hundred million dollars. With that, you can afford anything you want. You're an intelligent and experienced woman. Ellie, with your T and A and a hundred million dollars, you'll be a most attractive widow. You'll be beating suitors off with a stick."

Back in Pearl, Mike is riding a desk and waiting again for orders. He doesn't seem to fit into the normal routine. It's like they put him on ice until something unusual comes up. Then, he can almost hear them say, "Let's send Holmes on this one. He's good with the weird jobs."

On top of it all, reporting to Tweed is a monumental pain. He values saving money more than developing intelligence or carrying out covert operations. If he had been in the Continental Congress in 1776, America would still be a colony.

To keep himself from going crazy and feeling lost once more, Mike writes another unmailable letter to Grace.

October 28, 1971
Dear C. J.,
    I just finished a very interesting case on Kauai. A man fell off a cliff. We didn't have many suspects, and the solution was quite a surprise. I was able to draw out what happened from the night maid. It turned out to be an accident that was witnessed by her. She was afraid to tell us for fear we would accuse her of pushing him. That solved the case.
    Now I'm sitting on my hands waiting for my next assignment. I really wish I could hear from you. I don't like the thought that we are through, even before we barely started. Sooner or later I'm going to have to face reality.
    If I can't find you soon I just have to get off my back side and carry on.
Hanging on,
Sherlock

"I'm acting stupid. It's over. She's gone somewhere, and I'll never see her again. I've got to put that behind me and get on with my life. I'm thirty-four years old and alone. Those are the facts, so I better stop feeling sorry for myself. Courage, old man. Stiff upper lip and all that."

Months later, Mike's orders finally come through. He's assigned to the staff of the US delegation at the United Nations in New York City.

Chapter 22

Safe Harbor

September 1972
New York City

Mike's very impressed with the site of the UN's headquarters set along the East River of New York City. He thinks to himself, "I guess I'm still a naïve sentimentalist from North Dakota, but it gives me warm feelings of stateliness to walk through the UN building's several large meeting rooms and wide hallways. Often there are meetings in session. The walls are decorated with scenes and photos of men and women who have made history here." While he waits for his assignment, he sits in the visitor's galleries and watches the deliberations.

His favorite room is the General Assembly Hall. He stands at the back of that great space, marveling at the structure and recalling the historic events that have taken place there. This citadel of peace seats two thousand people in six sections, each with more than a dozen rows all angled downward toward the speaker's platform. Behind the speaker is a golden shaft about twenty feet wide at the bottom and tapered as it rises to the ceiling. It's the background for the UN logo. The large, dark wooden acoustical shafts on the side walls angle up and inward from the floor past the translator's windows to the ceiling. The entire focus is on the speaker's stand. It's truly a most powerful room.

The general assembly is not meeting today, so there's almost perfect silence broken only by murmurs from two men down in front working on some mechanism.

Suddenly Mike hears a voice. "Commander Holmes?"

He's startled because he's lost in thoughts about the atmosphere of this great hall. Then, it comes again: "Commander?" When he turns around, he's shocked—stunned. He can't believe what he sees just ten feet away. He tries to breathe but gasps at the sight.

"You're looking fit, Commander."

He can't speak. It's as if some mythic person is saying his name.

"What's the matter, Sherlock? Cat got your tongue?"

He's stuck. Finally, he takes a few steps toward her until they stand three feet apart. He's afraid to go any closer or reach out to touch her for fear this apparition, this dream, will vanish. "Grace, what are you doing here?"

"I'm a special agent of the state department and a member of the US delegation. I consult and advise on special projects related to Asia Pacific. My background seems to be highly valued around here."

"How long have you been here?"

"About a year. When I saw that you were coming here in a staff bulletin, my heart skipped a beat. It's the first I'd known that you were still alive. I could hardly believe it. I cried. I'd written you several notes, but they kept coming back. I would have come to see you earlier, but I was away on a mission for the past month. What happened to you? Where have you been? Why did you stop writing after the one about going on a secret mission of some sort? When I didn't hear from you again I thought that…that…I didn't know what to think."

"I don't know what to say. I thought I'd never see you again when my letters to you were returned."

"If you're unhappy to see me, I'll leave you alone."

"My god, no! It's just a shock for you to appear out of nowhere after all these years. Where is Jerry?"

"Didn't you hear? A month after you left Jerry was killed in a collision of two P3Vs flying between Moffett and North Island. I was in Honolulu taking care of my mother when he went down with his total crew. Then Mom died the same month. I wrote to you a few months afterward, but my letters were returned. I was devastated. In less than a year, I had lost everyone."

"I'm so sorry to hear that. I was in deep cover for over a year and never received your letters. When I was last in Hawaii, I tried to find you. I went to your mother's house, but there were other people living there. The neighbor didn't know where had happened to you. I called the realtor who sold her house and he had lost your forwarding address. I wanted to punch him out. Then, I went to the Chinese Cultural Center too. I remembered you said you worked there part time. Apparently it had been several months since you were there, and all they could tell me was that you had moved to the mainland. What happened?"

"With Jerry and both my parents gone and you missing, I was totally alone. I had time to think about the rest of my life. I decided to change my name back to my maiden name, mostly out of respect for my parents, who never liked Jerry. When I was about to marry him, my dad took me aside and said, 'That boy is self-centered, manipulative, and insensitive…just like Chiang.' He said, 'You can always come home. If he hurts you in any way, I have friends who'll turn him into shark bait. He'll never be heard from again.'

"So, Donaldson is gone, and Liu is back. I had decided earlier that the thing I know most about and truly enjoy is the politics and economics of Asia Pacific. So I went back to school at UH-Manoa to finish my master's in China Studies. I sold Mom's house and took an apartment near the campus. Again, given my experience and my previous studies at Stanford, they put me on a directed study track and I was able to finish my degree in less than a year. Somehow all that closed the loop for me. What happened to you?"

"I was sent on a special, top-secret mission that I still can't talk about. It lasted a year. I wrote to you before and after the mission, but I never heard back. I've continued to write to you and saved the letters because I didn't know where to send them. I just wanted to talk to you through the letters. How did you get here?"

"While I was at the cultural center in Hawaii, I shepherded a group from the United Nations that held a meeting in Honolulu. The deputy for Asia heard about my background and suggested I come to New York and talk to them about joining the staff. I had no reason to stay in Hawaii by myself. I thought it was time for a new life. So I did as he suggested, and they offered me a great position here. She smiled. "Any more questions?"

"I don't know what to say."

"I can see that. It's been a long time from Celia's party to now—just over six years, right? I think about our conversation all the time. I read and reread your letters and wish we had had more time together. An afternoon in San Francisco at the hospital and a couple weeks when you were at Tripler—that was it. I always think about kissing you on the beach at Maili and about our discussion later there when you asked if I could put up with the life of military wife. It was so romantic, so bittersweet."

"I shipped out ten days after our first meeting at Maili. I didn't call to say good-bye because we were so messed up that it seemed pointless. I didn't know what to say at that point. You asked me to write, and I did, but I didn't know how much that really meant. Then, when I was a Tripler and we had out picnic at Maili again I had hopes but no assurance that so long as you were with Jerry there was any hope."

"Men are so obtuse. Of course I wanted to stay in touch with you. Even though it looked hopeless, I still wanted to be in contact. I needed you in my life, even if only a little bit."

Mike drops his folder, steps up to her, and takes her hands. It's just like six years ago, but now things are different. They look at each other for what seems like eternity but is probably only a few seconds. He pulls her into his arms so brutally that it knocks the wind out of her. Then, he relaxes a little.

She leans back and takes a deep breath. Then, she says coyly, "Does this mean you still like me?"

"I've had a shrine in my heart for you since the night we met."

She slides her arms around his neck and gives him the softest, sweetest, most overwhelming kiss anyone has ever had.

"I say, that was a bit of all right."

"That's my boy, Sherlock. I'm happy to see that you're still silly." She moves back into his arms. With her cheek next to his, she answers his unspoken question: "Yes."

He can't speak.

She says it again: "Yes."

They hold each other tightly and breathe together softly.